CRUEL DECEPTION BOOK III

DEGREES of CONTROL

INTERNATIONAL BESTSELLING AUTHOR

VIA MARI

CONTENTS

Published by Book World Ink

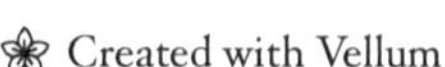 Created with Vellum

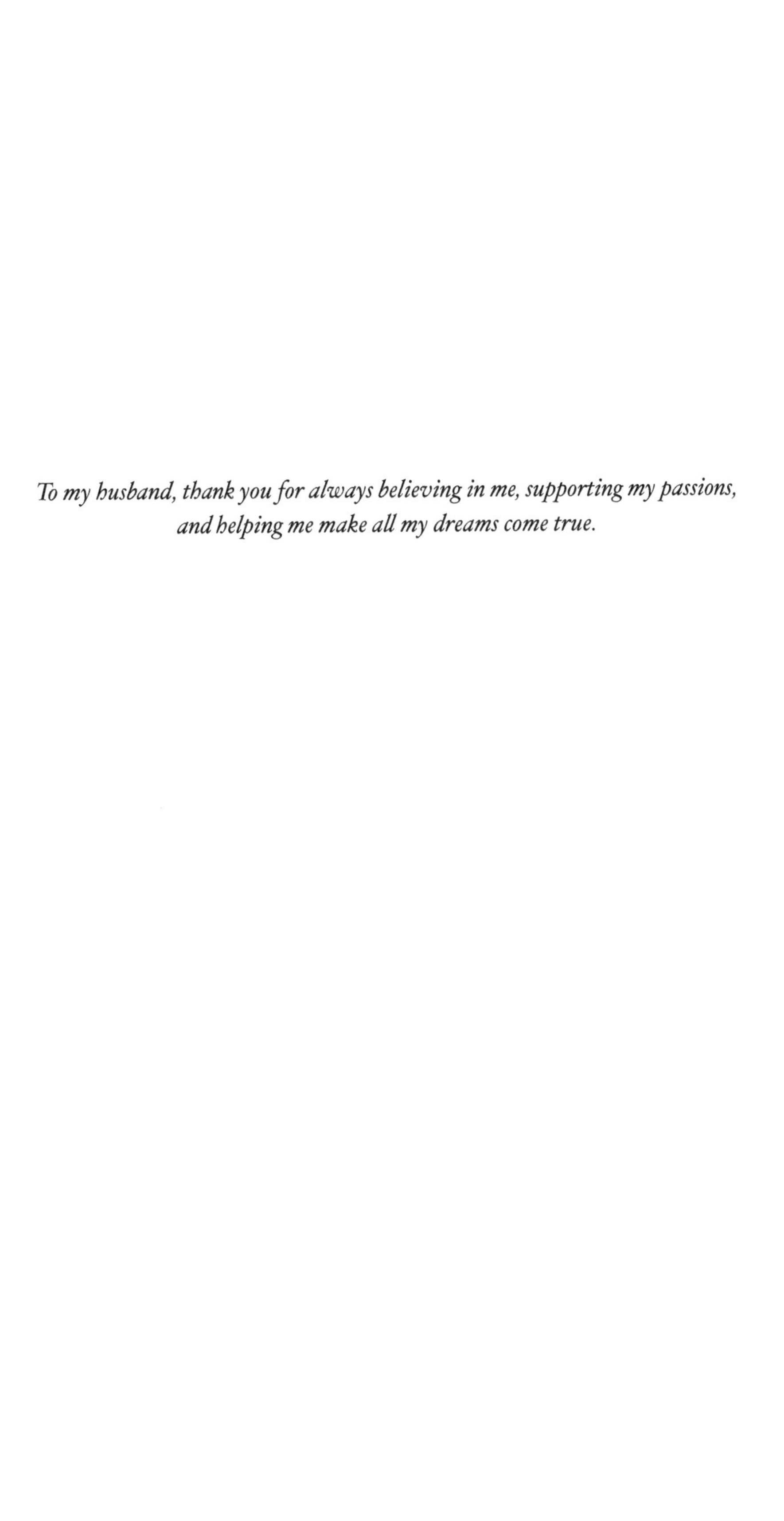

To my husband, thank you for always believing in me, supporting my passions, and helping me make all my dreams come true.

ONE

I can barely hear the sound of the band gently playing in the background over the pounding of his heartbeat as he holds me closely. The weight of the magnificent princess cut diamond he has just placed on the ring finger of my left hand is as heavy as the despair in my heart.

"Katarina, there's nothing that would please me greater than to call you my wife," he says, repeating his proposal, lifting my chin to meet the intent deep green eyes searching my own.

My heart is racing, and for the second time in my life, I find myself turning down a wedding proposal. "Chase, I care about you more than you will ever know, but I can't marry you," I say, sliding the ring from my finger and placing it into the palm of his hand. I cannot bear to look into his eyes as I close his hand around it, turn from the restaurant and head towards the ocean. My body is on autopilot and full of despair. I just need to move. I find myself walking faster, gaining speed as I head towards the ocean, but I can hear him behind me, and he quickly closes the distance.

"Katarina," he says, spinning me towards him just before I reach the coast. "Tell me what is wrong," he says, brushing the tears that have escaped and are streaming down my cheeks. I take a step back trying to gain a little distance. If I let him kiss me, I will succumb.

"Chase, please. I'll always love you, but you were right when you said that I don't trust you. I know that now, and if I don't, how in the world can we expect to live happily ever after?"

"Why do you say this?" he asks, eyes probing, deep pools of green. They are like magnets and I struggle to avert my gaze.

"I do not want to have this conversation here," I say, gesturing to the beach around us.

"Katarina, we are the only ones within hearing distance in the middle of an entirely private coastline. Tell me."

"My mom informed me about what happened in Miami the night you and my dad rescued her."

"What is it that you think you know about that night?" he says.

"You knew the men in that house would be killed, you and Carlos planned it, but yet you let me believe their deaths were an accident. I thought somehow things went wrong, or maybe it was self-defense, but it was planned, an assassination. You and my father have an entirely different set of values than I do. It's exactly why my mom ran twenty-six years ago. I can't make the same mistakes she's made."

He begins to say something, and I put my hand up to dissuade a quarrel. "I don't want to argue with you, Chase. I don't have the emotional strength. I know everything about that night and what happened to Ty. I can't even think about what transpired without feeling ill," I say.

"I see," he says, watching me. His eyes are hooded and controlled. "So, you would walk away from what we have, putting your principles above all else?" he asks.

"You said it best some time ago. If I don't trust you, over time it will manifest itself, and we won't have a relationship anyway. I don't know what else you want me to say. I can't pretend to condone the things that have happened," I say, swirling my foot in the sand.

"It's late, and you are emotionally exhausted. I'll let Jay know we're heading to the airport."

"Chase, I'm not even packed. We weren't planning to leave so soon," I say.

"We're leaving now. I'll have the team bring your things. They can meet us at the airport," Chase says once again in full command, on his phone, ordering people around and making arrangements. When we reach the Ridalgo, Jay has a car awaiting our arrival and opens the back door of the limo for us.

Jay leans into the open window to talk with the driver who I do not recognize and then turns his attention to Chase. "By the time the pilot's ready to take off we'll have your luggage and computer onboard. I'll meet you there," he says, closing the door. I have never met our driver, and Chase does not introduce him to me. As we pull away from the resort entrance, the privacy glass of the limousine slides into place, effectively eliminating him from our view.

Chase pulls the laptop tray down from the seat in front of him, boots up his Mac, and within moments is engrossed in his work appearing at ease with the distance between us. I don't know what I expected and resign myself to an uncomfortable trip back to the states. I decide to forgo hooking into the limo internet, and pull out my cell to message Jenny.

Message: We're on the way back to Chicago. Will let you know when we arrive.

Reply: Sounds good. I thought you were staying for a few days?

Message: Long story. Talk later.

Reply: Have a good flight. Call me tomorrow.

It is a relatively short drive across the island to the airport. Chase assists me up the ramp and into the jet entrance, his hand briefly on my back, a painful reminder of the palpable current which exists between us. He spends a few moments thanking the crew for making adjustments in the schedule before joining me in the cabin.

I glance around the multimillion-dollar Gulfstream. It is the same jet we took home the last time; his favorite by admission, designed to make him feel at home in the air with overstuffed leather couches and loveseats, a fireplace that crackles lightly giving off a warm ambiance and extending from floor to ceiling in decorative stone. We buckle up, and it is not long before the pilot is traveling down the runway, and we lift off, careening past the island perimeters and over the multicolored turquoise sea that surrounds it below.

"Katarina, you look exhausted. Why don't you go into the bedroom and get some sleep? It will take me the majority of the trip to complete the work I need to finish," he says.

I shrug my shoulders and try to avert my eyes, feeling dismissed, but at the same time thankful for the separation and space to be alone with my thoughts. The bedroom is an instant reminder of what we've been to each other, and it is difficult not to think about the time we've spent in this room. I slip out of my dress and pull the luxurious feeling white robe around me trying not to think of the times he has wrapped me in it after making love to me. My heart is aching as I climb into the oversized bed longing to talk to my mom who must have felt the exact same way years ago.

A brief knock startles me hours later before the door to the bedroom opens. "Katarina, we'll be landing soon. You will need to get seated and buckled up shortly," he says before closing the door.

I try to stifle the feeling of despondency as I slip my dress back on and shrug into the sweater Jay thought to bring along for the trip back to Chicago. I look around the room, drinking in the memories, before closing the bedroom door and buckling in across from him for the final descent.

He is still working on his computer and the silence between us is unnerving. "Chase, I'll plan to take a cab to Jenny's from the airport. I'm sure she won't mind me staying with her until I find a place to rent," I say, finally breaking the unbearable silence between us before we touch down.

"Katarina, things with Alfreita have escalated to the point that I have had to increase security for both of our families. It is not safe for you to be on your own right now. In fact, your mom and dad will both be staying at our home for the next couple of weeks. Let's not give them another reason for worry right now. You can sleep in the room we've been sharing, and I will move to one of the spare bedrooms. Your parents can use the guest wing which is on the other side of the house."

"I'm not sure what you're saying."

"Your father is aware I intended to propose and your parents will no doubt be anticipating a celebration upon our return. Expecting your acceptance, news of our engagement was leaked to the press in hopes of drawing Alfreita from hiding. I'm afraid we'll need to keep up appearances for the short term. In fact, the entire plan to attract him relies on it," he says.

"You want me to lie to my parents about our engagement?"

"If it makes you feel better, pretend that you said yes," he says, sliding the five carat princess cut diamond ring onto my finger. I flinch at the electricity his touch creates, but if he feels it, he does not give any indication.

"Katarina, it will be for a very short time. We have much to discuss, but right now, I need to finalize security details. I'll send you an email outlining all the announcements and particulars shared with the press. We can talk about them in more depth tomorrow." His eyes are hooded and controlled, and my heart feels as heavy as the new weight he has placed upon my finger.

The pilot announces the upcoming landing to O'Hare, and we've no sooner touched down than Jay has us pile into the awaiting helicopter. Chase hands me a pair of earplugs. I am both annoyed, and at the same time grateful, for his thoughtfulness putting them grudgingly into my ears before I pull on the regulatory headset. The ascent is smooth as the pilot hovers, lifts off, and navigates around the expansive sky-rises that are lit up against the dark of the night, over the lake and toward Chase's home in the country. It is a short flight and the pilot descends, hovers, and puts the helicopter down seamlessly on the helipad which is only a few hundred feet from the house. As we approach, Gaby greets us at the door with warm hugs and a gentle smile.

"Well I certainly wasn't expecting you two back this soon, but Chase tells me congratulations are in order," she says.

"Thank you, Gaby. Have Katarina's parents retired for the evening?" Chase asks, easily averting more questions about our engagement.

"Yes, they were tired," she says.

"Very good, I'll let them know we're back in the morning," Chase replies, walking into the kitchen.

"I have a few issues which require my attention, and I'm sure Katarina must be exhausted after the long flight," he says, giving me the perfect reason to retire before excusing himself to his study down the hall.

The clock on the nightstand registers one a.m., and I am emotionally exhausted. I wish it were not so late and was a decent hour to call my mom. She would understand what I am going through. It's hurtful that Chase has barely spoken to me, but I am the one that called it off, not him. I change into a nightgown, brush my teeth and curl into the bed that up until now, we have shared. My iPad dings with the alert of an incoming message.

TO: KMeilers@TorzialConsulting.org
   From: CHPrestian@PrestianCorp.org

THE ATTACHED DOCUMENT will provide you with the details of the announcement, along with the press release, times and dates.

C. **H. Prestian**
   Chief Executive Officer, Owner
   Prestian Corporation

THE MESSAGE IS as impersonal as he has been all evening, outlining media and press plans. He has included a well-written announcement by Nate Collins, the freelance journalist who now works exclusively for Prestian Corp. I reread it and close the email without responding, suppressing the desire to send Chase a scathing response about lies and deception. Instead, I lay the computer on the nightstand, curling up with his pillow. The smell of his cologne permeates everything around me. I pull it closer, breathing in the smell of Chase and his fresh-scented soap. The tears rush unwelcome and uncontrollably down my cheeks. He always knew it, even before I did. He is right, a relationship would never last without trust. I will do well to heed his advice to survive the next few weeks. I finally fall into a fitful sleep, tossing and turning, thinking of dark green intense eyes.

TWO

PRESTIAN

I wake early, after only a few hours, restless and unable to fall back asleep. Today, Chase will officially break the news of our engagement to my parents. Shortly after that, Nate will publicly release the engagement announcement of Chase Prestian, one of the wealthiest entrepreneurs in the country, to Katarina Meilers, a consultant hired by his company to assist with the design of the city's newest medical centers. It will be in all of the local social columns. Once the Associated Press pick it up I have no doubt it will necessitate dodging paparazzi attempting to get pictures to go along with the stories.

It is evident to me, that like everything else; this announcement was arranged down to the finest of detail weeks before Chase actually proposed. The awkward plane ride home, the need to appear engaged all seem like a bad dream, but here I sit, twirling the white band of gold that holds a stunning princess cut diamond around my finger, a magnificent symbolism of our lie.

I need to go for a run and clear my head. I send a quick text message to Jay.

Message: Leaving for a run in about 10 minutes.

Reply: Ok- Chase wants you to take the orchard route.

I frown at the fact Chase is always apprised of my every move. I will no doubt have a fleet of security guards trailing along with me this morning. I know my annoyance is misplaced, and I should be grateful after everything Jay and his team have done to keep me alive. I zip off a quick text to let him know that I will take the orchard path this morning.

The air is crisp and fresh with a hint of winter's imminent arrival. The sun is just starting to peek over the horizon creating a pink and purple mixed hue over the blue-gray lake ahead. I ease into my pace, pulling the tie of my hood a little tighter, slowly acclimating to the briskness of the breeze coming off of Lake Michigan compared to that of the warm Aruba runs of the last week. My mind immediately drifts to Chase's involvement in the Miami explosion and of Ty and his injuries. He did not deny it and doesn't appear the slightest bit remorseful. I just hope that Chase is able to resolve his issues with Alfreita quickly so that we can move on with our lives. It feels good to expend physical energy after all the emotional trials of the last couple days.

I'll give Jenny a call a little later in the day when I know more. Maybe there is another assignment she can give me and someone else that can take over the Prestian Corp accounts. I make a mental note to call the realtor and have her begin looking for apartments as I round the corner and see his home ahead.

I have exceeded my usual route, deep in thought, and am completely drenched as I head upstairs to the bathroom and strip out of my clothing. I turn the shower on, letting the warm water from the dual-headed shower cascade over me, removing the chill of the morning run before drying my hair and applying makeup. I rummage through the closet and contemplate what to wear. If I am going to deal with Chase head on, business attire is required. I slip into a gray and black skirt with a slit that shows off my legs, pairing it with a long sleeve black button down blouse and a classic style pair of Louboutin heels purchased from Saks. I grimace at my long wild auburn tresses, apply a little product and begin straightening the unruly locks. When I'm finished, it is shiny and sleek, spilling in long layers over my shoulders. I spin around in front of the floor length mirror, before heading downstairs to the kitchen to face Chase.

There is no sign of him or my parents, but Gaby has laid out an assortment of fresh fruit, pastries, and cheese for breakfast. I select muskmelon, honeydew and Dutch cheese taking my plate outside, opting to sit on the patio to enjoy the view of Lake Michigan. I am just getting ready to text my mom when Chase walks onto the balcony. He is freshly showered by the look of his damp hair and is wearing a Chicago Bears sweatshirt and a pair of jeans. They fit his body perfectly, not tight, but accentuate his powerful thighs. I quickly avert my gaze and try to suppress the blush that I feel rising to my cheeks.

"Good morning, Katarina," he says. I feel sure he can hear the racing of my heart across the table. His eyes capture mine, and I am unable to discern the emotion that passes through them. It is fleeting and soon replaced with aloofness.

"It's brisk outside," he admonishes, flipping a switch that controls the overhead heaters which keep the balcony and adjacent decks warm even on crisp autumn days such as this.

"Thank you, that feels much better. I was just getting ready to text my mom to find out where they are," I say, pouring another cup of coffee from the carafe.

"Carlos and I had breakfast together, and your mother took coffee in their suite. She's working on a press release and apparently needs to have it completed by day's end," he says.

I wonder with disdain if everyone's actions are reported to him on a play-by-play basis or summarized by the hour. "Don't you think it's a little odd that I haven't heard anything from them, but you apparently know everything about their plans?" I ask.

He raises his eyebrows in question, and the sides of his lips are upturned. "Your father and I had a very early meeting. I didn't think there was a need to wake you," he says by way of explanation.

"I didn't sleep well and went for a run. How long are we going to be under house arrest this time?" I ask.

He lowers his eyes at me. "We'll be on the highest level of security until the situation with Alfreita is resolved. It's unfortunate we weren't successful in getting to him at the same time we extracted your mom. That would have been ideal, but until we do, he is still a very real threat."

I cringe at the meaning behind his words. *What does it mean to get to someone?*

"You didn't really answer my question, Chase. Are we going to need to remain at the house or can we go into the office?" I ask.

He raises his eyebrows and his mouth quirks in outward annoyance at my continued questioning. "You should plan to work from here for the next couple of weeks. If you require anything in the way of technology or otherwise, let me know. If we're finished with that subject, I've asked your parents to meet us for lunch today. They will most likely want to congratulate us on our engagement," he says, taking a seat across from me.

"Chase, we need to discuss this further. I do not want to lie to my parents. Why is it so important for them to think we're engaged? I don't understand how our relationship has anything to do with Alfreita."

He sighs and leans back in his chair with his coffee mug. "We organized a celebratory evening to officially announce our engagement. A gathering of this magnitude is needed to draw him out, but I would like to discuss a few things with your dad before we talk in greater depth about it. He's finalizing the details as we speak and I should be able to explain everything to you this afternoon."

He looks exhausted, and I fight the bubbling urge to wrap my arms around him. "No news then on Alfreita's whereabouts?"

"No, I'm afraid not," he says, taking a sip of his coffee.

"You don't believe this is the last we've heard of him, though?"

"Unfortunately not. The leverage Alfreita had for moving illegal product was holding your mom hostage. Now that we've got her back, he's going to need to find a different way," Chase says.

"Why don't you just tell him that you weren't responsible for tipping Interpol last year?"

"Katarina, there were millions of dollars of narcotics in that shipment. It's not just him we are dealing with, it's the suppliers, too. He's trying to cover his own ass and will do whatever it takes to keep them happy. When our teams rescued your mom in Miami, even more of their production was lost. He's looking for retribution now," Chase says.

"Well maybe if you and my dad hadn't blown it up he wouldn't be out for revenge," I say.

He lowers his eyes at me. "Katarina, we can discuss this in greater detail after I've talked with your father."

"I guess we can talk about it later, then," I say, opening my Mac with an aloofness that I do not feel.

Gaby brings a fresh carafe of coffee and Chase takes it from her to top off both of our mugs. The deep rich aroma of Columbian beans wafts through the morning breeze. I take a sip and murmur my appreciation to her before she goes inside. It is aromatic and robust, and not the slightest bit bitter, the same coffee we drink when we are in Aruba. I feel his intent gaze upon me and look up. His eyes, deep green and molten, capture mine and it's hard to discern the fleeting emotion or turn away.

I pull my eyes away with difficulty; calling on my resolve, forcing myself to focus on the work at hand. I begin responding to emails, hoping Chase will leave me on my own. Instead, he sips his coffee and begins to concentrate on his MacBook. I steal a moment to gaze at him over the top of my computer. His eyes are hooded and controlled, focused on his work, seemingly unaffected by the distance between us.

I half-heartedly peruse my emails completely distracted. I see several from Jenny noticing she has been online extremely late each night. My heart hurts knowing she is recovering from a brutal attack endured at the hands of her boyfriend.

The sound of Chase's phone pulls me from my reverie and I look up to see him watching me intently. I don't know how long I have been in thought. "Hi Dad," he says, pausing to listen for a few moments. "No, Brian's got everything under control operationally. His father would be proud of the man he has become. I know, I'm going to miss having him around, too, but it's time." He pauses for a moment before responding. "Yes, we've got security tightened for everyone. I know it's an imposition for her family, but it's necessary, and it will only be for a short while," he says before laughing out loud. "So true, Dad. By the way, did the attorneys get back to you with information on Torzial?" he asks.

I look up at the mention of Jenny's company and connect with his watchful gaze. "I'm glad that Jenny and her company have been cleared of any wrongdoing," he says before disconnecting.

"Jenny and Torzial were officially exonerated?" I ask.

"Yes, it's over for her. She will never be at the mercy of Ty's blackmailing or vicious attacks again," Chase says.

"It's hard for me to know what to say. On the one hand, I appreciate that you took care of it and on the other, well, you know..."

The sound of my father's ringtone on Chase's cell phone interrupts us and he picks up the call. "Chase here. No, we'll meet you for an early lunch and then I'd like to discuss something with you privately afterward," he says. I look up and he is still watching me. "Yes, she's working with me right now," he says.

"Your parents will meet us for lunch a little later," Chase says.

"That will give me enough time to catch up a little bit," I say, just capturing a glimpse of his upturned brows before lowering my eyes. After a couple hours, I am no longer able to concentrate, so I power down my laptop and decide to ask what has been weighing on my mind.

"What are you and my father meeting about? I know it has to do with Prince Alfreita, but why do you have to talk to him before you tell me what's going on?" I ask.

He looks at me with a strange intensity and I watch as a mix of emotions play across his features. His jaw is taut and I can feel the tension radiating off of him from across the table.

"Katarina, it is impossible to keep you sheltered from things when you ask me a question like that. You may not want to hear the truth," he says.

"I'm pretty sure I already know the worst. I just want our lives to go back to the way they were without fear that our family will be kidnapped or come under attack. I know whatever you and my father are doing is for the long term safety of our family, but that doesn't mean I have to agree with the manner in which things have been handled to this point," I say.

"You want everyone we love and care about safe, don't condone what needs to happen to ensure it but still want to know what is being planned?" he asks, eyes raised in challenge and inquiry.

I sigh. "I don't think that's too much to ask. I'd like to know what to be prepared for. Right now, I feel like you and my father are making plans that I won't agree with but that I'll be expected to be involved in. Chase, for as long as we've known each other you've told me that I need to be open and honest with you. I'm trying to do just that. I want to be included in the strategy if I'm expected to be part of the plan," I say.

He nods and I see a moment of uncertainty flash through his eyes. "Let's eat lunch with your parents and after I meet with your father we can talk about the details," he says, rubbing his thumb thoughtfully along his bottom lip. It is distracting, and I hope he is unable to tell the effect it is having on me.

He stands up and pulls my chair out for me taking my hand in his. "We are just newly engaged. It would seem appropriate to be holding hands as we walk in to meet your parents," he says by way of explanation. They are sitting at the table, his arm draped casually around her shoulders and she is softly laughing. My mom is the first one up as we walk into the room and sweeps me into her arms. "Congratulations on your engagement. I'm so happy for both of you," she says, looking from me to Chase.

"Thanks, Mom," I say embarrassed by her exuberance. "It's good to see you, Carlos," I say, as Chase guides me to an open chair with a hand on the small of my back and then pushes it in for me as I am seated.

"Yes, congratulations to both of you," Carlos says, pouring each of us a glass of wine from the bottles that are nestled in a basket on the table. "I couldn't have been more pleased when Chase asked me for your hand. Our families have been friends for years, and I can't think of a more suitable man to marry my daughter than Chase. Donn and I are ecstatic with the arrangement," he says, placing his arm on my mom's shoulder.

I look from my father to Chase trying to sort out my feelings about this. I understand why Chase talked to my dad before he asked me to marry him. The families have been friends for years, and it would probably have been rude not to do that, but I am a grown woman, and I've had a father for about five minutes of my adult life. He certainly doesn't have any right to say yes or no to who I marry. While he probably didn't mean it that way, having a father is new to me, and I am still unclear of his involvement in the Miami incident. I hope in time to feel less awkward in his company.

A hand on my thigh brings me back to the present. I look up at Chase, and he raises a brow in question as he continues to regale my parents with highlights of our trip. My mother is inquisitive, asking the one question I was hoping to avoid. "So, have you two set a date? We were a little surprised you were coming back so soon, until we learned you wanted to share the news with us before we read it in the papers. That was really sweet of you, Katie," she says.

"We're still talking about it, Mom," I say, trying to avoid the penetrating green eyes that are regarding me warily. Nothing escapes my mother, and she is not to be put off. "So what's there to talk about?" she asks.

I inwardly sigh and glare at Chase who has left this awkward explanation up to me and does not appear to be coming to my rescue. I don't want to lie to my parents and decide to take the honest approach.

"Mom, our life is in constant turmoil right now. I just found out that I have a dad and an entire family that I've barely just met. I always envisioned needing you to walk me down the aisle having no male relatives in my life. It's all changed in the matter of a few weeks, and I'd like a chance to get to know my father a little better before our big day. I don't think there's any rush," I explain. I look up and feel guilty as I see the emotion in my father's eyes and feel the magnetism of Chase's intensity. I don't have to glance at him to know the look I will see, it is emblazoned on my memory.

"Katarina, the family is having a gathering at our home Saturday night in honor of your recent engagement and Karissa's return. I'd like very much for you and Chase to stay the weekend with us. There is plenty of room and Donn and Emily will also be in attendance," he says.

I glance at my mother. "Mom, how do you feel about that? The last time we spoke you were frightened to death of anyone knowing of your existence," I say.

"Your dad talked to the family about why I left. Suffice it to say, I am no longer worried and we've put that chapter behind us," she says, glancing at my father. I am embarrassed by the intimate look that flashes between them and avert my eyes, only to have Chase capture my gaze with his own.

"Katarina, Jay, will have teams in place to ensure everyone's safety if that makes you feel any better," Chase says.

"While I can't say I'm a huge fan of all the security, it does make me feel better after the last few weeks, especially with Alfreita still out there. I'd like to stay the weekend if that's okay. The uncles and cousins I met last week were so busy trying to find out who kidnapped mom that we really didn't have much chance to talk or get to know each other," I say.

"Perfectly fine with me," Chase says.

"Excellent," Carlos says, squeezing my mom's shoulders. I feel the magnetism of his eyes on me and look up. Chase is watching me intently and his mouth quirks in that way I have come to know. The tension between us is palpable and raw and it takes a concentrated effort to avert my gaze.

A light lunch of arugula, tomatoes and cucumbers is served with a fillet of grilled salmon that has been lightly marinated in olive oil and cracked pepper. When we finish our meal, Chase pours each of us a glass of wine. "Ladies, Carlos and I have business to discuss. We won't be long," he says, before leaving us to catch up.

"So, it appears that you and Carlos have gotten a lot closer during the short time Chase and I were away," I tease, smiling at the blush rising on her cheeks.

She looks wistful. "We have a second chance to be together, but I need to know that you're okay with this," she says.

I contemplate her question. It is clear that he loves her. He has kept her portraits over his fireplace at his home in New York for all these years and helped Chase invoke a full-blown mission to find her and bring her home to me. "Mom, I just want you to be happy, and it's clear to see how much you care about him. I'm thrilled that I have a father and in time we'll get to know each other better," I say, hoping that I will not always feel so suspicious, uncomfortable and awkward in his presence.

"I didn't think I was going to make it and all I kept thinking about was the chance to see you and your dad again," she says, wiping a single tear that has escaped and is gently running down her cheek.

The trauma of her recent kidnapping has apparently taken its toll and I feel a sense of anger at the man responsible for this. "Mom, please don't cry. I love you, and I am thrilled that you have a second chance with Dad. It's clear he's as much in love with you today as he ever was," I say. She dries her eyes and I squeeze her hand from across the table.

"Do we know what the plans are for Saturday?" I ask, diverting her attention to the family gathering being organized in New York for our engagement.

"Carlos has had a planner taking care of the details but they are planning to fly both families in for the celebration. I haven't seen some of them since my wedding and many of them I don't know at all.

"It's heartwarming to see you so happy, Mom," I say.

"Thanks, Sweetie. I couldn't be happier, and I'm ecstatic about you and Chase. I'm looking forward to this weekend, but I don't have a thing to wear," she says.

"Oh, sure says the lady with two walk-in closets full of clothing," I say.

"I'm pretty sure I'll need to go shopping for a new dress before the weekend," she says.

"I think you'll probably need some help," Carlos says, as he and Chase return, taking their seats at the table. He squeezes my mom's shoulder and she blushes. I roll my eyes skyward and glance at Chase. He smiles, but it does not reach his eyes and his jaw is tense.

"Ladies the travel arrangements are set. We'll fly into New York Saturday afternoon and spend the weekend with the Larussio family," Chase says.

He glances at his phone. "Now, if you will excuse us, Katarina and I have a conference call for the Prestian Medical Facility project that we need to sign into," he says, taking my hand. I don't recall seeing anything on my calendar for this afternoon but follow in his stead. The door to his office is barely closed before he pulls me into his arms. He does not kiss me and it is not sexual. I look up and his eyes are tremulous. He brings his lips to my forehead and smooths my hair.

"What's the matter, Chase?" I ask.

"Come and sit with me," he says, pulling me to the couch along the window that overlooks the shore of Lake Michigan. I follow silently, and my mind conjures up all sorts of things at the moment. *Did someone find out that he and my dad were behind the explosion in Miami?*

I pop off my shoes and tuck my feet under me on the sofa in an attempt to warm myself from the chill that has set in. Chase sits on the love seat across from me and I eye him warily. *What is he going to tell me?*

"Katarina, I needed to speak with your dad before we talked to make him aware that I was going to fill you in on the details of what's been planned since he is involved." He does not give me a chance to comment. "While this is still against my better judgment, and he is in complete disagreement with me sharing this with you, I understand your need to know the truth," he says.

I feel my heart catch. *How much more is there, is it worse than what I already know?* "Tell me," I encourage, hoping he does not see through my false sense of bravado.

"You already know that Prince Alfreita is behind the kidnapping of your mom. What you don't know is why."

"I thought he was trying to get you to deliver a shipment to replace the one they blamed you for reporting last year."

"That's part of it, Katarina," he says.

"Alfreita has been working with a member of the Brazilian cartel for some time supplying the Middle East, but the shipment confiscated last year was intended to undercut your family's business in the United States. We don't know who he is working for or why, but we do know, now, that the head of the Brazilian cartel is not aware of his intent to try to gain a foothold in your family's market, only that they expect Alfreita to get the shipment he lost back and recover their losses. He received advancements for the job and did not return the money, instead he made assurances that he would get another shipment through."

"How does he intend to do that if he no longer has my mom?" I ask.

"I'm sure that's exactly what he's trying to figure out right now. We need to draw him out with the opportunity to do just that. We meant to locate him the night we rescued your mom, but our plan was thwarted by a mechanical aircraft difficulty outside of Saudi. We had to turn the plane around or the crew would have never made it." He shakes his head. "We were that close, Katarina," he says wistfully.

"We've had people working around the clock to locate him, but he knows we have significant intel, so he is extremely cautious. The element of surprise when we rescued your mom no longer exists. It means we have to create it or we will be the ones surprised."

"How do you intend to do that?" I ask.

"The only way we have right now is to create a window of opportunity. He realizes that I know who he is and that we were able to locate your mom through an extremely advanced intel system. After Miami, he must understand the Mafia is helping us and that they are aware of his plan to infiltrate the United States." I raise my eyebrows with his reference to my father and uncles as Mafia, but let him continue.

"If he thinks this, he has two choices. They will hide or come after us first. My assumption is he will do the latter, which means we need to act fast," he says.

"And you have a plan?" I ask.

"Yes, we do, and that's what we need to talk about. Katarina, we need to find Alfreita fast, and we'd like to use Saturday night as that opportunity," he says.

"What exactly would it involve?" I ask, hoping I appear relaxed and unflustered.

"It means we intentionally make sure Prince Alfreita is aware we will be moving a large shipment of drugs into the United States. If he can confiscate the product, he can repay the Cartel what they lost last year. If we dangle the carrot, I will put money on him going after the shipment," he says.

"I think it sounds risky and dangerous. Besides, you said you weren't a drug trafficker."

"Katarina, I told you I wouldn't lie to you. It obviously comes with risks, but I have to weigh the alternatives and we need the element of surprise. I am not a drug trafficker, but as you're aware, your father's family is more than heavily involved in the movement of the product."

"Chase, this was already planned before we went to Aruba, before you knew that he would elude your teams."

"It was a mitigation strategy we hoped not to need," Chase says.

"I see. Everything planned down to the greatest level of detail."

"Katarina, backup plans are essential. Prince Alfreita has been trying to overtake some of your family's territory both in Europe and now with shipments to the United States. While it's unclear why, he made a huge mistake when he took your mother hostage. You heard your father. He will not rest until he is no longer a menace to the family. You have to know that I feel the same way. If the threat is not removed, we will be looking over our shoulder for the rest of our lives," he says.

"How do you plan to make your intentions known? I would assume you don't just ask Nate to run an article that you are planning on moving a large shipment of illegal drugs into the United States," I say.

He narrows his eyes at my sarcasm. "Katarina, it's the only way and no we do it very carefully and thoughtfully. We will make the public aware we are having a party to celebrate our engagement, but will not release it until later in the week. Alfreita's team will not have time to compose a strike, but it should give them time to get as close to the property as we let them," he says as my eyebrows rise.

"What do you expect he will do?" I ask, trying to appear calm as I desperately try to control the fear that has immediately overtaken my senses.

"There's no doubt in my mind that he will put together an attempt to at least gather information. We won't give him enough latitude to make a play, but they'll know where we are and will no doubt deploy communication drones to gather intel, which means they will know what we are saying," he explains.

I shake my head. More James Bond espionage toys, no doubt. "Chase, what if they're listening now? What if while you're telling me your plans they can hear us and are one step ahead of you?" I ask.

"Katarina, our homes have protection against that type of breach, but Saturday night Carlos will have it disarmed. They will be able to hear us talking and will learn about the shipment."

"Chase, you're scaring the hell out of me. You mean that we are going to be sitting ducks," I say, even more upset now that I know what he intends.

"There will be more protection around his property than a small country. They know that, but it's going to be an opportunity they can't pass up. Besides, you will not be there," Chase says.

"Chase, talk to me. This is our engagement party, right? You don't want me to be with you, so I just wait for you and my parents to get attacked? What the hell are you thinking? You're just going to give away your position and let them come after you?"

"Katarina, we need to sign on to the conference shortly, but we're not going to be in danger. Trust me," he says.

I scowl at him. "We've already had this discussion, and right now I'm not even sure if I understand your plans well enough to even contemplate trusting them, or you. If you ask me, they're completely fucked up!" I exclaim.

His eyebrows rise. "Such language," he says, and his lips are upturned as he tries to suppress a smile.

"What is so funny to you?" I ask, furious at the level of criminal activity and danger swirling around me.

"I'm not laughing at you, Katarina. I just don't think I have ever heard that word come out of your mouth before," he says.

"You are going to hear it a lot more if you continue putting yourself in danger and keeping me in the dark!"

"You asked me to tell you. Please don't make me regret my decision," Chase says, closing the distance between us, pulling me into his arms, and kissing me with a passion that takes my breath away. "I love you, Katarina. There isn't anything I wouldn't do to make sure you and our families are safeguarded," he says, capturing my lips again. I know I should not succumb, but my body has a mind of its own, shamelessly pulling him closer, relishing in the feel of his arms around me.

I am breathless as he takes my hand, urging me onto the couch, pulling my skirt up as he eases me onto his lap. I balance myself, straddling his body, my legs bent on either side of his thighs, leaning forward to capture his lips with mine, caught up in the desire of the moment. He breaks our kiss gently, holding my face in his hands. His eyes are a storm of emotion. "Baby, I want you so badly, but not like this. Not just physically," he murmurs against my ear. My body is overcome by desire and passion and I shut out the images of death and injury that haunt my dreams.

"I don't know how we get there with everything that has happened but I don't think I can give up trying. We have things to work on but I want us to be together, not just physically either," I say, out of breath, kissing his mouth.

My lips part and he takes that moment to explore further, finding my tongue and deepening our kiss. He audibly groans and I gasp as he slides his hands underneath my skirt, grasping my hips and ass underneath my panties. I am helpless against my need for him, more than ready, wet and slick. He rocks me back and forth, his zipper comes down, and his hands position me upward, sliding my panties aside as he slowly brings me down... hard, allowing me to feel the entire length of cock.

"We were meant to be together, Baby," he says, shifting so that he is firmly and deeply rooted. I audibly gasp at the feel of his length in my lower belly. "Stay quiet, I want to see all of you," he says, as his fingers deftly unbutton my blouse. He takes his time and it is hard for me not to shift against him. "Still Baby, just feel me, deep inside of you," he says as my desire flares with need. He pushes my blouse from my shoulders and lets it slip away, and with one click of the front closure bra, my nipples are exposed to his gaze. They are erect with want, the brisk air and the intensity of his scrutiny. "So beautiful," he murmurs as his mouth finds them, sucking each one, in turn, warming them and making me squirm shamelessly. They are hardwired to the most intimate part of my body and I feel it deep in my core. It is hard for me to stay still. I balance myself, my hand on top of his muscular shoulders, and his hands on my hips steady me, keeping me in perfect rhythm as I glide over the top of him. He pulls me back onto him, deeper each time. I am right there, but he holds our rhythm, right on the brink, not allowing me to gain momentum. Instead, he pulls my hips flush against his body, rubbing deep inside of me.

I moan with need. "Baby, you're so close," he says, grasping my hips, pulling me onto him deeper and faster. We are climbing and climbing, he tells me to cum, his warm breath blowing in my ear, driving me over the edge and I can no longer hold back, climaxing around him, shaking and trembling as he grinds into me, prolonging my pleasure as he releases deep inside of me. I collapse against his chest, breathless, listening to the strong, steady heartbeat as he holds me close.

"Do you know how much I love you?" he asks, kissing me gingerly and pushing the hair out of my face.

"I love you, too, Chase, that was never the issue. I can't bear the thought of you in danger. Regardless of everything, I love you with all my heart," I say breathlessly, dismayed at the cracking in my voice and the command he has over my heart and my body. He knows me more intimately than anyone, emotionally and physically. I have gone a day without him and it has seemed like an eternity.

"This will be over soon," he says, kissing me warmly on the lips before his office line rings.

"Chase here," he answers, smiling widely as he tries to balance me on his lap and reaches over to hit the desk intercom.

"Chase, I have you dialed into the conference. It should start momentarily."

"Thanks, Lois," he says, putting the call back on mute while we quickly take turns freshening up in the adjoining bathroom. The conference lasts a couple hours and I find myself enthralled with the conversations around the expansion of the model and projected outcomes on a national level.

"Now I understand why you wanted to develop an infrastructure for the design work," I say when the conference is over.

"Yes, the effort you've put into the model will provide the platform, but this is going to be no easy feat," he says.

"If it were, we'd be doing the wrong work," I say.

"Indeed," he says.

"I'm glad you included me in the conference. Do you know when we'll need to have work completed for the other communities interested in the model?"

"No, I thought your teams could help with the timeline development and rollout," he says.

"They can. We've already hired an excellent group of project managers," I say, avoiding reference to my involvement in future projects. I had intended to make a clean break. Who the hell was I kidding? I can't stay away from him for two days, much less a lifetime.

"I honestly don't think I've been this excited about a project since I first heard about the Prestian Medical facility," I say.

"I'm glad you're pleased, Katarina."

"We'll have to step up the pace on the structure Jenny and I put together for the Torzial Division of Prestian Corp. We laid out most of the details before we left for Aruba," I say.

"I need to send Jenny a note to bring her up to speed on the negotiations, but I'll leave the details to the two of you."

"Sounds good. I was going to give her a call a little later in the afternoon. We've been talking every day since the rape, but I haven't heard from her yet today," I say.

"She's been working long days at the office, but has been seeing the psychologist she told us about." he says.

"You have someone assigned to Jenny's security?" I ask, knowing the answer before he replies.

"I do, I don't think it's likely that Ty will try to see her again, but he's in bed with some pretty rough characters and I want to make sure she's safe," he says.

I hug him to me tightly and kiss him on the lips. "I think I'm going to get a little work done and give Jenny a call," I say, trying to keep my thoughts at bay with his reference to bad characters.

I head toward our bedroom to find my phone. I'm not sure where we now stand, if anything, it's just become more complicated. Nothing about what Chase has done has changed, but I know that I don't want to be without him. The sun is shining brightly through the windows. I open the french doors and walk out onto the balcony. The air is a little brisk, but nice, and I settle into one of the patio chairs.

"Siri, call Jenny."

"Torzial, this is Jenny," she says, answering on the second ring.

"Hi there."

"I was just wondering when I would get my daily call," she says.

"I'm just worried about you."

"I know, Kate."

"How are you doing today?" I ask.

"Just trying to keep busy," she says.

"Anything you feel like talking about?" I press gently.

"No, day by day it's getting a little better. Now that all the legal stuff with Torzial is over, I'm just focusing on the company," she says.

"Did Chase send you an update on the project, yet?"

"Yes, in fact, I was just skimming over it when you called. It seems to be moving rather quickly," Jenny says.

"Chase was right, since the national outcomes from the Houston model came out the phones haven't stopped ringing."

"They certainly should be," she says.

"The design phase for the Chicago facilities is coming along nicely. We demonstrated the exam room simulation to the project team before our trip. I included the cost of each model, not only to build but to run in terms of energy consumption. They settled on the option we were hoping they would. The savings came in well above what was projected. We'll end up saving approximately 3.5 million for the Chicago project alone," I say.

"Kate, that's wonderful. What an accomplishment," she says.

"Thanks, Jenny. The second facility in Chicago will be modeled off the first, and as we've discussed, should significantly decrease the amount of effort we need to put into that phase. I sat in on a conference with Chase today and we reviewed the Houston data. It's delivering some pretty fantastic quality outcomes. There is significant interest and Chase has asked us to put a long-term strategy and project plan together for the national expansion," I say.

"I didn't think it would happen so quickly, but we should be in good position to move quickly. We're definitely going to need more space, though. Chase sent me a note while you were in Aruba, letting me know The Prestian Corp towers in Chicago and New York both have floors that could be utilized for Torzial. He thought it would be ideal, since he envisions the two of you traveling to New York quite often," she says.

"I agree. It would make perfect sense for Torzial to have a location in both Chicago and New York," I say.

"Christy has already started the process of screening applications for a few of the additional positions we'll need, but we'll require much more support.

"How did the conversation go with Chase about keeping her on as head of human resources?" I ask.

"Good, actually. The entire department will become Prestian Corp employees, and we'll lease services instead of having duplicate units. Christy will remain in charge of our division, with a bump in pay and a new title. She was pretty happy about the arrangement and has already started coordinating interviews for the expansion. I asked her to reach out to you to find out how you wanted to handle all of your open positions," she says.

"Sounds good, Jenny. I'd like to get the lean consultants on board as quickly as possible. In the meantime, I'll put the finishing touches on the training material. On a personal note, Chase and I are engaged if you haven't heard already," I say, smiling at the squeal on the other end of the phone and filling her in on the details before disconnecting.

THREE

The wind off Lake Michigan is beginning to pick up and the temperature is starting to drop. I reach for the remote control and turn on the overhead heaters on the deck to warm the air. A couple hours later, I feel satisfied that the training and onboarding plan will allow for quick and efficient expansion. I change into one of my new dresses, a long sleeve, cream colored sweater number that fits the curves of my body perfectly. I couple it with a large brown leather belt and my new brown slouchy boots before wandering downstairs.

I find Chase and my father in the great room deeply engrossed in conversation. They look up as I walk in and the exchange immediately discontinues. I try to hide my annoyance, but I see Chase's eyebrows raise in question. I turn towards the bar and pour myself a glass of wine before taking a seat beside them.

"So, do we have a script for Saturday night or are we just going to wing it?" I ask.

Surprise flashes over my father's face and Chase attempts to hide his amusement from my dad.

"Carlos, your daughter likes to be made aware of situations so she isn't taken by surprise. Reminds me a lot of you at times," Chase says.

"Katarina, we haven't finalized plans for Saturday, but there will be a set of guidelines for people in attendance and scripting for individual conversations," he says, watching me guardedly.

"Were you working on the plans for Saturday night when I came in?" I ask.

"We were talking about Saturday night, but not with any degree of detail. We have a lot of work to do to ensure things go smoothly," my father says evenly.

I raise my eyebrows in question and swirl my drink. Chase is watching us, amused at the exchange and father-daughter standoff. I am about to question him further when Mom walks into the room. She has changed into a clingy bright blue cashmere dress with black boots. Her short auburn hair is spiky, and her blue eyes are shining brightly. It's clear that Carlos has lost interest in anything but her.

Chase comes to stand by my side placing his arm around me, caressing the top of my shoulder blades with his thumb. The tension I feel at being kept in the dark begins to subside and I find myself leaning into him as my body starts to relax and heat under his touch. I start at the sound of my mother's voice. "What do you think, Katarina?" she asks. *Think about what; Chase's hand rubbing my body and my moistening panties? Jeez, pay attention.*

"What did you say, Mom?" I inquire, attempting to suppress a scowl at the smile on Chase's face.

"I was asking if you would like to go shopping for Saturday night?" she says.

I am at a loss for words. They have obviously not made Mom aware of the plans, and I would prefer not to be the one to tell her. I feel Chase's hand squeeze my shoulder and look up. He moves his head side to side slightly. *Is he telling me not to go?* How does he know what I'm thinking?

"Mom, I just went shopping with Jenny before Chase and I went to Aruba, and as you can imagine, I have plenty of clothes. You can't shop with Jenny and walk out of a store empty-handed. Besides that, I've taken a lot of time off work lately, and Jenny and I are in the middle of finalizing the structure for the Prestian Corp division of Torzial. Maybe you and Dad could go shopping this time," I suggest.

Chase looks down at me and winks, while his fingers extend around the back of my neck underneath my hair, spreading warmth throughout my body. My lips part and I can feel my body's physical reaction to him. I barely comprehend the overall conversation as he guides me into the dining room behind my mom and dad.

My parents are talkative and lively at dinner. I find myself relaxing and even laughing at a few of my dad's silly jokes and some of the tension from earlier dissipates. Chase and my dad have known each other for a very long time, and it's clear that both respect the other a great deal. Carlos knows a lot about Chase's business successes and talks about his accomplishments with evident pride, sharing stories about his earlier adventures with my mom and me. I am becoming much more comfortable with them being together after tonight.

I look over at Chase and his lips are twisted in a smirk. I wink at him, and he raises his eyebrows in inquiry. I am awarded an amused smile.

My cell vibrates.

Message: Are you flirting with me?

Reply: I am...

Message: I have delicious punishments for just this type of behavior.

It is my turn to raise my eyebrows in inquiry. Just what does Chase have on his mind? I narrow my eyes at him, but he is not giving anything away. My mom is asking a question and he controls his smile at my obvious disadvantage. I have not been listening again.

"Katarina, your mom was asking if you wanted to attend any of the bridal shows in New York," he says, coming to my rescue.

I answer my mom, grateful for his catch, and wonder how he manages to follow the conversation when we are bantering back and forth. The long day, filling meal and wine are starting to take effect. I suppress a yawn and it does not go unnoticed. Chase says good night to everyone and excuses us for the evening, putting his arm around me as we head upstairs. As we enter the bedroom, he pulls me into his arms capturing my lips with his own. "Do you want me to go, Katarina?"

"Stay with me, Chase. I don't know how to move forward after the last few days, but I'd like to try," I say.

"You need only ask once, Baby. Let's get you out of this dress and into bed. I want to feel your bare skin next to mine," he says, before lifting my dress over my head and discarding it on the floor. He takes his time, tracing his finger from my lips, down the side of my neck and then softly caressing my already erect nipples. "So beautiful, Baby," he says, lifting me effortlessly and placing me on the bed before he undresses himself and lies down beside me. He pulls me close, his powerful thigh sliding in between mine, entwining me and drawing me near, skin on skin so that I can feel the rigidity of his arousal against my belly. His lips are warm against mine, and he holds me close.

"Katarina, I don't want to rush this. You mean more than that to me, Baby. I need you to talk to me, to tell me what you're feeling," he says, brushing the hair out of my eyes.

He cares enough to ask. I know I need to be honest with him, but I don't know how to put it into words. There is a pregnant pause before he takes my chin in his. "Tell me, whatever it is," he says.

"When I walked into the dining room you and my father stopped talking. It makes me feel like you're hiding something. I'm scared Saturday night is going to be another repeat of Miami and people are going to get hurt, and that you and my father may be the cause of it," I say, finally, trying to discern the emotion stirring in his eyes.

He keeps me held tightly against his lower body with his thighs but lifts up onto one elbow so he can look down into my eyes. "Katarina, your father and I were talking about Saturday night, but no one is going to get hurt. We've already leaked news of a pending shipment which is what will draw them to us. Alfreita and his teams will most likely be able to hear everything that goes on within your father's compound, but that's all. His men won't do anything to disrupt the shipment, only learn about it, which means they will be listening and reporting back what they hear. I promise you, nothing will happen on Saturday, except for an orchestrated exchange of information," he assures, kissing my forehead with his lips.

"My dad didn't want to talk about it with me," I say.

He sighs. "No, he didn't Katarina. Your mother learning the truth about his criminal activities is why she left. He doesn't want to take a chance that either of you would discover the extent of his past activities for fear of losing you. You have to know I have the same reservations about sharing too much with you, Baby," he says, capturing my thighs as he rolls on top of me. His lips find mine and his hands begin to explore my body and I soon find myself overcome with longing and succumb to his slow and unhurried lovemaking.

FOUR

The clock on the nightstand registers five a.m. I pull on a robe and go in search of Chase, finding him at the kitchen table engrossed in his Mac. He is drinking a tall glass of orange juice in his sweats and a t-shirt.

"I woke up and you were already gone. Good workout?" I ask.

"Yes, couldn't sleep so I thought I'd get a little work done," he says, barely looking up from his computer.

"What's wrong?" I ask.

"Lot's going on, but nothing that should concern you," he says.

I scowl at him, but he doesn't notice, intent on whatever it is that he is reading.

"Chase, I thought you were going to keep me apprised as things came up," I say.

He looks up and his eyes capture mine, softening. "Baby, I'm sorry. It's not my intent to keep you in the dark. There are a lot of small details and logistics involved in Saturday night's effort, but nothing for you to be worried about. You and your mother will be safe here until your father and I return.

"Yeah, about that," I start.

"Katarina, your safety is priority one. You are not going to be anywhere near that house when this goes down, Baby," he says, pulling me into his lap.

"How can you tell me in one breath not to worry about anything, we have more security than a small country, and then in the next say I'm not going to be anywhere near it? Clearly, it's going to be dangerous if you don't want me there. What about you and my dad?" I ask.

He regards me warily, and his eyes take on that hooded and controlled look that I have come to know so well. "Baby, I would never allow your mother to be put in harm's way. She will need to stay home and care for her ill daughter. As for your father, he will be with me," he says.

"If you two have everything planned down to the very detail, instead of making me wonder about this stuff, why didn't you just tell us? My mom thinks she is going to our engagement party and she's excited, Chase. She's even going out to buy a new dress," I say.

"Katarina, the plans are coming together nicely, but not everything is finalized. I thought you were okay with this last night," he says, nuzzling my forehead with his nose.

"I was, I mean, I am... but, I guess I just want to know the details. I can't help thinking that this could turn out very badly. I'm scared, Chase." He pushes the hair out of my eyes and captures my lips with an intense and feral need, parting them, invading my mouth with his tongue. My body responds shamelessly, all thought of argument tossed aside as desire sparks deep inside of me.

"Baby, I will keep you safe and protected. It frustrates me greatly that you don't understand that," he says, rubbing his thumb across my lower lip. I am entranced and capture his thumb in my mouth, sucking it, licking it with my tongue and then nipping it with my teeth, hard. The sexual tension between us is palpable. His eyes darken, molten and hot as he scoops me up and carries me to the elevator that opens into our master suite. My body is pressed tightly against his, my legs wrapped around his waist as we enter the bathroom. When he lets me down, it is slow and deliberate, like a well-choreographed dance step. I slide along the length of him and he holds me close, letting me down easy while pressing my body against the evidence of his arousal. My mouth is dry, and I feel myself moisten under the intensity of his gaze. The passion in his eyes is riveting as he pushes the robe from my shoulder and slips the white lacy nightgown over my head, tossing it carelessly onto the vanity. I am standing nude before him, left without panties after last night's tryst. He kisses me roughly, finding my tongue, exploring deeply while rubbing the sensitive and erect tips of my nipples.

"Baby, stand right where you are. I love looking at you," he says, as he undresses. His body is a mass of lean and sinewy muscle. When he moves his thighs flex, and the muscles in his abdomen ripple as he bends down to start the whirlpool. He pours my favorite chamomile scented bath oil into the bubbling waters, gets in and dips below the water, rinsing off before taking my hand to steady and guide me into the swirling bath. He pulls me into his lap, straddling his body, my legs on either side of his powerful thighs. I take him in my hands, just below the water and stroke his hardness, relishing in the rigidity and girth, feeling his growing need, along with my own.

"Baby, I want to be deep inside of you," he says, guiding my body up and over his cock. He lowers me and I slowly engulf his length, gasping, as he slides deeper inside of me until he is firmly rooted. He brushes the tips of my nipples and then takes one into his mouth, warming me and then sucking harder. I can feel it deep in my core and moan softly, attempting to rise and shift against him, but he keeps me held firmly.

"Slow, Baby, just let yourself feel this," he says as his finger grazes my clit, just lightly underneath the water, teasing me gently before beginning to stroke her. He is unhurried, watching me intently as he takes turns suckling both nipples while caressing me. I can feel the throbbing and fullness of his cock deep inside of me and yearn to move my body against him.

"I'm right there," I murmur, unable to suppress the building need any longer.

"Baby, this is going to be over much sooner than I wanted. God, I want you," he says, moving me up slowly, allowing me to feel his entire length before sliding me down hard on his cock, deep and fast, over and over as we climb out of control and are left holding each other breathless and spent. I rest my head on his chest and listen to his rapidly beating heart. He pulls me close and kisses the top of my head, before turning the faucet to warm the water around us.

"Lean back and relax for a few minutes. I'll pour us both a cup of coffee," Chase says, getting out of the whirlpool. He wipes the beads of water running down his torso, buttocks and down the back of his thighs with a towel before securing it around his waist. My eyes are riveted on his masculinity, and when I look up, his mouth is turned up in a quirk and his eyebrows are raised.

"It'll keep until later," I murmur, attempting to keep the embarrassment from my voice at being caught checking him out so intently. I slide deeper into the aromatic water relishing in the feel of the bubbling jets around me and can't help but smile.

He returns with two mugs of coffee. The bold Columbian aroma and hazelnut extract he has put into mine wafts through the air as he places both cups on the ledge and slides into the whirlpool behind me. He pulls me against his body and maneuvers his legs on top of mine, pulling them apart under the bubbling silky water.

"There, now let yourself relax while we talk about Saturday night. I want to make sure every question you have is answered and that your fears are put to rest for good. I hate that you're so upset," he says, nuzzling my neck.

"You will see an article written by Nate about the engagement party in the newspaper on Thursday. We didn't want to give Alfreita's men too much lead, but enough so he can get organized. They will know we have security in position, and more than likely, will be watching and listening from a distance with multiple broadband communication devices and drones. You will unexpectedly take ill and be unable to attend. Your mother will need to stay with you, and as you know, she is not yet aware of this."

"Is that why you didn't want me to go shopping with her?" I ask, leaning back against the strength of his chest.

"No, it's because I don't want you in public with Carlos until this dies down and I knew he would want to go with her."

"I don't understand. Why don't you want me out with my father?" I ask, taking a sip of the coffee.

"Katarina, Carlos is the head of the largest crime syndicate in the United States. While he may no longer be active in the transfer of the supply, your family very much is, and his demise would undoubtedly make things a lot easier for Alfreita and his men right now," he says.

I sigh. "I wasn't thinking along those lines. I take it Dad has adequate security," I say.

"He does, but I'm not willing to take any chances with you and your mother. Carlos and I will attend the celebration. We'll make our apologies for the evening and let everyone know that another gathering will be arranged when you are feeling better."

"Did you invite, Nate?" I ask

"I did. In fact, I'll be meeting with him soon to go over some of the press release highlights," he says.

"So you intend to handle things down to the smallest of detail? That doesn't surprise me in the least," I say.

"Carlos is flying all of your family in for the event because it has to look real. He and I will have a quiet conversation, which if I were a betting man, will undoubtedly be picked up on their telecommunication devices. Once they confirm what we leak about the shipment is true, they are going to want to learn more. In fact, Alfreita will demand it. This will allow us to draw him out, track and find him. Right now he has gone off the grid, and our teams can't locate him. That's all that is going to happen on Saturday, Katarina. The real work begins once they take the bait. The shipment will lure him out, but he'll be careful, and our intel teams will need to monitor the waves twenty-four hours a day to find him. Jay's working to get the units in place and setting up the communications teams and logistics as we speak. Once we know they are interested in the shipment and we can track them..." He shrugs. "Then, the rest is easy," he says.

"The rest of what is easy?" I ask.

He nuzzles the back of my neck and pushes my legs farther apart with his own. The scent of chamomile drifts through the air as the bubbling water stirs. His hand covers my mound under the water, and his fingers begin to explore. "Baby, I think you've had enough story time for one day," he whispers in my ear.

FIVE

The next day is a whirlwind of activity. I sign onto the video conference, and after a few moments, Jenny appears on the screen. "Sorry I'm late, Kate. You're never going to believe this, but it looks like we are going to be neighbors sooner than we thought. Apparently, Chase put some pressure on the company remodeling the Torzial floor of Prestian Corp. Sounds like it will be move-in ready in about two weeks."

"That's great, Jenny."

"We'll move into the Chicago facility first, and as we hire, we'll expand into the New York City offices," she says.

"You sound excited," I say, delighted that she is so animated.

"I am, I think it's just what I need right now. It's going to be great to work together in the same place again. You know going out to lunch, taking long walks on beautiful days," Jenny says.

"Absolutely."

We begin working on the new Torzial structure, along with the plan to transition Torzial and all of its employees from its current location into the Prestian Corp Towers.

"We've been working for hours," Jenny says. "Why don't we take a break and sign back on in an hour? I could use lunch," she says.

"Sounds like a good idea. Gaby is cooking something that smells delicious," I say before we sign off. I find Gaby in the kitchen just bringing out a bubbly golden apple pie from her stainless steel Viking oven.

"That's what smelled so good," I say.

"If you're looking for Chase, he and your father have been locked in the study for most of the day. They didn't even come out for lunch. I told Chase I would bring it in for them, but he said they would get something a little later," Gaby says, shaking her head in obvious disapproval.

"I'll take them something," I say, lifting the lid on the crockpot which is full of chicken noodle soup. The steam escapes, releasing the pungent smell of thyme, sweet carrots and freshly roasted chicken into the air. I begin ladling the thick soup full of egg noodles into bowls while Gaby cuts a few slices of fresh warm bread and starts to spread it with sweet Irish cream butter. I reach over and select a piece, savoring the taste, earning a playfully stern look from Gaby before sending Chase a quick text to warn him of my impending interruption.

Message: Gaby tells me you haven't eaten yet.

Reply: I have not. Is that an invitation?

Message: Behave yourself! Aren't you with my dad?

Reply: He has it under control. I'm interested. I know how sweet you are.

I smile, moistening at his last comment and quickly turn my attention back to the task at hand. Gaby pulls a serving tray from one of the lower cabinets, and we load the soup, bread and two large slices of freshly baked apple crumble pie onto it. It is still piping hot, and the aroma of cinnamon and nutmeg permeate my senses as I carry the food into the study. Sid is on speaker phone talking about communication devices and the latest technological advances and my dad and Chase are sitting across from each other with computers open in front of them.

"Sid, hold onto your thoughts for a moment. Katarina took pity on us and has brought us lunch," my father says smiling at me. I try to hide my disappointment at his blatant attempt to curtail the conversation, and Chase looks up to catch the exchange, winking at me.

"Carlos, my fiancée is quite ingenious. See, she has brought us bowls of hot soup, fresh bread and Gaby's homemade apple pie to find out what we are doing behind these walls. She is ever curious about our operations and hates to be left in the dark," he says, smiling at me with that imperious quirk.

"So, are you going to fill me in?" I ask, ignoring his fiancée remark and scowling at his attempt to placate me.

"Katarina, right now we're just in the initial stages of planning the communication stations and devices the teams will need. Sid and his overseas crew have ears and eyes on many of Alfreita's known hang-outs, but we've got nothing so far. He's very careful. We're hoping to have a well-laid-out plan by the end of the day and then we can fill you in on the details," Chase says, ignoring Carlos's upraised eyebrows and apparent disapproval.

"Katarina, Chase is right. We just don't know enough right now," my dad says, attempting to soothe me.

"Very well, I'll leave you to your spy fun. I need to get back to work developing the infrastructure that will support my fiancé's financial ventures," I say, unable to keep the smile from my lips at the look of surprise on my dad's face and Chase's wide tooth grin.

I turn and close the door to the study, serving myself a bowl of soup and helping of bread in the kitchen before heading toward the library to get signed onto the video session with Jenny. By the end of the day, we have all the structural components and plans in place for both phase one and two of the Torzial expansion and have even set key milestones and criteria for beginning expansions into New York City. We finish up the details and chat for a little while longer before I sign off and go in search of my mom who I find pouring a glass of wine for herself in the great room.

"I wasn't sure if you were finished working today or not," I say.

"Yes, I just ended the last call. The entire day was spent developing a campaign for a new client. When I first took him on he seemed pretty low-key, but he's turned out to be quite cantankerous and high maintenance. A real pain in the ass," she says, taking a sip of her wine.

"Have you seen Chase or Dad?" I ask, laughing at the wild stories about her new client.

"No, but your dad sent me a text a short while ago and said they may be working late," she says.

"Well we should probably head to the dining room before Gaby sends a search party after us," I say.

"The men are eating in the study again tonight," Gaby informs us with a shake of her head as my mom and I sit down to dinner. She serves roasted Cornish game hen on a large platter encircled with parsley leaves, baby Yukon gold potatoes and green beans. She has paired the meal with a white chardonnay that has a floral character mixed with a sweet intensity of fruit.

"Where are the servers?" I ask, recalling Chase's insistence that Gaby stop doing so much.

"Shh... don't get him started on that again," she says, sashaying out of the room and back to the kitchen.

"If she's not careful Chase is going to renegotiate her contract and give her more help than she ever wanted," I say, laughing at the thought.

The meal is delicious, and by the end of the evening I am quite relaxed and a little tired after such a full day. "I think I'm going to retire a little early and catch up on some reading," I say, hugging my mom before heading upstairs.

I am freshly showered and sitting up in bed when Chase enters the bedroom. He looks tired, and I wonder how much they have accomplished, and while I am curious, I try to curtail my curiosity.

"Did you get something to eat... for supper," I clarify, blushing as I recall our earlier banter.

"Gaby brought dinner in for us, but it was not by any means what I was hungry for,"

he says, taking in the low cut bodice of my white negligee while removing his tie and jacket.

"I find your outfit quite enticing, but it may be missing something," he says, sitting on the bed beside me.

"What would be missing?" I ask as he lifts my hair, kissing the sensitive skin of my neck.

"You see, I envision you gilded in the finest jewelry and lace, moaning as I do shocking and stimulating things to you," he says, holding up a delicate necklace of silver and diamonds, adorned with circular rings that match the circular charms on my bracelet.

"Chase, it's magnificent," I say, fingering the strand of diamonds and brushing over the loops and clasp.

"Lift your hair and let me place it on your beautiful body," he says, clasping it behind my neck as I do.

"I'm going to take a quick shower now, Katarina. I want you to lay here and think about the meal I'll have when I return," he says, smirking as the blush rises onto my cheeks. I fluff my pillow and look into the ceiling mirror above, trying to keep the giddiness and anticipation of the night from getting to me, but when he walks back into the room, everything is lost. The light of the moon is shining into the bedroom and his skin glistens with droplets from his recent shower. He takes another step into the room to retrieve something from the dresser while I follow the view of his broad shoulders, enjoying the way they taper into a V shape down to his slim waist. My eyes are drawn to his powerful buttocks and thighs. He turns toward the bed, erect and masculine, watching me intently as he moves toward me and positions himself on the bed beside me.

He fingers the four dangling silver and diamond bracelets that adorn my left wrist, and with a twist, he separates them and holds them up for me to see. Each bracelet has an accompanying ring, and he swivels them around. My mouth is dry as he pulls the covers from the bed.

"Give me your ankle, " Chase says, rubbing the instep of my foot with his chin before securing it with one of the diamond bracelets and affixing it to the bed. "And the other," he instructs, doing the same with it as I offer it to him. "As pretty as this negligee is, I want to see all of you, Baby," Chase says, pulling the nightgown over my head. He captures my lips in a passionate kiss while securing my wrists to the headboard of our bed with the remaining two bracelets.

He moves slowly, kissing and sucking my lips, then my neck, moving leisurely down my body until he finds my erect nipples. His tongue teases one, while gently squeezing the other, the pressure going straight to my core.

"You like that don't you, Baby," he says, capturing the tender flesh with his teeth before sucking on it. He takes his time, nipping and sucking, flaming the desire that is already molten.

"Do you remember how it felt last time we played with hot and cold, on the verge between pleasure and pain?"

"Oh, God, yes," I murmur, recalling how he rubbed my nipples with ice and then heated them with rope.

"Patience, Baby. I think you need something to cool you down a bit first," he says, reaching toward the nightstand and placing a cube of ice on my sensitive nipple. He rubs it over me, swirling it in circles, traveling slowly from one to the other erect nub. My nipples are hardwired to the most sensitive part of my body, and I feel the heat deep in my core. I moan, and my hips rise from the bed.

"Still Baby," he says, rubbing the cubes from my breasts towards my navel and leaving it there. "I want you to see what I'm doing to you. Watch, Katarina."

I concentrate on the mirror that stretches from corner to corner in the tray ceiling above us. I have never felt more exposed and vulnerable as I do at this moment, but I am more turned on than I have ever been.

This is exactly how I envisioned you looking when I had these made," Chase says, fingering the delicate strand of diamonds and unclasping it from behind my neck. This jewelry was custom designed for you, Baby. You see, it is actually a nipple chain, and the clasps have a dual purpose. They are intended to hold the strand of diamonds around your neck by day, and meant to adorn your breasts at other times," he says, fingering one elongated nipple as he speaks.

My hips rise, but my restraints leave me immobile as I feel the heat of his touch and intensity of cold in my navel. "Easy, Baby. I want you to watch," he says, moving the ice cube along the length of my abdomen to trail across my nipples.

"Chase," I moan, as he rubs the sensitive skin with the frozen cubes.

"Shh, almost ready, Baby. I don't want you to experience any pain when I put them on you for the first time," he says, rolling the cube around my elongated nipples. "Are you ready?" he asks, placing the ice back in the glass beside him.

I can only nod, mesmerized as he places one of the clasps over my nipple. I feel a small degree of pressure as the diamond nipple ring snaps in place. "How's that, Baby?" he asks.

"So good," I say, acclimating to the pressure of the clamp, the icy prickly cold of my skin, and the warmth it's creating below.

He affixes the remaining ring to my other nipple before laying the silver and diamond chain over the swell of my breasts and across my skin. "So beautiful, Baby," he says, running his hands slowly over my waist, and around my hips. He is agonizingly slow in his journey, and I find myself rising to meet his touch.

"Patience, Baby," he says, tracing the two circular diamond rings that now adorn my erect nipples, before tugging lightly on the diamond strand.

I audibly gasp at the wave of sensation it causes.

"Shh..." he says, trailing his fingers and lips lightly over my heated skin, traveling lower and gently circling my mound, never touching my clit, but driving me wild with the heat of his breath. I feel myself continue to moisten, and my hips rise unashamedly, but he has secured me well, and his hands hold my hips still as he lowers himself between my legs.

"Watch, Baby," he whispers, and I can hear myself softly panting, my breathing heavy, anticipating his touch. He nuzzles his nose among the soft hair, stopping to inhale my scent, before finally caressing me with his tongue. He barely touches her, but it causes me to moan softly with need.

"Slow, Katarina," he says. He is gradual, unhurried and I squirm as my desire climbs. He holds me still, gently pulling at the long delicate chain attached to my nipples, stoking my need even further. I gasp at the intensity as he pulls the jewelry off forcing me to climax, trembling around him. He is merciless, taking my clit between his lips, drawing everything I have to give before releasing the bracelets that hold my ankles. He pulls my hips toward him and lifts my legs around his waist. His eyes are glazed with passion as he penetrates me, filling me completely. I moan at the depth and he pulls out agonizingly slow only to enter me again, deep. "Feel me inside of you, Baby," he says, sliding into that one particular spot, teasing, in and then out, back in, dipping slowly and leisurely renewing my desire.

He has not let go of my hips and when he quickens his pace he penetrates deeply, over and over against that spot deep inside of me until I hear myself moaning aloud, as we tremble with the force of our climax. He gently releases my wrists and curls in behind me, holding me close as our breathing returns to normal.

"Now, time for a little story," he says, turning me around so that I am resting on his chest. "The entire day was spent getting communication networks and intelligence in place for next week. It took coordination to get overseas teams onto ships in the areas we believe Alfreita may travel to. He's been careful, so we had to create a wide net, but I think we've got monitoring in place for land and sea signals now," he says.

"I'm surprised you're telling me all this," I say.

"It's against my better judgment. I'd much prefer to keep you sheltered, but as you so aptly pointed out you have a right to know," Chase says, kissing my forehead. "Your father and I also discussed the conversation we will have on Saturday night. We're certain after Alfreita hears the exchange, he'll be communicating with members of his alliances and we'll be able to locate him. That's all we did today," he says, holding me close.

"I don't like that my dad wants to keep me in the dark. He actually had the audacity to stop the conversation. Did he think I wouldn't notice?" I ask.

"Katarina, he cares how you feel about him and doesn't want to give you or your mom a reason to think poorly of him. Give him a chance, Baby," he says, brushing the hair out of my eyes.

"I guess, but it's so annoying."

"You'll need to talk to him and tell him how that makes you feel once this is all over. Trust me. He's organizing things to the best of his ability under the circumstances and doing nothing that should cause you angst," he says, holding me close against his chest, rubbing and circling his hand on my back, relaxing me. That is the last thing I recall as I fall into a restful sleep.

SIX

I come in from my run the next morning and see the Midwestern sitting on the kitchen table next to Chase's laptop. The newspaper is bulky and has been flipped open to the social columns where anything worth knowing about the who's who of Chicago is found. I pour myself a ceramic mug full of coffee, add a little hazelnut creamer from the fridge and sit down to read the article.

CHICAGO MIDWESTERN
> **Chase Prestian Engaged**
> **Nate Collins**

A LARGE CELEBRATION is planned for Chase Prestian, CEO and Owner of Prestian Corporation and his fiancée Katarina Meilers. Ms. Meilers is highly specialized in lean methodologies and has been working closely with Prestian and the Martel and Son's Architectural firm to design what is anticipated to be the most patient-centered and cost-effective facility that health care has to offer. It is expected they will officially announce their engagement and possibly a wedding date this Saturday. The event is being held at the home of a long-time friend of the Prestian family, Carlos Larussio. Karissa Meilers, Katarina's mother, will also be flying in for the occasion.

Chase walks into the kitchen freshly showered, dressed in denim jeans and a t-shirt with hair that is still damp. He kisses me lightly on the lips before sliding into the seat beside me.

"So, Nate published the article according to plan," I say.

"Yes, things are coming along nicely. The announcements have been made and security is in place at your dad's. He'll be heading back to New York tomorrow morning since most of the family will be arriving in the next couple days. He plans to let your mom know later today that she won't be attending the event on Saturday," he says.

"I wonder how she'll feel about that. They haven't really been apart since she was kidnapped," I say.

"He's a little nervous. It's a big step for him. He doesn't want to lose Karissa again," he says, before his cell phone rings.

"Chase here," he says, a slight scowl crossing his handsome features. "Dig into it a little more and keep me posted. Thanks, Sid," he says. I can't help wondering what the conversation is about. *Am I always going to feel like I need to know every little thing?*

"That was Sid. They've got some leads and a few communications that are coming in from Spain. We need to learn a little bit more about them," he says as if reading my mind, answering my questions before I even have a chance to ask him.

The rest of the day and Friday are a blur with Chase, Jay, my father, and Sheldon sequestered in the study with Sid. My mom is quieter than usual, reading a book in the parlor when I find her. "You okay?" I ask, slipping into one of the reading chairs across from her.

"I'm trying to be. Carlos told me they intend to entice Alfreita out of hiding with the engagement party tomorrow evening. Your father and his family are not men to cross. I'm afraid that this is not going to end well for anyone," she says.

"Chase talked to me about it. I was more concerned before he told me that it was just intended to have people overhear a conversation and they don't expect anything else to occur, but it's still unnerving," I say.

"We can only hope that it will be over soon I'm afraid," she says. I feel like there is more she is not saying, but she'll talk when she is ready. In the meantime, she regales me with the details of her newest marketing launch until we are both ready to turn in for the evening.

"It's four in the morning; you're just coming to bed?" I ask groggily as I wake to the sound of the door hours later. The room is dark, but I can discern his shadow from the light of the bedside lamp.

"Sorry I woke you, Baby," he says, tossing his discarded clothes over the armchair before curling in beside me. He pulls me close and I relish in the warmth of his body next to mine.

"I'm worried about later and I couldn't sleep well," I say, nuzzling into his chest, listening to his heartbeat.

"There's nothing to be concerned about, Baby. Everything is going according to schedule and all the security teams are in place. I'll leave here about noon so I can spend some time with my father. He's going to come over to your dad's a little early and bring Emily."

"Why is it safe for her and not for me?" I ask.

"Baby, I want you and your mom here, where I know you will be safe. Alfreita's men have arrived in the United States. The grounds here are as secure as the White House. You know how to navigate the safe room and Jay will have the highest level of security here with you and your mom," he says.

"Chase, I'm not concerned about me, I'm worried about you," I say.

"Rest for a few hours, Baby," he says.

It is midday Saturday when Chase and I join my mother for a late brunch of omelets, cantaloupe, and Havarti cheese. We visit with her for a short while before she excuses herself to sign onto a web conference. I glance at the clock and know it's almost time for him to leave for New York. I push the remainder of my food around my plate. "I don't want you to go. What if they have intelligence and know what you're planning and you and my dad end up being targets?" I ask, after a long pregnant pause. He pushes his chair back from the table and comes around to sit next to me.

"They may have advanced intelligence, and in fact, we're counting on it. That's why we sent out information about a significant product move. Alfreita's men don't have anything to gain by harming us. They need to learn more about the shipment. That's what tonight is about... that's all, Katarina," he says, lifting my chin so my eyes meet his own and kissing me gingerly.

"I want you to stop worrying. I'll be back before you can miss me," Chase says. I look up and see Jay standing in the doorway, waiting, and he kisses me one last time. My heart is heavy and as much as he has assured me, I cannot put the thought that he is walking into a trap out of my head.

"Text me when you get there," I say as he leaves.

He raises his eyebrows, and his lips turn up in a smirk at the smile that passes over Jay's features. "As you wish," he says, before they walk out of the kitchen together.

It is hours later, and I am on the treadmill when I receive his text.

Message: In NYC

I glance at the time and realize he must still be at the airport.

Reply: Taking the helicopter to Dad's?

Message: Just boarded.

Reply: Text me when you get there?

Message: Stop worrying!

Reply: Trying.

Message: Remember cell phone connections will be down once I get closer to your

Dad's. Security knows how to reach us if needed. I'll text when I'm back in the air.

I frown at his last message. Sheldon, Matt, and Dereck have been left with me and my mom and I know they have entire teams surrounding the perimeter this evening. I try to focus on the music, but my mind keeps wandering to Chase and my dad. I finish my run and head back upstairs to shower and change for dinner. I do not feel like dressing up and instead pull on my yoga pants and a t-shirt and go in search of my mom.

She is in the great room admiring one of the paintings that adorns the wall when I walk in. "Would you like a glass of wine before dinner?" I ask.

"Yes, please," she says.

I pour a glass for each of us and curl up in the oversized tan leather chair, stretching my legs out onto the accompanying ottoman as she takes a seat on the matching loveseat.

"Have you talked to Dad at all today?" I ask

"He called a little earlier before they reconfigured the perimeter control. He told me he would call me after everyone left tonight," she says.

"Chase mentioned that I wouldn't be able to contact him on his cell phone, either. You're so quiet tonight, Mom. Are you sure you're okay?" I ask.

"I guess I wasn't prepared for how I would feel being away from him," she says.

I look up at Gaby as she enters the room. "Anyone for dinner?" she asks.

"We should probably eat something," my mom says as we take our glasses and follow Gaby back into the dining room. She has prepared dill seasoned halibut, baked potatoes and a salad with a zesty lemon basil dressing. My mom is still unusually quiet throughout dinner and I know she is as worried as I feel.

"The paparazzi have been going crazy since news of my illness hit the wires. Did I forget to mention that not only am I engaged, but am home sick due to pregnancy?" I ask, sharing with my mom just one of the many stories that have circulated since the announcement. My attempt to lighten the mood with a little humor draws only the smallest of smiles, but it does not reach her eyes.

"Mom, they are going to be fine. Chase and Dad have done everything they can to prepare. Jay and his teams have plans in place to mitigate anything that may arise," I say, trying to alleviate her concerns.

"I know they've taken precautions, Sweetie. I'm not sure how to broach this with you, but I should probably tell you before you learn about it from Chase," she says.

"Learn what, Mom?"

"Your father has asked me to move back in with him after tonight is over," she says.

"Are you having reservations about that?" I ask, trying not to appear surprised.

"No, maybe that's the part I need to reconcile. I don't know what's changed, but what your father has done in the past is no longer of any consequence. I've spent years away from him on principle and at the end of the day I still love him, Katie. I'm just concerned with his involvement in the plans for this shipment they're talking about. I don't really know any of the details and my mind is running away with me a little bit right now," she says.

"If it makes you feel any better, Chase told me Carlos is just using his connections to set up a ploy to draw Alfreita out, that's it, as far as I know," I say, trying to relieve her anxiety. It has been a long day, and we both have a lot on our minds. We finish our glass of wine and I hug her tight to me before we retire to our respective bedrooms.

I am sitting in the overstuffed chair in our bedroom contemplating whether to sign onto emails or read for a while. The apprehension I've felt ever since Chase left for New York is getting worse if anything. I try losing myself in a good book, but am unable to focus. I am restless so I call Jenny.

"Hey," she says, answering the phone on the first ring.

"What are you up to?" I ask.

"Just watching a movie," she says.

"I can talk to you tomorrow, then," I say, not wanting to interrupt.

"Don't be silly. How are you feeling? According to the newspaper you are home pregnant and sick. Where are you?" she asks.

"I came down with a bug and wasn't able to attend," I say, blanching at my lie.

I hate keeping secrets from her, but I can't tell her anything, just yet. "I also wanted to see how you were doing since I haven't heard from you all day," I say.

"I'm okay, I guess. I retained a new lawyer to work through the contract with Chase and his attorneys and when I was at his office one of the paralegals mentioned that Ty lost his job and was offered a corporate position in L.A. It helps to know he didn't get off scot-free, but it sounds like he landed on his feet. At least he'll be on the other side of the country," she says.

"And I still can't convince you to press charges?" I ask.

"Kate, we've been through this. I'm trying to get it out of my head.

The last thing I want to do is tell a bunch of strangers about the incident while he's staring at me from across a courtroom," she says.

I make a note to talk to Chase about Ty's new job. I have still not broached the conversation about his injuries and Chase's involvement.

"So, how's life with Mr. Intense?" she says, changing the subject.

"Definitely never a dull moment," I say, laughing.

"So did you set a date, yet?" she asks.

"Jenny, you're not going to hound me, too?" I say, not sure how to explain the events of the past few days. "I'd like to get to know Carlos a little bit better, so it actually means something to have him walk me down the aisle. Right now, he's still a stranger to me," I say.

"I completely understand, Kate. Tell Chase to get some patience then and we'll have a wedding when you're ready," she says, causing me to laugh.

"That's what Chase is always trying to teach me, patience and anticipation," I say, talking for a little while longer before disconnecting for the evening. It's only nine p.m., and I don't expect Chase to call for at least another hour or so. I open my book but find it difficult to keep my mind off what may be happening in New York City. The swooshing sound of my phone awakens me a short time later and I reach over for it groggily, surprised I've managed to fall asleep.

Message: Just boarded. On my way home.

I am filled with relief, and my heart swells with the love I feel for this man.

Reply: Great news!! This bed is lonely without you.

Message: Try to rest. You'll need it later.

Reply: Glad I wore the white lacey thong...

Message: I'll be thinking of nothing else all the way home. Now sleep!

Reply: You're always so bossy!

Message: That's not likely to change, Baby.

I smile and decide to text my mom in case she is still awake.

Message: Chase is on his way home.

She is awake and her reply is almost immediate.

Reply: Your dad texted me before he left. Everything went well and he wants me to fly out tomorrow.

Message: NYC?
Reply: Yes
Message: Are you going?
Reply: Yes, I miss him.
Message: Do Chase and Jay know so they can arrange security?
Reply: Carlos and Chase discussed it earlier tonight.
Message: I'm sure arrangements have already been made then.
Reply: They are a little domineering, aren't they?
Message: Slightly! When would you leave and for how long?
Reply: Won't fly out until after breakfast.
Message: Sounds good. See you in the morning.

I discard my nightgown but leave my thong on before falling into a relaxed sleep.

The feel of his hands on my backside awakens me, caressing, tracing a path from my hips and to my cheeks. His lips and tongue follow, and I delight in the building desire. It is hard to hold still while his finger teases me, exploring the wetness below.

"I love how ready you are," he says, adding another and slowly curling his fingers, rubbing deliciously. My hips push into him on their own accord.

"Baby, hold still, or I will restrain you," he says, nipping one of my exposed cheeks. I squeal, half in shock, laughing, unable to stop squirming as I try to anticipate where he may bite again.

"You moved," he says, pulling my hips toward him, capturing my wrists. I hear the faint click of the bracelets, and they are now connected to my ankles, rendering me face down with my ass in the air and on display.

"This is all I have been thinking about since you texted. Your beautiful ass adorned only in this sexy white lace," Chase says, fingering the path of my thong, caressing, and teasing before his tongue begins to explore. I am tense, awaiting the feel of his teeth as his lips graze me, but instead, he trails kisses along my heated skin.

"Baby, you're breathing hard and so wet for me," he says, leisurely gliding his fingers in and out. I suppress a moan, moving my hips and feel a quick nip to my ass causing me to gasp.

"Still, Katarina, absorb the pleasure," he says, sliding one more finger inside of me, stretching and circling. I push against his fingers and am rewarded with another nip, causing me to cry out.

"Next time you move, you will leave me no choice but to punish you," he says, tracing the top of my thong. "So lovely, but I think as pretty as this is, it will just be in the way," he says, sliding the white lace over the top of my hips and down my thighs. I feel the warm oil, drizzled, following the same pattern his fingers have traced. He swirls it around the sensitive bud of my ass and it takes every ounce of self-control not to push back.

"Well done, Baby," he murmurs.

"Now, let's see how well you do with this," he says, entering me with his finger. I groan as he sinks all the way in and then slowly draws out.

"More ?" he asks.

"Oh, God, yes," I say, softly panting.

He moves his finger, stretching me, allowing me to acclimate, before adding a second, slowly inserting them deeper. I moan aloud, fraught with need and push back against him.

"Baby, you moved," he admonishes. I anticipate a nip on my ass, but instead, he removes his fingers and gently rubs a rounded object against my skin.

I can't help the smile, knowing his intent. "This is going to feel like last time we trained," he says, drizzling more of the warmed oil, rubbing it against my heated skin before slowly inching it forward. He pauses and allows it to stretch me before advancing the device inside of me.

"How are you doing, Baby?"

"Good," I say as he waits momentarily, allowing me to acclimate to its girth before finding a slow and sensual rhythm.

I rock against him slowly, my breathing ragged with need. "Don't stop, Chase."

"Anticipation and patience, Baby," he says, teasing me for some time before gradually slowing the motion. I hear a faint clicking sound in the background and he pauses but leaves the butt plug in place.

"Chase, Honey," I moan.

"Shhh, this is going to feel much different than anything you have experienced. Take a deep breath and relax. Your body will instinctively wish to move and I want you to remain still and focus on the intensity. Absorb all of its pleasure, Baby."

He presses another object forward and I gasp at the width— sizable and thick— as it enters my vagina. He advances it until it is rooted deep inside of me and I moan breathlessly and unashamedly, pushing back against him, wanting it inside of me as far as it will go.

"Baby, you moved," he admonishes, and the butt plug begins to vibrate. I gasp. The vibration is slow, rhythmic, pushing and pulling inside of me, intrusive and hot.

"Honey," I moan as he glides the dildo in and out, along the length of the butt plug. The intensity is too much and after a short time, I hear myself softly moan as wave after wave begins, leaving me trembling uncontrollably, gasping at the magnitude of my climax.

"Shh Baby," he says.

"Baby, you moved, again," he says, nipping my ass. I jump and am rewarded with a firm slap on the ass before I feel the rigidity of his cock slide into me.

I gasp at the feeling of him inside of me. "Chase, right there Honey," I say, pushing back to meet him. He grasps my hips, sensually teasing me, over and over, pushing my body until I am panting and climbing again.

"I want to be deep inside of that tight little ass of yours tonight," he says, pulling out of me and rubbing his rigidity against the entrance of my ass.

"Chase, I want you," I murmur.

"Patience, Katarina. We've trained well, but we still need to go slow. I don't want to hurt you," he says, pushing gently, teasing me, but holding himself in check at the anal ring.

"Okay, Baby?" he asks.

"I'm so ready," I say heated with desire, but he barely inches forward, allowing the ring time to stretch and accommodate his size. The rhythm of the vibrator suddenly intensifies and wave after wave begins to pulse and this time he effortlessly slides past the anal ring and I feel his cock moving inside of me.

I gasp, "Chase it feels so hot. Oh, God, so much better than the toys, Honey," I moan breathlessly.

"How are you doing, Baby?" he asks.

"Chase, this is so hot, don't stop, Honey," I pant, grinding into him as he pushes deeper, fully rooting himself inside of me. I can barely catch my breath as he grasps my hips and begins to drive his cock over and over into my ass.

"Chase," I moan.

"Baby, cum with me," he urges, and I am lost at his command. My entire body convulses around his cock at the same time he releases deep inside of me.

I wake up and the sun is spilling into the bedroom from the french patio doors. The clock registers nine a.m., and I stretch, feeling slightly stiff, but wonderfully relaxed after an incredible night of sex. I look over at the empty bed and shake my head. He runs on such a small amount of sleep. I reach for my robe and go in search of him. He is in the kitchen reading a news article spread out on the table. I slide onto his lap and capture his lips with mine.

"Missed you while you were gone, yesterday," I whisper against his mouth.

"Baby, I missed you, too," he says against my lips.

"It was hard to concentrate on anything else knowing you might be in danger. We seriously need to talk about the future at some point," I say.

His eyebrows raise in question. "What would you like to discuss?" he asks right before Gaby walks in and I slide out of his lap and into the seat next to him.

"Did you already read this?" I ask, changing the subject as Gaby goes about her business in the kitchen.

"I just finished before you walked in. Nate did an excellent job capturing the evening without adding a lot of unnecessary detail," he says as I begin to skim the article.

Chicago Midwestern
Chase Prestian Engagement Announcement Postponed
Nate Collins

A LARGE CELEBRATION was planned for Chase Prestian, CEO and Owner of Prestian Corporation and his fiancée Katarina Meilers at the home of Carlos Larussio. It was anticipated the couple would officially announce their engagement. However, Katarina was taken ill and unable to travel from Chicago to New York City. Her mother, Karissa Meilers, stayed in Chicago to tend to her daughter while Chase and her father Carlos spent time with guests who had traveled in from out of the country. In attendance were Chase Prestian, his father Don Prestian and special friend Emily Hartsway, along with Carlos Larussio, and many of their family.

CARLOS LARUSSIO SPOKE OPENLY to family, friends, and reporters gathered at his home this evening in a heartfelt announcement. He and his estranged wife Karissa, presumed to be dead for the last twenty-six years, are happily reunited. He told attendees they are looking forward to the union of their daughter, Katarina Meilers to Chase Prestian, a long-time friend of the family. The plans for another celebratory party are already underway for the happy couple.

"I LIKE the articles he writes about us," I say, closing the paper. "Why is it that you read everything else online, but you like reading the newspaper?" I ask.

"My parents used to spend Sunday mornings with coffee and a large newspaper and I would get the comics and sports pages. You can't get dirty hands from an article on the computer and there's no possibility at all of getting an imprint to stick to Silly Putty," he says, laughing as his eyes light up in childhood memory.

"That's great! Maybe we should buy some for next Sunday," I say, laughing at his antics.

"We might have to do that," he says.

"So what happened last night?" I ask, pouring the steaming coffee from the carafe in front of us into ceramic mugs.

"What would you like to know, Katarina? Things went as planned. Carlos and I had a quiet conversation that was picked up by some advanced listening devices. As a result, Jay and his teams were able to get a pretty good lock on devices and put tracking mechanisms in place. We have a team monitoring things around the clock and they've already identified a little radio traffic," he says.

"So, now you just sit and wait?" I ask.

"Yes," he says, watching me.

My mom interrupts my thoughts as she enters the room and joins us at the table for breakfast. "Good morning, Karissa. I take it you slept well last night. Jay has everything arranged for your travels to New York," Chase says.

"Thank you for doing that. I'm so glad things went well yesterday. I was more than a little worried. I felt much better once everything was over and you were on your way home," she says.

I flash a sincere smile at my mom. It is clear she likes Chase and I feel fortunate the two most important people in the world to me like and respect each other.

"Ladies, if you will excuse me, I need to make a couple of phone calls. I'll return as soon as possible," Chase says.

"So, if you move to New York, what happens to your job, Mom?" I ask.

"I can work from anywhere, as long as I have my computer and the ability to travel every once in a while. I'm actually surprised how much more I get done when working from home compared to constant interruptions in the office," she says.

"I'm going to miss you after you leave. It's been nice having you here," I say.

"It's a quick flight and Chase and Don are always flying between the two cities. You know your dad is going to want to continue to get to know you better," she says.

Chase walks into the room and slides into the seat beside me squeezing the top of my thigh under the table as he does.

"Chase, I was just telling Katie that we'll see a lot of each other. New York City isn't far away and your father lives there, too," she says.

"He does indeed. I'm sorry you weren't able to see him yesterday. He was looking forward to it, but there will be plenty of other times. Are you all packed and ready to go? I just got off the phone with Carlos, and he's anxious to have you in the air," he says.

My mom's face lights up. "I just need to finish a few things and then I'll be ready to go," she says, excusing herself from the table.

"Mom is clearly a little excited," I say.

"She's not the only one. I could hardly get Carlos off the phone," Chase says.

"What were you talking to my dad about, besides Mom?" I ask.

"Intel was able to get some leads during the night, so we are deploying teams outside of the country," he says.

"They found Alfreita that fast?" I ask.

"No, Baby. He's more careful than that. The information is getting moved around and scrambled, but we have an excellent team and our equipment is superior to most. We'll find him," he says confidently.

My mom enters the room carrying a small overnight and her laptop bag. I hug her tight. We've gotten to know each other so much better the last couple weeks and now she will be living in New York and I'll see her even more. She pulls Chase into a big hug and thanks him for his hospitality and everything that he did to save her from her captors.

"Will we see you soon?" she asks.

"It won't be long, Karissa. We'll be out in the next week or so and plan to get together then," he says.

I look up in surprise. Chase hasn't mentioned a trip to New York that soon.

"The helicopter has been cleared and ready to take off whenever you are," Jay says, walking into the dining room. I hug my mom one last time and Chase puts his arm around me when they leave.

"It's going to be a little quieter around here," Gaby says, clearing the table as she talks.

"Indeed, but I'm pretty sure we can count on having company more often," Chase says, kissing the top of my head.

"Katarina and I are going to take a tour. I spoke with the president of the Boys and Girls Club earlier and it sounds as though it will be a full house this year," he says to Gaby.

I laugh as we go outside. Chase has had two bright shiny red bicycles brought around for us. "And just what are these for?" I ask, eyeing the contraptions warily.

"I thought we'd ride to the camps," he says.

"I haven't been on one of these things for years," I say.

"It will come back to you," he says.

I narrow my eyes at Chase's unsuccessful attempt to disguise his laughter at my awkwardness as we reach four identical two-story wooden cabins. "I'll give you a quick tour," he says, showing me into a living area that has a stone fireplace on one wall, a small kitchen off the main living room and four couches and a sectional. There is a big screen TV, a bookcase filled with books and board games.

"The cabins were built for the Boys and Girls Club in addition to the local bonfires and salmon fishing events we hold for the community," he says, guiding me down a long hallway and opening another door.

"This is one of the units," he says, leading me into a large room with four wooden bunk bed sets, overhead large screen monitor and adjoining bathroom.

"We try to keep the kids busy with activities like boating, kayaking, swimming, biking, and riding ATV, but sometimes, if we get bad weather it's nice to have movies to fall back on," he says.

"Incredible," I say, taking it all in.

"We have four chaperone rooms in each cabin, but furnished with double beds instead of the bunks," he says, guiding me downstairs, through another living space and into a large game room. It is equipped with foosball, pool and ping-pong tables, in addition to various electronic stations and a popcorn maker in the corner.

"Chase it's amazing. Are the other cabins the same?" I ask.

"Identical, except for mine. Each can house up to sixteen youth and four chaperones. In total, we can accommodate sixty-four children, and I'm inclined to add another unit or two based on the overlapping requests lately," he says, taking my hand and guiding me outside and towards another small cabin.

It is simplistic, furnished with a large brown overstuffed leather sofa and matching recliner with quilts adorned with bear and deer patterns lying on the backs of both.

He waves his hand around. "All you need," he says, gesturing to the kitchen equipped with a refrigerator, coffee pot, stove and microwave before leading me to the master bedroom. There is a whirlpool in the corner with a stone ledge.

Chase turns me around and kisses me. "The bonfires tend to go late sometimes and we routinely have early morning activities planned. I like to stay in the cabin and give the counselors an extra hand," he says. "Right now, though, I would like to show you my bed."

We are lying naked curled in each other's arms after our mid-day tryst. My head is on his chest, and his arm is wrapped protectively around me. I can still feel the faint pounding of his heart. "So what future did you want to talk about before Gaby walked in, Katarina?" he asks, before the sound of his cell phone interrupts us.

He scowls and looks down at the incoming number. "Baby, I have to take it," he says to me before hitting the accept button to engage the call. "Chase here," he says, leaning up on his elbows slightly. "Run some scramble exercises. They're either playing with us or are more desperate to get to the shipment than I thought. According to Carlos, he's been trying to undercut the family's business for quite a few years. We're not certain what the relationship is but we know he was paid to run the shipment last year and provided verbal assurances to the cartel that he would get the product to the supplier in their area."

He pauses and shakes his head slightly. "No, it's not about the money, his family is worth billions. There's something we're missing. We know he wants into the Larussio's territory and while it appears he may be running their supply, our understanding is that the head of the cartel is not aware. Even if they were, they wouldn't be this careless with communications. Play with them for a little while, and in the meantime, see if we can find out what the connection is with Alfreita," he says.

My interest is peaked, and I roll over on my side listening to him intently. He is watching me, warily, gauging my reaction and I see the uncertainty registered in his eyes.

I wink at him and pull the cover down, slowly revealing my breast to him. I see first the look of surprise, relief and then amusement reflected in his eyes. He rubs the tip of my nipple, which is firm and erect with the tip of his finger while he finishes his conversation. He disconnects, rolling on top of me, capturing my lips with his. His kiss and the need for me are feral, and the look in his eyes is palpable. I am grasped with the depth of his passion and need as he finds his way inside of me. I moan as he pushes in deeply and my hips rise to meet him. "Baby you were made especially for me," he says, as our passion ignites and this time it is slow and unhurried.

It is hours later when I wake to the feel of him pulling me close. I am comfy, lying in the crook of his shoulder and look up to meet the deep green intensity of his eyes watching me.

"You were asleep for quite some time," he says, pushing the hair out of my eyes.

"Hmm... You took all my energy," I say.

"I'm interested in what's altered your view of the world Katarina? I thought for certain you would have been upset by what you heard on the phone earlier."

"I don't know, Chase. Prince Alfreita is still at large and his alliance with the cartel is at stake. That scares me."

"I know, Baby. I'd like nothing more than to shelter you from this, but the reality is he will continue to come after our family with everything that he has if not stopped."

"Every time I think of how they treated my mom when she was there, or what they would have really done to her if you hadn't intervened..."

"That's not going to happen again. Your mom has our security teams and your father's assigned to her," he says.

"Are we ever going to be free of him? What did you mean when you said it wasn't about the money?"

"Initially it appeared he was attempting to save face and regain the money lost in the bust, but at this point, he would have already settled the debt and moved on. There's something more," Chase says.

"I just hope it will be over soon," I say.

"Soon, Katarina. Now it's time to get out of bed and head back. Gaby probably has dinner waiting and you've taken all my energy. I need to replenish," he says, swatting my butt.

EIGHT

When we arrive home, we find a piping hot crockpot full of chili thick with meat, beans, onions, and macaroni noodles. I proceed to ladle it into ceramic bowls and smile at Gaby's note. I open the oven door and a cast iron skillet of freshly baked cornbread is already cut and waiting for us. I carefully remove the pan and place a few pieces on a plate to take to the table as Chase answers an incoming call.

"Good news, Jay. I'll let Carlos know that you'll be contacting his teams. Tell the men, thanks."

"What happened?" I ask.

"They've got a lock on the communication signals and are close to getting locations pinned down. It means the real work begins, Baby. I'm going to get a bite to eat and then I'll be working in the study most of the evening," he says, sitting down at the table across from me.

"No problem. I've got plenty of work to keep me company. In fact, I should start reviewing the resumes that came back for the additional staff. I also told Jenny I would help her move some of the lighter stuff from Torzial to her office at Prestian tomorrow," I say.

He raises his eyebrows in inquiry. "Does Jay know the plan? I don't recall him mentioning anything about that," he says.

I scowl at him. "Chase, it's so annoying having him report my every move to you! Seriously, I didn't mention it, yet. I was planning to ask him tomorrow, but I suppose I should let him know tonight," I say, remembering that I've given him my word to try and take my security more seriously.

"Thank you, Katarina. You shouldn't be annoyed with Jay or at me for that matter," he says, lowering his eyes at me. "We are both trying to keep you safe," he says, kissing my upturned lips on his way to the stove for another piece of cornbread.

"I know, I'll try to be more tolerant. Jenny has a company moving most of the heavy stuff on Friday, but we were going to take some of the prints and personal stuff over ourselves. I suppose I don't have to go, but I was looking forward to seeing her," I say.

"Text Jay and let him know you're planning to go to Torzial and then to Prestian Corporation, but I want him and his team with you. He can leave others here at the house," he says.

"Thanks, Chase. I'm excited to have her in the same building. Do you know which floor Torzial will be on?" I ask.

"They'll be two floors below us. The layout of that space is very similar having been prepared for office rentals. Jenny completed a walk through last week with the realtor and it sounds like she was pleased with it. I'll try not to be too late," he says, kissing me gently on the lips before heading to his study.

I finish the rest of my chili and head upstairs, slipping out of my clothes and underneath the warmth of the inviting rain showers, letting the water wash over me until my body is refreshed and ener-gized. The smell of the aloe butter wafts through the air as I apply it to my skin and I luxuriate in the silky way it makes me feel.

I slip into my robe while my skin absorbs the moisture and settle into the overstuffed chair to read the latest on designs and cost model associations. We are well under budget having successfully avoided the overbuilding of waiting space and exam rooms. It appears the designers are deliberating over the correct placement of the facility on the land. I send Terry a decision-making tool that includes data around impor-tant criteria for patients such as natural lighting, elements minimizing patient steps to services, and total staff footsteps to assist with the final decision. The pinging sound of an incoming email catches my attention.

TO: <u>KMeilers@TorzialConsulting.org</u>
  From: <u>CHPrestian@PrestianCorp.org</u>

I LIKE that you want to make the decision based on attributes for the patient and not overall cost.

C. **H. Prestian**
  Chief Executive Officer, Owner
  Prestian Corporation

TO: <u>CHPrestian@PrestianCorp.org</u>
  From: <u>KMeilers@TorzialConsulting.org</u>

DO you read EVERY email you are copied on??
  In these particular models the cost is minuscule, so in my humble opinion, we should focus on getting the patient experience correct.
  Kate
  Kate Meilers
  Project Consultant
  Torzial Consulting Firm

TO: <u>KMeilers@TorzialConsulting.org</u>

From: <u>CHPrestian@PrestianCorp.org</u>

I DO AND WE SHOULD.

C. **H. Prestian**
   Chief Executive Officer, Owner
   Prestian Corporation

UNTITLED

To: <u>CHPrestian@PrestianCorp.org</u>
    From: <u>KMeilers@TorzialConsulting.org</u>
    Are you going to be much longer?
    Kate
    Kate Meilers
    Project Consultant
    Torzial Consulting Firm

To: <u>KMeilers@TorzialConsulting.org</u>
    From: <u>CHPrestian@PrestianCorp.org</u>

Unfortunately, yes. Don't stay up too late.

C. H. Prestian
    Chief Executive Officer, Owner
    Prestian Corporation

To: <u>CHPrestian@PrestianCorp.org</u>
    From: <u>KMeilers@TorzialConsulting.org</u>

Why can't you work up here with me? I'm lonely.

Kate
> **Kate Meilers**
> **Project Consultant**
> **Torzial Consulting Firm**
> **To:** <u>KMeilers@TorzialConsulting.org</u>
> **From:** <u>CHPrestian@PrestianCorp.org</u>

Baby, I've got the whole team in my office. It's going to be a long night. Get some sleep.

C. H. Prestian
> **Chief Executive Officer, Owner**
> **Prestian Corporation**

I try not to worry, but my mind keeps wondering what may be occurring downstairs. I decide to text my mom.

Message: How was your flight?

Reply: Relaxing. Read a book in the back bedroom on the way here.

Message: Did Dad tell you they found Alfreita?

Reply: He did, but not much more. He's been wkg in his office for a couple hrs now.

Message: Chase, too.

Reply: Hope they get done soon.

Message: Better get back to work. Good night!

Reply: Night, Sweetie.

I scour through the emails, reviewing the informational items and placing the things that need to be done into my calendar. I sign off, slip under the covers and decide to read a book, but find myself rereading the same paragraph again for the third time, unable to concentrate wondering what's happening downstairs. My phone signals an incoming message from Jenny.

Message: What are you doing?

Reply: Reading. What are you up to?

Message: Can't sleep. Can you call?

I hit Jenny's number, and she answers almost immediately. "What's the matter?"

"I just need to talk for a while. Is that okay?

"Of course it is. Ty didn't try to contact you, did he?" I ask.

"Kate, he didn't, but... well, it's hard to talk about. I haven't been sleeping that well. You know, at first, I was just scared, hurt and angry. Then when the police found Ty roughed up, I felt a little avenged. After that, I was able to sleep a little," she says.

"And now?" I ask, still uneasy about Chase's involvement in that.

"I feel like I am always looking over my shoulder. I'm jittery, Kate. I've never been scared to be alone, but now I can't sleep through the night. I'm petrified he's going to come crashing through the door any minute. I just need sleep," she says, softly sobbing on the other end of the line.

"Jenny, I am so sorry." I wonder how many nights she has lain awake at night scared to be in her own home. "I'll come over and stay with you tonight."

"I don't want to bother you," she says.

"Stop, Jenny. I'll get someone to drive me into the city," I say.

"Kate, I didn't realize you weren't staying at the condo in the city. Seriously, we can talk tomorrow," she says.

"Jenny, it's not a big deal. Why don't you try to relax and I'll be there shortly."

Message: Chase, I need to go to Jenny's. How?

Reply: What happened? I'm on my way up.

Message: I need to spend the night with her.

I have barely sent the text before he appears in the doorway.

"What's the matter, Baby?" he says, walking into the bedroom.

"I just got off the phone with Jenny. She's scared to death and hasn't gotten any sleep for nights. Meanwhile, the monster that did this is living it up in Hollywood," I say.

"Baby, I can assure you he's not living it up by any means. Now that Jenny's started counseling routinely it may be bringing all of the issues to the forefront. We'll take the helicopter and I'll fly with you," he says.

"Chase, you can't leave everyone here. I just need a ride," I say.

"The team is coming with us. Matt can stay with you at Jenny's. Jay will coordinate putting another team on the perimeter. I'll stay at the condo tonight with Jay and get the rest of the plans wrapped up from there," he says.

"Okay," I say, knowing he has already worked through it. I shake my head at the need for such stringent security, throwing some clothes and personals into an overnight bag.

It is a matter of minutes before we are soaring over the dense forest, skirting Lake Michigan, and heading for the city. Chase is on the radio, but my headset has been muted, and I can't make out what he is saying. It is a quick flight and when we land Chase escorts me to the limousine. Jay, Matt, and Sheldon are not far behind conferring with each other as we reach the car. Chase holds the door open for me and I recognize the driver who retrieved my mom's computer in Naples. Matt gets in the front seat beside him.

"Keith, nice to see you, again," Chase says.

"Likewise, Mr. Prestian. I was thrilled to get assigned to the Chicago area for a while."

"Please, call me Chase. Jay mentioned your wife is due with the first child and he's been trying to keep you close to home. We need our most skilled and trained employees stateside right now, but either way, we would have made sure you were close to home for the arrival of the little one," he says.

"Greatly appreciate that, Chase."

"Can you drop Katarina and Matt off at the address Jay gave you and then take me to the condo? Sheldon and Jay will meet me there. After that, take the rest of the night off. Jay already has another team watching the apartment," Chase says.

"Thanks, Chase. My wife will be thrilled."

"Once the baby is born, you'll have a month of paternity leave with full pay. After that, if you're interested, it appears we have full-time employment right here in Chicago," he says.

"I'd love to work in the city, but you know I'll go wherever you need me," Keith says.

"I do know that and you're most welcome. I have your number programmed into my cell. Jay or I will contact you if we need some extra help, but otherwise, enjoy your time off," he says.

"Thank you," he says, before the privacy glass slides into place and Chase answers his phone. "Excellent work! I'm not getting any connection, so I'll wait until you call me back," Chase says.

I raise my eyebrows in inquiry. I'm sitting right next to him and I could clearly hear the conversation. *What the hell?*

His phone buzzes and he answers it, watching me as he speaks.

"Carlos thanks for taking my call. Jay and the intel team have broken through and they've got the location. Everyone needs to stay on silent from here on out. Have your teams stay off the main channels; no cells, texting, email or skyping, absolutely nothing, we have to be especially careful with the overseas lines. Have them dial into the secure line and get patched into the quiet lines."

He pauses and looks down at me. "No, Carlos, she's with me. You remember the friend we discussed a few weeks back? She had a setback and we're on our way to look in on her. No, she won't be alone. I've got security with her," he says, pushing the hair out of my eyes. "Will do," he says, before disconnecting.

"What was that all about?" I ask.

"Your dad just wants to make sure you are safe and although I try to ensure that, myself, I understand having a daughter is new to him, so I'm trying to give the guy a little room," he says laughing.

"He asks you about me?"

"Baby, that's an understatement. He's interested in everything that you're doing," he says.

Keith pulls up in front of Jenny's, and Chase kisses me goodnight. Call me if you need anything," he says, before giving Matt instructions for the night.

"Thank you," I say, kissing him soundly on the lips.

"She may not be able to be on her own for a while. See if she is open to having someone move in with her or if she wants to stay at our place for a while," Chase says.

"The way you protect me, our family, and friends is beyond belief."

"Remember to text me, so I know everything is alright," he says. Matt is the first one out of the car and he opens the back door for me, as Chase kisses me one last time.

NINE

I ring the doorbell and Jenny answers. I am taken aback by her appearance. It is clear she has not slept for a while. Her eyes are bloodshot and she has dark circles around them. I take her in my arms, holding her close. "Jenny, I am so sorry. Chase flew back into the city with me and doesn't want us to be without security. This is Matt. He's been with Chase for over ten years and was part of the crew that helped me in Aruba. He's going to be staying with us tonight. Would you mind if he settles in downstairs on the couch instead of outside?" I ask not mentioning that he has had someone watching her around the clock or that there is an entire team watching the premises.

"Oh, yes, most definitely. Come in," Jenny says, moving past the doorway. "I'm sorry the place is such a mess, but... well, I haven't been feeling the best," she says.

"It's nothing to worry about, Jenny. We can go upstairs and let Matt get comfortable down here," I say.

She walks around the living room and soon returns with a pillow and comforter, placing them on the larger of the two tan leather couches. "Make yourself at home, Matt. The bathroom is right around the corner to the right and the remote is somewhere," she says, looking around the end tables scattered with tabloid magazines before she uncovers it.

"Thanks, Jenny. Let me know if you need anything," he says as we head upstairs. I take in the wine bottles sitting on the nightstand along with glasses which are either empty or partially full.

"Jenny, how long has it been since Sara came in to clean?" I ask, looking at the dirty clothes scattered across her bedroom.

"I told her not to come anymore. I can't sleep or function right now. I couldn't stand the thought of her seeing the house such a mess," she says.

I can't believe the son of a bitch has left scars this deep on my friend, but hold my tongue. "Jenny, curl up in bed. I'm here now and Matt is downstairs. No one is going to get into your house or harm you. We'll talk in the morning," I say.

She does not argue and slides into her bed, snuggling into her pillow. My heart expands with the love I have for my best friend as I cover her with the soft down comforter. No sooner has she laid her head on the pillow than she is out.

I change into a pair of yoga pants and a t-shirt before settling into the oversized reading chair in the corner of Jenny's room. I text Chase that Jenny is asleep.

Reply: Night Baby. Call me in the a.m.

I have barely fallen asleep when I am jolted awake by a blood-curdling scream. My feet hit the floor and I am instantly by her side. "Jenny, wake up, it's only a dream," I say.

She awakens groggily, and I pull her into my arms just as Matt bursts through the door.

"Matt, it's okay, it's a dream," I say. He looks around the room, pulls the curtains back to glance outside and checks the bathroom.

"What are you doing?" I ask

"Protocol, Kate. Let me know if you need anything," he says before leaving.

"Thanks, Matt," I say, hugging Jenny close. She is sobbing softly, and I hold her close, rocking her gently until she falls back asleep. I am wide awake now and begin gathering her glasses and emptying the contents into the bathroom sink, before carrying them downstairs to the kitchen.

"Is she okay?" Matt says.

"I wish she were, but right now she's a mess. Even in her sleep, she's afraid. Hopefully, she'll be able to rest for a little bit now," I say before heading upstairs.

I make a note to ask Chase about female security and to talk to Jenny about the cleaning lady before I curl up in the armchair. I am almost asleep when her nightmares begin again. They have not fully awakened her this time, she is just fitful and restless. I rub her back, she seems to calm and in a short while has fallen back into a rhythmic pattern of sleep.

I awaken stiff and sore from sleeping in a crooked position all night. She is sound asleep. I put on a bra and new t-shirt before gathering my belongings as quietly as I can. Matt is already up working on his laptop when I enter the kitchen.

"Morning," he says with a broad smile.

"Good morning, Matt. Thanks so much for staying last night. She's still asleep. She must feel a lot more secure with us in the house," I say.

"Not a problem, Kate. I'm glad she was able to get a little rest," he says, as I scope out the breakfast options in the refrigerator. I grimace. There is not much to choose from. "Matt, would you mind staying with her while I run to the supermarket?" I ask.

He looks hesitant. "If you like, I can get one of the security guards to come inside and I'll go to the store with you. The other options are to see if Chase or Sheldon will go with you or give one of the security hands the shopping list, but I'm pretty sure you going by yourself is definitely out of the question," he says grinning.

I smile, enjoying his sense of humor. "I'll text Chase. I'm pretty sure *he* will love to go shopping!"

Message: Need to grocery shop. Matt won't let me go by myself.

Reply: Glad to hear that! We'll be there shortly.

"He's on his way. He's seriously the biggest control freak I have ever met," I say to Matt who does his best to hide his amusement.

"Do you mind staying with Jenny? She might be a little scared of being alone with you once she wakes up," I say, hoping that it won't frighten her too much.

"Not a problem. I'll try not to be too scary," Matt says.

I hear a soft rap at the door and Chase is in the doorway when I open it. "How is she?" he asks, pulling me into his arms for a kiss.

"She's a mess; hasn't slept in days and is having nightmares."

"She needs to make sure her counselor is aware."

"I'll talk to her about it a little later, but right now I need to get some food into this house. It's hard to say when she went shopping last. I feel bad that I didn't realize she was struggling. She sounded fine on the telephone when we were working and just said she was trying to keep busy," I say, as we make our way to the car.

The supermarket is not busy when we arrive and we are in and out fairly quick. Jenny is still asleep when we return and Matt has made coffee and is pouring himself a cup. I set about making blueberry pancakes, scrambled eggs, and bacon for everyone. We are about to take our seats at the table when Jenny comes down the stairs wearing a long robe and sheepish smile.

"That smells absolutely amazing. I am so hungry," she says.

"Take a seat and I'll pour you some coffee," I say.

Chase passes her the pancakes. "Did you get a better night's sleep, Jenny?" he asks.

She nods, and swallows, her mouth already full with a bite of pancake. "I slept really well. I just needed one good night's sleep," she says.

"I can stay as long as you need me to, Jenny. Otherwise, Chase and I thought you might want to stay with us for a little while," I suggest.

"That is so nice of you both, but I called my niece last night while I was waiting for you to arrive. She still lives with her parents and just got a job offer here in the city, so she's going to move in with me until she can afford to get a place of her own. It will work out well for both of us short term. In the meantime, I should probably be a little more open with my counselor, but it really didn't get bad until about a week ago," she says.

"I'm so glad to hear that, Jenny. Let me know what I can do," I say.

"Kate, you've done plenty already and thanks for cleaning and grocery shopping. I just haven't been myself lately. I've been like a seriously sleep deprived biatch," she says, laughing at herself.

"Well, I have to admit you looked pretty frightful when you answered the door yesterday. I was like, 'Who are you zombie lady? What's up with the bloodshot eyes and dark circles,'" I say, teasing. She tosses her napkin at me playfully and I am delighted to see a little spark back in her eyes this morning.

"When is your niece supposed to arrive?" I ask.

"She's planning to be here this afternoon and will stay with me tonight. My brother-in-law will help her move all her belongings in on the weekend."

Chase glances down at his cell and scowls. "Chase here," he says, muting his phone.

"Excuse me, ladies, I need to take this," he says, getting up from the table and walking outside. We have just finished clearing the dishes when he returns. I raise my eyebrows in inquiry, but he does not say anything, and his expression gives nothing away. Jenny and I begin to load the dishwasher while Chase begins filling Matt in on the call.

"Do you want me to stay with you today? I brought my computer and I can work from here so you can nap," I offer.

"No, really, I'm fine until I try to fall asleep. Could you just hang out while I jump in the shower, then I'm good?"

"Go shower, we'll hang out here," I say, as she heads upstairs. I'll ask her later why she wants us to stay while she showers, but for now, I'm just glad she seems to have gotten some well-needed sleep and won't be alone.

"So, what's on the agenda for this afternoon, gentleman?" I ask as I walk into the living room, ignoring the amusement playing over Chase's features at my question.

"Well, we're going to wait for you and then fly to New York," Chase says.

"Why are we going to New York?"

"We've got a location tip on Alfreita and some of your family are flying in to help set up the mission," he says. I glance at Matt who is engrossed in his laptop and does not appear to be paying us any mind.

"That's a good thing, right? Are we staying at your dad's?" I ask.

"Well, that's up to you. I was planning to, but Carlos extended an invitation for us to stay with him and your mother. I'll need to spend lots of time with him and your family, so staying there may work out better, logistically, but it's really up to you, Baby," he says.

"Let's stay at my dad's. At least then mom and I can visit while you're working," I say.

Jenny comes downstairs looking refreshed and pours another cup of coffee. "I seriously can't tell you how much I appreciate you taking care of me last night, Kate. Matt, thanks for staying with us too," she says.

"Not a problem at all, Jenny. Your couch is very comfortable," he says, grinning.

"Jenny if you are sure you're good we'll get out of your hair. Chase has meetings in

New York and I'll work from there," I say, giving her a big hug.

"Thanks so much for coming, Kate. I really, really needed some sleep," she says.

"Remember to call the counselor and let him know what's going on," I say so only she can hear.

"I will... I promise," she says, giving me a squeeze back.

The mid-morning traffic is heavy, but Matt navigates it well. Chase puts his arm around me after we get into the back seat, kissing the top of my head, pulling me close, so that I can snuggle into the warmth of his chest. His phone buzzes and he answers it while keeping his arm firmly around my shoulders.

"Hi, Dad," he says pausing for a brief moment. "No, we're on our way to the airport. Jay flew out this morning to help the crews get organized. He'll meet us when we land," he says. I can't make out what his dad is saying on the other end. "No, Katarina's with me. She didn't get much rest last night. I'm pretty sure she'll sleep on the plane. Sounds good, we'll see you when we get there," he says as we arrive at the airport and he disconnects.

It does not take long to board and we have no sooner taken off than Chase unbuckles his seatbelt and leans over to do the same for me. "Come on, Baby, you look absolutely wrecked," he says, leading me into the bedroom of the plane and closing the door behind him. "Arms in the air," he says, lifting them over my head. He pulls my t-shirt off and unclips the front fastener on my bra, exposing my breasts to his eyes and the cool air of the room. They are immediately erect. He takes turns kissing the upturned nipples, lingering momentarily, before sliding my yoga pants down, along with my panties. I balance on his shoulders as he pulls them over my feet. He stands and scoops me into his arms placing me into the plush king-size bed. I reach for him, but he shakes his head as he covers me with satiny sheets that feel cool against the heat of my skin. "Sleep, Baby," he says, pulling the light down comforter over me.

I am disoriented when I wake. I look around, acquainting myself with the master bedroom of the Gulfstream. There is a flat screen nestled into the mahogany frame that sits atop the stone fireplace which is glowing softly, emanating warmth throughout the room. I drowsily get up, redress and head into the bathroom. I shake my head at the opulence of the granite dual sinks and stone shower in an airplane and finish freshening up. I go in search of Chase and find him working on his computer at a table next to a window and slide into the leather chair across from him.

"I was planning to wake you up," he says, so only I can hear him.

"Maybe I should go back to bed and pretend I'm still asleep," I tease.

"Later, now buckle up your seat belt and behave yourself, we'll be landing soon," he says as his mouth quirks up in amusement.

TEN

When we land, Jay is waiting for us in a long black stretch limo. He fills Chase in on the security progress as he heads out of the city and towards my dad's estate north of the city. Carlos and my mom greet us as we pull into the semi-circular drive in front of his home. He shakes hands with Chase and I hug my mom and then him shyly. It is still all so new to me having this person in my life.

"A lot of the relatives have already arrived, Katarina, but some are still traveling in," he says, guiding us into the great room. I recognize many who helped Chase and Carlos rescue my mother. They are friendly and warm, inviting me into their conversations, sharing family stories with me and my mother throughout the afternoon. Chase, my father, and many of my uncles have been behind closed doors all afternoon. I am anxious and wonder what they are up to, becoming progressively irritated by late afternoon. The men rejoin us for cocktails before dinner and afterwards many of the family members depart to guest quarters that adorn the property.

"So are you going to tell me what you and my father were doing all day?" I ask as we reach our bedroom suite.

"Not this time, Baby. Give it a little time to play out," he says.

"What, I am not to be trusted with the information?" I ask,

sullenly undressing and climbing into the old fashioned four poster bed.

"Nice view," he says.

"Do not try to distract me, Chase. I have a right to know. My mother and I are part of this and it could be dangerous. You just give me small bits of information, and you keep major parts of the story out of what you tell me. It sure doesn't feel like you trust me right now," I say petulantly.

He watches me warily while undressing. His tie comes off, and he unbuttons his white dress shirt, tossing it carelessly over the chair revealing his long, lean torso as he does. The muscles in his abdomen ripple as he unzips his dress pants and lets them fall to the floor. The dark patch of hair trailing from his navel to the top of his briefs is mesmerizing, and I find it impossible to avert my eyes as he slides them off and steps out of them. He is fully erect, masculine and I will myself to look up and into his eyes.

"Baby, I trust you completely," he says, sliding into bed. "You really want to know what's happening?" he asks, leaning on one elbow so that he can look down at me.

"I really do. I was waiting all afternoon for you guys to come out of that stinking study."

"Jay and his teams got a confirmed lock on Alfreita's position. He is in the city of Najran and his yacht has been spotted in the Arabian Sea just off the coast of Oman." I am intrigued and sit up, positioning myself on two pillows.

"I don't even know where that is," I admit.

"It's on the southern border of Saudi Arabia. Our guess is Alfreita is attempting to make his way south through southern Saudi Arabia and into Yemen. We believe he will try to board his yacht at that point. Once he does that, your dad's men will have him," he says.

"Are you or my dad in any danger?" I ask.

"No, we have teams positioned in Yemen, Oman and boats in the Arabian Sea with several teams standing by," he says.

"Do I even want to know what's going to happen and what they are going to do?" I ask.

"No, Baby you do not. In fact, story time is over. Now I want to tell you another kind of story," he says, before turning the light out and capturing my lips with his own.

When I awaken, Chase is already up and gone. I look out the window; the sun is shining, and the trees surrounding the property create a majestic backdrop of yellow, orange, red and green as the leaves fluttering to the ground hint at winter around the corner. I am restless and decide to go for a run before breakfast. I send a message to Jay.

Message: Jay, can someone go for a jog with me?

Reply: Any chance we can get you to settle for the treadmill?

Message: It's BEAUTIFUL outside.

I know it's not his fault, and it's for my protection but I want to go for a run. I don my running gear and head downstairs just as I read the incoming message.

Message: Baby, they are just trying to keep you protected.

My anger softens as I reach the bottom of the stairs and see Jay and Chase consulting. I think back to the time on the Aruban beach when I was assaulted by three hoodlums. If Jay had not been following me, I don't know what would have happened.

"It's a beautiful day and Katarina wants to go for a run outside. You think it's safe to have her out there?" Chase asks my father who has just walked into the room.

"There are teams around the entire perimeter, as well as the interior paths and trails. No one is getting onto the property without being seen," Carlos says.

Chase nods his consent to Jay and I try not to show my displeasure at everyone's control tendencies. "I know everyone is trying to keep me safe, but seriously, it's all a bit too much. I promise to stay on the main road," I say, ignoring Chase's amusement at my outburst and the look of surprise on Jay's face.

"Give me a minute while I change," Chase says, raising his eyebrows at my look of inquiry.

"Chase, I'm going to pull in another team while you get ready and I want to make sure you both have GPS synced before you leave. I just need a few minutes," Jay says, but avoids looking in my direction.

I eye Chase warily. "Are you planning to guard me yourself?" I ask.

"I think the security teams have that under control, but I am going to jog with you. I had an early conference call with Sid and haven't had a chance to get a workout in," he says.

"You've never gone running with me before," I counter.

"First time for everything, Baby," he says as he heads upstairs.

My parents come into the kitchen while I am waiting for Chase. She is wearing a long baby blue silky robe tied at the waist and pours a cup of coffee for herself and Carlos. "How did you sleep, Honey?" she asks.

"I slept fine, but the bed is so high I almost fell out of it when I got up to go to the bathroom," I say.

Carlos laughs out loud— a deep belly laugh, and my mom scowls at him. I've never heard my dad laugh like that and his eyes light up with his amusement.

"What's so funny about me almost hitting the floor?" I ask, placing my hands on my hips in mock annoyance.

"Your mom fell in love with that bed when we were younger and in a moment of stupidity, I bought the damn thing," he says, smiling at my mom's look of sheer disapproval.

"Well, if you had used the steps that came with it there wouldn't have been a problem now would there?" she asks, smiling at him sweetly.

"She was upset when she learned I put it into the guest room and bought a different one for our room after she left," he says, looking down at her. I look away, embarrassed at the raw and carnal gaze that passes between them.

"Well personally, I think you should put the damn bed back into your room and get one for the guest room that I don't keep falling out of," I say. He laughs out loud again and Mom scowls at me playfully. Chase comes bounding down the stairs in his running pants and hoodie, just as Jay places a GPS band on my arm. "It's been synced with the security system, so we should be all set. Well, as long as someone doesn't take it off," he says while adjusting it.

I can't help but smile as I recall the time I put the device on a park bench and him and his security team ended up following a skateboarder through the city when I needed time alone and wanted to give security the slip.

"Thanks, Jay. I promise I won't take it off. It was a stupid thing to do and I won't put you through that again," I say to reassure him.

His eyes light up with a smile. "Don't even worry about it, Kate. The team had you in our sights and we knew as soon as it started moving in the opposite direction that you were trying to give us the slip," he says.

"I guess I'll have to get a little more creative next time," I say, secretly pleased with Jay's look of shock.

Chase takes my hand and tries to hide his look of amusement at our bantering as we go outside. "Do you run with music?" I ask, as I put one of my earbuds in.

"No, Baby, it messes up my rhythm. I usually run while I'm going over stocks or just get in sync with my own breathing. I tend to pace myself to the music instead of my breathing, otherwise. Go ahead and listen to your music," he says.

"I've heard that from other joggers, but have never been able to run without tunes," I say, selecting my playlist and hitting shuffle. His stride is longer than my own and it takes me a few minutes to settle into my pace as we venture off. The grounds are surrounded by impressive tall green pine trees which embellish its perimeter and the lawn boasts of towering maples, all in a variety of red, green, yellow and orange color. The property is well cared for with manicured hedges along the walkways and several burning bushes scattered throughout the yard. I am finally getting into sync with my own breathing at this pace when Pink's Raise Your Glass comes on. I am abruptly pulled out of my reverie by a hard brisk tap on my shoulder. Chase captures my hand and turns us around; his pace has quickened. I look up and see a large helicopter and then two, hovering above us. In a matter of moments, we are blanketed with security men, all carrying large rifles. Chase has a steady grasp on my hand and pulls me forward. It is a struggle to keep up with his stride as we run toward the house, but the security guards have us enclosed, leaving me no choice but to keep up until we are inside the house and he has closed the door shut behind us.

I take my headphones out in the foyer. "When will our life be normal? Alfreita will stop at nothing," I say, still shaking and out of breath.

"Nothing you say is untrue, Katarina, but I need to confer with your father right now," Chase says.

"I'll be upstairs," I say, turning to climb the stairs to our suite and shedding my clothes on the way to the shower. The warm water is relaxing, raining over me until the chill of the brisk air and fear finally subsides. I take my time getting ready and finally decide to go in search of Chase.

I stop dead in my tracks, mid staircase at the commotion. "How the fuck did they get that close, Carlos?" Chase says. I cringe at the angry, ominous tone contemplating whether to go into the study or head back up the stairs.

"I've got my best people looking into it. They'll have answers soon," Carlos says.

"They couldn't have missed them. Jay realized they were flying too low for normal aerial movement and brought the helicopters and snipers out. Who knows what could have happened if he hadn't. We handled it your way Carlos, but going forward Jay runs intel—with teams I can trust."

"Chase, think about the implications."

"If Interpol wants to come after me, so be it," Chase says.

"Son, you're talking with your heart and not your head. You don't want to give them any more reason to suspect you at this point," Carlos says.

"Today was too close. Alfreita's men were looking for a shot before the copter came in or were sending a pretty significant message."

"Neither makes a damn bit of sense if their goal is to come after the product they think we'll be moving," Carlos says.

"Exactly, they can't do that if we're dead. Jay will get it sorted it out. In the meantime, I am taking Katarina home where our teams can keep her protected," Chase says as he pulls the door open wider.

"I was just coming up to check on you," Chase says, leading us back upstairs to our suite. He's barely closed the door to our room before he takes me into his arms. "You must have been scared to death. We'll get to the bottom of it," he says, stroking my hair, holding me tightly against him.

"I overheard you and my dad talking. Why doesn't he want you running the intel operations?"

"Baby, it's a long story. Right now, I am taking you home where my teams can protect you. Jay will have us up in the air within the hour," he says.

"What about my mom?"

"She's welcome to join us. Why don't you talk it over with her. I need to take care of a few things before we leave. I'll meet you down-stairs once you're done," he says, taking my face in his hands and kissing my lips tenderly before he leaves.

I finish packing and go downstairs to talk to my mom. She is reading a magazine and looks up as I come in and take a seat beside her, pouring myself a cup of coffee from the carafe on the table. The smell of the french roasted coffee wafts under my nostrils and I breathe in its scent.

"Your dad just told me what happened," she says.

"What did he say to you, because to be honest I'm still not sure what the hell happened."

"I think you know as much as we all do. Your dad said there's no reason Alfreita's men would want to harm anyone connected with that shipment. He's conferred with his head of security, and they're investi-gating, but it's best if Chase takes you home," she says.

"You won't come with us?" I ask.

"No Sweetie, I need to be with your dad right now," she says, as Carlos walks into the kitchen.

"Katarina, I am sorry about what happened today. I promise you, we'll get to the bottom of it," he says, taking a seat next to my mom as Chase walks in.

"Morning, Karissa," he greets my mom. "Carlos, Jay's all set. The helicopter will put down in a few minutes. He's been working with your head of security and they have the joint meeting of our groups scheduled later this afternoon. You've got a couple teams in Belize that are having communication difficulties, so he's working to rectify that before we can scramble the channels," he says. Carlos lifts his eyes in question, glancing between my mother and me, but says nothing.

Chase scans his cell, and I know it's time to go. We say our good-byes, and I hug my mom, conflicted at leaving her behind and the apparent discord between my dad and Chase. The helicopter is much larger than the one we've been using between home and airports. It is a sleek bright blue model, which proudly displays the Prestian emblem on its side. As we step into the cabin, I am shocked at the design. It is customized with white leather seating, around what appears to be a coffee table of sorts and is completely walled off from the front of the helicopter. Jay is the last one in and closes the door.

"Is this your dad's helicopter?" I ask, wondering again at the opulence of the lifestyle.

"No, Baby, it's mine," he says, smiling widely. "I thought the increased frequency of travel between Chicago and New York warranted it. The design will be much more comfortable and it's soundproof, so no need for the ear plugs or headsets," he says.

"Chase, it's like a mini living space. A coffee table?" I ask.

"I think the designers needed a space to store things," he says, lifting the lid to display the collection of iPads, wireless keyboards, walkie-talkie looking devices, and GPS bands.

I reach for the remote and a push of the power button engages the large monitor in the corner overhead. "It appears you've spared no expense," I say, taking in the plush leather seats, mini-bar and all the amenities of his limos.

"It's only money, Katarina. Don't let it bother you," he says.

"We'll be off the ground shortly, Chase," Jay says, taking a seat in the leather chair across from us.

"I want a detailed report from each of the teams with a play by play of what transpired, along with a thorough gap analysis including miti-gation strategies on my desk by tonight," Chase says.

"Already working on it," Jay says.

"Good. I didn't know you had the helicopters on standby," Chase says as we lift off. The tone of his voice makes me look up.

"I can give you a more in-depth brief once we get the team's reports compiled," Jay says. Chase's jaw is set and his eyes are hooded and controlled. He appears on the verge of saying something, but does not. The tension between the two men is unmistakable.

Our helicopter has just lifted off and is climbing over the Larussio property, clearing the tree line when I notice the shadow of another copter quickly approaching. "Chase, the helicopters," I shout, as another one flanks our left side completely surrounding us.

"Baby, they're with us," Chase says, unbuckling our seatbelts, putting his arm around me and pulling me close. I look to the left and right of us cringing at the sight of men with guns in each of the helicopters.

"Chase there's a frikken army out there," I say, trying to get a handle on my emotions, but failing miserably.

"I'm sorry, but it's necessary, Katarina," he says, pulling me closer to his side.

The flight to LaGuardia is short and the escorting helicopters begin to divert as we head in for the landing. We are accompanied by multiple security guards carrying weaponry as they lead us into the Prestian Corp jet that is awaiting our arrival. Chase keeps his arms around my shoulder as we board and buckle in. The door of the airplane has barely closed before the pilot is announcing our takeoff and we are soon taxiing down the runway, gaining altitude, high above the city below.

"I think I'm going to rest for a while," I say, excusing myself attempting to avoid the questioning look in his eyes as I head to the back of the plane. I love this man, but I want children. Can I knowingly bring them into a situation like this? Will they live in constant danger? I am plagued by this and everything that has happened, absolutely physically and emotionally exhausted. I climb into bed and drift into a fitful sleep and barely recall transferring from the jet to the limo in Chicago. I am awakened suddenly by the sound of Jay's voice.

"Send in aerial support. Repeat, send in aerial support now," Jay says.

"I look around and the car is surrounded by our security and we are driving very fast.

"Chase, what's happening?"

"We've got two cars heavily armed trying to get around our security.

The car is secure, Katarina. Jay is calling in support to remove the situation if need be," he says.

"Oh, my God," I say, as the shadows of two large helicopters come into view, hovering right above us.

"They're slowing down, Jay," says a voice over the speaker system.

"Jay, they're taking the exit ramp."

"Aerial, maintain visual and presence until we're home."

"Rodger that."

"Ground support, stay with them until we know where they're heading," Jay says.

"Rodger that."

"Chase, this was too damn close."

"Rodger that," Chase says, pulling me close against his body for the remainder of the ride home.

ELEVEN

Gaby is busy in the kitchen ladling steaming clam chowder into oversized ceramic-handled bowls and tops them with fish-shaped crackers. The sandwich maker on the counter buzzes and she opens it to reveal sizzling, golden browned, overflowing grilled cheese sandwiches. "You must be starving," she says, as she places them on matching square ceramic plates on the table in front of us while filling us in on the local gossip, blissfully ignorant of any of the day's activities.

I am distracted with my own thoughts. I look up and Chase is watching me intently, warily. The tension between us is palpable and the silence is almost deafening. I take a sip of my soup and a bite of my sandwich as it cools, but I do not have much of an appetite. Gaby pulls a peach pie out of the oven and while the heavenly aroma of the cinnamon and nutmeg permeate the kitchen, not even Chase has an appetite for dessert today. He finishes his soup and sandwich and gets up from the table. "I have a lot to do this afternoon, Katarina. Try not to worry," he says before heading into his study.

I finish as much of my lunch as I can and head upstairs to call Jenny. She answers on the first ring.

"Hi," she says.

"Hi, yourself. How are you feeling?" I ask.

"Much better, my niece is all settled in and I was able to sleep again last night. I had another appointment with my counselor and this time I let her know what was going on," she says.

"So, how's New York?" she asks.

"Actually, we're back at the country house," I say.

"Oh, I didn't realize you were planning such a quick trip," she says.

"No, we weren't. There's something going on with security and Chase freaked out and flew me back home."

"Mr. Intense taking control again?" she asks.

"You don't know how good it feels to have someone to confide in," I say, kicking off my flats to curl up in the reading chair and beginning to fill her in on the recent drama.

"Kate, your dad can't be in the position he's in without having some pretty impressive security. Something must have happened that he didn't expect. He's not going to intentionally let something happen to her, or to you, for that matter," she says.

"I don't know, Jenny. I heard my dad tell Chase that the Prestian intel division was far superior to the Larussio's, but they clearly decided instead to use the Larussio team. I can't figure out why."

"What did Chase tell you about it?" Jenny asks.

"I asked him about Dad's reference to it and got absolutely nowhere. He just skirted the entire question," I say.

"Kate, he's been pretty forthcoming lately about everything else, hasn't he?" she says.

"I thought so, but after today... I think he picks and chooses what he tells me and we still haven't had a heart to heart about what happened in Miami."

"I thought you were going to talk to him?"

"I tried, then we were interrupted and the moment just sort of passed and now all the doubts and fears I had when I first learned that Chase had been accused of drug trafficking are just multiplying," I say.

"I can understand your concerns, especially after today," Jenny says.

"The people he's dealing with are ruthless. They're probably the same men that kidnapped my mom and could have killed us in broad daylight today."

"You know, maybe everyone is overreacting. It wouldn't be the first time that Chase has reacted excessively where your safety is concerned."

"I wish that were the case, but those helicopters moved in fast, Jenny. It was really scary. I don't even think Chase knew that Jay had helicopters and snipers on standby," I say.

"Maybe Jay is the one overreacting. I know Chase really trusts him, but it would explain why he didn't tell Chase about the plan to have the helicopters out," she says.

"No, he may have been overreacting about the helicopters passing over this morning, but the cars following us were armed," I say. "If Jay hadn't called in aerial support who knows what would have happened?"

We chat for a while longer about Torzial's move into the Prestian Towers and the upcoming work week before disconnecting. I am still restless and sign on to email noting the progress of the medical center expansions. State approval has been received for the two building plans in Chicago and key stakeholders for the lower Illinois project have been identified. Brian, Chase's chief operations officer, is in negotiations with two more facilities. I send him the culture survey which will be used as part of the standard readiness assessment before signing off.

I take my time getting ready for the rest of the day. I pull on the rust-colored cashmere sweater dress my mom bought me last year, with tights, flat brown boots, and hoop earrings and go in search of Chase.

His study door is closed, which is unusual but I decide to go in. I open it tentatively and he waves me inside. He is on speaker phone, and puts the call on mute. "Sid's doing all the talking, as usual," he says with a grin. He seems much more relaxed than earlier. I take a seat on the leather couch in the corner and try to follow the conversation.

"We've got confirmation that he's in Yemen and heading south. There's no doubt he intends to board the yacht. Everything is in place, now we have to be patient and watch and wait. In the meantime, I'm more concerned with what's going on in the states," Sid says.

"Me, too. You and Jay keep me posted," he says, before hanging up. He is watching me intently. I'm not sure how to articulate what I feel about everything that has happened.

"I heard what you said to my dad earlier today. I wasn't trying to eavesdrop, but I couldn't help overhear the conversation. Are you going to let me in on what's going on?" I ask.

He sighs, cupping his chin with his hand while his thumb slowly runs across his lower lip. "Alfreita is making his way south through Yemen where we believe he will try to meet up with his ship, which is, as we speak, just south of Oman and heading west. He doesn't know we have a lock on his whereabouts or he would have discontinued the journey south."

"So he's taking a chance on getting picked up by the communication waves because he desperately needs this shipment."

"Yes, exactly. That's what I can't reconcile. If he is so driven to get the shipment moved, the last thing in the world he would want is for something to happen to us right now. The incidents today do not make sense on any level," he says.

"Do you think Jay was overreacting?" I ask.

"No, Jay is seldom, if ever, wrong. We've learned a little more today and I should bring you up to speed," he says.

"I'm listening," I say.

"Jay overheard part of a conversation between your uncle Joey and someone else when they were working together to get your mom back. Let's just say it made him suspicious, so he put tracers on all of your uncle's communications."

"My dad was okay with that?"

His eyebrows raise. "Your uncle Joey has been in almost constant contact with secure radio channels off the Gulf of Mexico. It is very likely that your father is being double crossed by his younger brother."

"You think my uncle Joey is behind what happened today?" I ask.

"Baby, we're not positive, but it does appear that he may be working with Alfreita. Your grandfather left the family business in entirety to Carlos, knowing he would ensure the well-being of the family over the years and there was some family resentment about that decision, Joey taking it the hardest. This will be all-out war if we are correct," he says.

"Do you think he meant to do us harm or just scare us?" I ask.

"It would appear the helicopters were just attempting to get some aerial shots of the property and trying to find a communication leak, and Jay's still running intel on the drivers from this afternoon."

"This is unbelievable."

"Jay's still working on pieces, but we've got communications locked down where Alfreita is concerned. If he had gone through his normal channels, we would have seen it coming, Katarina. Jay is convinced it was your uncle's crew, but maybe at the direction of Alfreita. We just don't know enough, yet," he says.

"Does my dad know?" I ask.

"I talked to him just a little bit ago. He doesn't want to believe it's his brother, but everything is pointing in that direction. He's a man of few words, but I'm sure it's hard on him."

"What are you going to do now? I ask.

"There's really nothing to do. Jay has close surveillance on your uncle and security on your mom and dad. In the meantime, his teams will continue to feed Alfreita information which should help flush it all out. I'm going to need to spend a little more time with the teams though," he says.

"I have plenty of work to keep myself occupied," I say.

"It would appear you do. I saw the emails about the designs. It looks like the expansion of the facilities is progressing nicely," Chase says.

He looks down at his cell. "Excuse me, Katarina," he says, answering the call. "Chase, here," he says, pausing to listen to the person on the other end. "No, that's okay, Sid. Nice work. Let us know once he's on board," he says.

"Alfreita?" I ask.

"Yes, he's just changed transportation and is south of the center of Yemen. It won't be long before he's onboard and will assume the ship's safe communication lines are just that. Jay's teams have been able to infiltrate them, though, so communication should be invaluable," he says, pouring me a glass of wine from the bar in his study.

"I'm surprised you are telling me all of this," I say, taking a small sip.

"Katarina, you know I would prefer to keep you sheltered from this, but as you so aptly pointed out, it's your safety and you have a right to know what's occurring," he says.

Gaby's voice interrupts my thoughts from somewhere overhead. "Dinner ready in five," she says.

I look around not seeing her. "Intercom system," Chase explains, answering my question before I've had a chance to ask it. "Shall we," he says, opening the door for me. His hand is on my lower back as we walk from his study into the dining room and it is hard to think about anything else.

Gaby has made a rack of lamb with roasted potatoes, and a salad. Chase pulls my chair out for me and sits next to me as we proceed to enjoy the meal she has prepared. The smell of garlic and rosemary waft from the serving platter as Chase serves each of us. The lamb is tender and juicy, seasoned with crushed garlic, rosemary and lemon zest.

"Gaby, this is fabulous," I say as she walks into the dining room.

"It's one of Chase's favorites," she says and I look up to see the twinkle in her eye.

I roll my eyes at him when she has turned around and am rewarded with an uprising of his eyebrows and the quirk of his jaw.

"Gaby, Katarina and I will be working from home for the next few days," Chase says.

"Glad to hear it," she says. "Now if you'll excuse me, I have a couple pies to make for *tomorrow*," she says, sashaying out of the dining room and into her kitchen.

"Apparently we've been warned off the pies tonight," I whisper.

"It would appear we have. We'll have to see what we can do about that a little later," he says, winking at me.

"You're incorrigible."

"Probably," he says, bringing me up to speed on some of the national expansion efforts of the health care facilities. We have barely finished dinner when his cell phone vibrates.

"Chase here," he says. "No, give me a minute," he says, standing up.

"I'll give you some privacy. I have plenty of work to do," I say, leaving the table before he can excuse himself.

I head upstairs and rummage through the dressers for a change of clothes. The soft suede handcuffs are lying in my panty drawer, where they were left. The material feels soft and sensual in my hands, and I place them back in the drawer where we keep all the other toys.

I try to push the distrust out of my head. I know that I need to have a conversation with Chase and either let these feelings go or move on. I open the drawer again, staring at its contents recalling all the conversations we've had about trust. I light the candles in the room and message him.

Message: Be up shortly?

Reply: Soon.

His response is not what I was hoping for so I decide to change tactics and message him again.

Message: I ran across our handcuffs.

Reply: Did you now? Whatever crossed your mind?

Message: Umm, being tied up, deliciously punished, among other things.

Reply: I might need a little hint on, "other things".

He's clearly going to make me come right out and say it. I feel myself beginning to moisten at our exchange. Embarrassment be damned, I want this. I need this.

Message: Getting spanked...

There is no reply. I wait, anticipating him walking through the door, but ten minutes pass and he has not replied or come upstairs. I assuage my disappointment, pouring myself a glass of white wine and selecting a playlist from the digital monitor in the bathroom.

The gentle sounds of Adele begin to float through the sound system as I take another sip of wine, slip out of my clothes and adjust the temperature of the shower before getting underneath the warmth of its spray. My body begins to relax to the sound of the seductive music. The water is sensual and gently cascades over my body, raining down my spine and over the curves of my hips.

I rub the fragrantly scented shampoo into my scalp, luxuriating in the rich lather before rinsing it and applying a deep conditioner, allowing it to soak into my long tresses while I shave my legs smooth before rinsing it out.

I begin to soap myself with the spongy side of the loofa, losing myself in the music and sensuality of the warm water and bubbles, as my fingers glide lightly over my skin, across my navel and gently through the delicate hair covering the most intimate part of my body. It is with a light touch that I rub, gently caressing my clit, enjoying my slowly growing desire until I become heated with full-blown arousal.

I sense his presence and instinctively stop rubbing, opening my eyes. He is standing before me, completely nude, watching me, and he is fully erect. His eyes are glazed over with the passion reflected in my own.

"Don't stop, Baby. Show me how you pleasure yourself, but don't cum," he says hoarsely, as my fingers slide across my clit. I am close and it is difficult to watch him stroke his own body and restrain myself.

"You wanted to get tied up and punished tonight?" he asks, moving under the shower with me. It is now that I see the suede handcuffs in his left hand. "Arms up, Baby," he instructs, as he moves me back toward the wall of the shower. "Turn around and close your eyes," he says.

Everything south constricts and I am so close that I can only nod as I face the shower wall and close my eyes. He takes his time, layering kisses along my spine as he moves my hands above my head securing them to the shower. "Spread your legs, Baby, I want to see you completely open for me," he says.

I am beyond turned on and he continues flicking his tongue along my spine. He has soaped the loofah and begins to rub it against my skin, the spongy soft side massaging me as he slides it along my skin. He reaches in front of me, washing my breasts with the softness of the loofah, and then turns it around to the abrasive scrubber, ever so gently, brazing it against my taut nipples. I can feel the sensation deep within my core and audibly moan as I try to restrain the desire coursing within me. "Honey," I moan softly.

"Don't cum yet or I will punish you," he says, as he continues his ministrations. I am on the brink, about to spill over when he changes course and begins rubbing my navel with the soft side of the loofah. "You almost didn't make it," he whispers into my ear, kissing me along the sensitive lobes of my ears.

"I'm sure I need to be spanked," I say.

"One day, again, Baby," he says.

"Honey, I am so close," I moan into the wall of the shower.

He turns me around so that I am looking into his eyes.

"Wrap your legs around my waist, do it now," he instructs, grasping my hips, lifting me onto his rigid and protruding manhood. His deep green eyes hold me captive, lifting me, bringing me down hard onto his rigid cock. I am watching him, our eyes locked, as he continues this rhythm, over and over, enduring this punishing pace until we no longer can and are left trembling around each other. He holds me tight to his chest before slowly letting me down so my feet are once again on the floor.

He looks tired and I can't help remembering other nights when he had the same look, after we flew to Florida to bring my mom to his home, or when he and his security team stayed up round the clock for days to secure my mom and rescue her after she was kidnapped. I put my arms around him, pulling his face toward mine and kiss his lips gently.

I get out of the shower first and walk nude to the corner whirlpool, bending over to start the water. I rise, intentionally slow, feeling his eyes on me from across the room, taking a sip of my wine, before adding chamomile scented crystals to the tub and turning to watch him finish rinsing. He steps out of the shower, gloriously male, regarding me warily, as I step into the warm bubbling water and slide into its sensual depths.

"Come and join me," I say, feeling bold as he walks toward me.

He slides into the water across from me, carrying a glass of wine that he must have brought into the bathroom with him.

"I thought we could talk about a few things," I start.

"What would you like to discuss, Katarina?" he asks.

"Our relationship, the issues we're having. We're together, but not really. Things aren't quite the same," I say, dismayed at the hoarseness in my voice.

"I can't disagree with anything you've said," he says.

"I don't know how we move forward, Chase. We can't just keep pretending that this invisible wall is not between us. It's killing me," I say.

"Katarina, what is it that you need?" he asks.

"I want things to be the way they use to be, but they're not. Even the sex, which I never thought would be different, is," I say.

"What do you think is different about the sex?" he asks, taking a sip of his wine.

"Well, you know. I feel like ever since we've been back, things have been different in that department. I know we've been together, but you know we haven't done the things we normally do," I say, trying to conceal the blush that is starting to warm my cheeks.

"I think the sex has been incredibly satisfying and I thought you were happy with the way things had progressed," he says.

I feel the warmth rising to my cheeks. "Chase, I didn't mean that. The umm... training, well that was way beyond astonishing," I say, taking a sip of my own wine.

"This is the participative part, Katarina. I need you to tell me what exactly it is that you miss in the way of sex," he says.

"The sex is always great, but you already know that, it's the other stuff we do that transcends the ordinary, Chase. You know what I'm talking about."

"I thought last night having you give up your ass was pretty extraordinary," he says. I am embarrassed talking so explicitly about our lovemaking, but I swallow and try to continue.

"It was unbelievable, but that's not what I'm talking about."

"You don't think what we did involves trust?"

"It's definitely a different way of making love, but as good as it was, it's not the same as when you punish me. There's a difference that transcends what we normally do. I sent you the text about spanking me and you pretty much turned me down flat. No response."

"Katarina, the things we experimented with were a result of the trust we shared with each other. People can't possibly be in a sexual relationship like that without a great deal of trust in their partner. I can't spank you, or punish you otherwise, when I know that the essential component is missing," he says.

"It seems that it always comes back to this for us, and I really don't know how to change it, given the facts," I say.

"Yes, the facts. Would you like to talk about those, Katarina?" he asks.

"Chase, I don't think I'm prepared for this depth of conversation, even though I thought I was. I don't know what to say about everything that's happened. Maybe this wasn't such a good idea. I'm exhausted and you look as tired as I feel," I say, stepping out of the water onto the bath mat, pulling my robe protectively around me as I leave the bathroom.

I dry off in the bedroom, putting on a nightgown before crawling into bed. I hear Chase opening and closing the dresser drawers, but keep my eyes closed waiting for him to join me, but instead, the bedroom door softly closes behind him.

I toss and turn trying to get to sleep, waiting for him, wishing that I could have shared my feelings, and at least gotten things out into the open. Instead I send a message to Jenny.

Message: You awake?

Reply: Of course, do I ever sleep?

Message: Not funny!

Reply: What are you doing?

Message: Chase and I aren't in a good place.

Reply: The trust thing again? Miami?

Message: Among other things. There are a few things I haven't mentioned.

Reply: You wanna talk?

I hit the Facetime feature and her image appears on the screen. "Jenny, what the hell is that on your head?"

"Oh, my God, I forgot I was wearing this. It's the latest in micro-toweling, pulls the moisture right out of your hair," she says.

"Great look!"

"Okay, enough with the idle chat. What's going on?"

"I'm not sure if we're going to last. He gave me every chance to ask him what was on my mind and I couldn't do it. Maybe I should have insisted on making a clean break, security be damned."

"Kate, I've never known you to be cryptic. Tell me what's bothering you."

"I told you about the issue with Interpol, and you know about the shit that went down in Miami. That is the stuff that keeps replaying over and over in my mind," I say, avoiding reference to Ty's injuries.

"Why didn't you ask him?"

"I don't know."

"Maybe you're not asking direct questions because you fear he's going to tell you what you don't want to hear," she says.

"Jenny, how can I marry a person when we will always be dodging people like Alfreita?"

"Kate, if you haven't forgotten, his team saved you from Martel who tried to kill you multiple times. He didn't have anything to do with Mark's vendetta against you."

"I know and I still feel bad that I thought he did."

"I think you only have one thing to decide. If he did what they accused him of, will you stay, is it a deal breaker?"

"Jenny, I love him, but I don't want my children growing up in fear or having to deal with this," I say.

"Kate, you should talk to your mom. Think about how many years she's regretted her decision. What a lonely life she had. What if you never fall in love again, never have children?" she asks.

"God, Jenny, I can't even fathom a life without him, but I'm so conflicted."

"Don't make any rash decisions, Kate. Get some sleep and think long and hard about what is important to you," she says before we say goodnight.

TWELVE

I wake early feeling groggy and unrested. I glance at the clock on the nightstand and it is not even four a.m. The covers on his side remain untouched and I slip into my robe and head downstairs to find him. He is in his study, drinking a cup of coffee and listening to Sid on the speakerphone. His face is creased with a slight scowl and I enter hesitantly, but he looks up and his face softens as he places his coffee on the desk and gestures me into his arms. I climb into his lap tentatively and he puts his arm under my legs to support me, kissing the top of my hair and drawing me close. My head lays naturally into the crook of his shoulder and neck, and I breathe his scent in deeply. It is profoundly calming to me after a long sleepless night filled with doubt about our future.

I have not been paying attention to the conversation until I hear Sid mention my father's name. Chase captures my eyes with his own, and the question and intensity within them surprises me.

"Sid, I agree. I'll discuss it with Carlos. In the meantime, let's stick with the plan. Katarina and I will be leaving for Aruba in a couple hours."

"Sounds good, Chase. If calculations are correct they'll be traveling through the Indian Ocean and won't hit the Southern Atlantic for a few days. They'll head directly north at that point. We've got teams positioned in Argentina and Brazil in the event they head out into the South Pacific, but it's highly unlikely. If I were him I'd be traveling straight up to the Northern Atlantic and if we're right, our teams will be in good position just outside of Venezuela, Morocco, and Spain. They'll want to get as close as they can to the U.S. before things go down, and based on the communication feeds, Joey Larussio and his crew are gathering forces just outside of Morocco."

"Great work, Sid. I'll see you soon," he says, before disconnecting. His eyes are still holding mine in their gaze and I see a brief look of uncertainty pass across his features.

"What's happening, Chase?" I ask, shifting in his lap.

His finger runs the length of my face, down my cheek and across my lips. "Alfreita is onboard his ship, and as we anticipated, he'll make the trip across the ocean to be as close as possible when Joey's men try to overtake the shipment. He believes that Carlos and your family will be moving it through the Caribbean Sea north to the United States," he explains.

"You were wrestling with how much to tell me?" I ask.

"You're quite right, but I gave you my word that I would keep you informed," he says.

"I'm glad you told me, Chase. So we're certain it's my uncle?" I ask.

"Yes, unfortunately, Sid's team confirmed what we initially thought. I still need to let your father know. He was hoping that it wasn't his brother, but at least none of your other family members appear to be involved."

"So, why are we going to Aruba and what are you doing with Sid?"

"We're going to Aruba because it's a central location to where everything will happen and I travel there often. It will not appear suspicious to anyone watching. I'll be meeting with Sid and Jay, along with your father and his teams, to discuss logistics as we learn more about Alfreita's travel and you are going because I don't want you out of my sight," he says.

"You have an uncanny way of explaining things in a way that doesn't tell me much," I say, ignoring the rise of his eyebrows as I move off of his lap and onto the couch beside him.

"Why do you say that, Katarina?" he asks.

"I think you purposely avoid the details. I'm pretty sure we're not traveling all the way to Aruba so that you can talk with men who are a phone call away," I say.

"And these details are important to you?" he asks.

"I don't even know how to respond to that right now, Chase," I say quietly. The sinking feeling in my stomach lets me know that we are once again balancing on the slippery edges of trust.

"I see," he says, shifting his gaze from mine before answering the call on his cell phone while I take the opportunity to head upstairs with my thoughts and pack for the trip.

The quiet is unsettling as the limousine driver navigates his way from the house in the country to the O'Hare airport, clears security and pulls onto the tarmac. The driver navigates as close as he can to the Gulfstream jet awaiting our arrival.

The plane is much larger than the others we've taken and proudly bears the black and gold Prestian Corp logo. Jay, Matt, Sheldon and the other security guards board the aircraft with us, talking to the flight team a few moments, before situating themselves into the cabin behind the pilots. Chase guides me past them into a large living space. The privacy door between the security cabin and ours is closed and we buckle into the soft cream colored leather recliner-styled seats situated around a small table by the windows. There is a matching crème sofa in the middle of the room facing a natural stone fireplace that extends all the way to the top of the plane's ceiling. It is gently glowing and radiating warmth throughout the entire room.

"This is absolutely amazing, Chase," I say, looking around.

"You like it?" he asks.

"It's beautiful," I say, watching out the window as we taxi down the runway and lift off.

"It's one of our newer planes. The other teams have our smaller units this week," he says, as he pulls his Mac out of his travel bag.

His reference to the other teams brings my thoughts back to the reality of why we are going to Aruba. He has already started working on his Mac and appears oblivious to the tension and uncertainty between us.

I inwardly sigh. We are no further along than when we arrived back in Chicago earlier in the week. We have the entire living space of the plane to ourselves, so after we take off I unbuckle, take a blanket from the overhead, and curl up on the couch in front of the fireplace to read a book.

The five-hour flight from O'Hare to Orangestad airport is relatively uneventful, but the security team dutifully surrounds us as we make our way down the plane's ramp and into the awaiting car. The man in the driver's seat gets out and Matt takes the wheel while Jay slides in beside him. Sheldon gets into the back seat of the custom extended silver Lincoln facing Chase and myself. The commute between the airport and resort is only twenty minutes and traffic is minimal, but we have a car full of guards in front of us and another in the rear. When I look to the right and recognize the face of another security guard in the vehicle beside us, I realize just how much protection we have in place.

"Chase, we have security guards around the entire perimeter of the car," I whisper.

"There's no reason to be alarmed. They are doing their job, taking precautions and keeping us safe," he says, as we pull up to the prestigious Ridalgo Resort. Jay and Sheldon open the doors for us and escort Chase and me through the opulent front entrance to the elevators that will take us to our penthouse suite in the Mayan Towers section of the resort.

"My dad sent me a text. They arrived a few minutes ago and are just heading up to their suite," I say to Chase as the bellboys place the suitcases in our room.

"Good. I have some things that I need to go over with him. Alfreita is on the move and not that far away," he says, giving the young men a tip before he closes the door behind him.

The tension between us has been uncomfortable the entire trip and I finally decide to ask what's been on my mind since earlier in the day. "When you find Alfreita what's going to happen, Chase?" I ask.

The deep green eyes turn murky and his jaw is tense. "You really want to know?" he asks.

"I don't know, time and time again you've told me that we need to be open and honest and I finally got the courage to ask," I say.

"I think story time has ended, Katarina. I presume you have already determined what possible endings may exist," Chase says, walking toward the door and closing it behind him as he leaves to find my father.

I don't know what I expected, for him to suddenly turn forth-coming about his activities? He will continue to keep me in the dark, but at the same time hold the trust issue over my head.

I try to focus on unpacking my belongings before jumping into the shower. The soft warm spray of the water rinsing over my tired body is relaxing, and after a few moments begins to wash some of the day's anxiety away. I get out of the shower and apply a liberal amount of the islands aloe butter onto my skin, relishing in the silky way it leaves me feeling. I select a melon color sundress that ties around the neck, slip on a pair of white panties and a pair of white thong sandals. I leave a note for Chase to let him know that I have gone to spend time with my mother and will be back before dinner.

Matt is outside the room. "Where are you headed, Kate? Chase thought you would be unpacking, at least for a little while?" he says.

"Did he now?" I say.

"He did, I know you find security a little invasive, but I can't let you leave without me. Orders from the big guy," he says, jovially.

"I'm going to see my mother; would you like to accompany me?" I ask, holding my sarcasm in check.

"I thought you would never ask," he says with a wide-toothed grin.

My anger softens. "Fine, follow me if you like," I say, entering the elevator that will take us to my parents' suite. It is the same room I stayed in the first time I was at the resort, right below the penthouse Chase and I are staying in. My mom answers my knock and greets me with a hug. "No wonder you and Chase love it here so much. It's absolutely breathtaking," she says.

"Yes, it's a lovely island and I've really come to appreciate its beauty and simplicity," I say, following her through the living area to the dining room that overlooks the ocean.

"Would you like a cup of coffee? It smells delicious," she says.

"Yes, let's have a cup. This is the coffee you had when you were staying with us. They import if from Brazil and it's amazing," I say, pouring her a mug from the carafe on the table.

"Have you seen, Chase?" I ask, taking a seat at the table and pouring a little cream into my coffee.

"He came down to talk to your dad a short while ago, but didn't stay long. He seemed agitated. Katie is everything okay between the two of you?" she asks.

"Things are strained right now." She's so perceptive and my heart aches with the weight of our deceit. "Mom, we're not really engaged. When he asked me to marry him in Aruba, I told him that I couldn't," I say, watching as genuine surprise and then concern register in her deep blue eyes.

"Sweetie, I don't understand," she says.

"I know, Mom. Chase expected me to accept his proposal and had already planned the engagement party as a means to draw Alfreita out. I'm sorry we lied to you."

"Katie, it's more than obvious you're in love with the man."

"I can't get past the violence, Mom. When he and Dad went to free you from Alfreita I knew people could get hurt, but there's a big differ-ence between rescuing you or protecting one- self, and what they did. I know they were holding you hostage and I am so grateful that they were able to get you out, but what gives them the right to be God? They intended to kill those men before they even left that night. It was cold, calculated and intentional murder," I say realizing this is the first time I've said it out loud.

"Katie, Sweetie, listen to me...," my mom starts.

"No, Mom. You raised me with to believe in wrong and right, and you can't just undo that. They beat Jenny's ex to within an inch of his life. I'm very glad they were able to clear her name, but don't you think with all Chase's money he could have figured out a way to put him behind bars where he belongs? Keeping our family safe I understand, but they don't stop at that," I say, wiping the tears that have escaped my eyes.

"Katie, I am so sorry. I didn't realize," my mom says, squeezing my hand.

I feel a presence in the room and look up. The intensity of my father's gaze captures my own. His deep brown eyes are wary, glancing hesitantly towards my mom and then back to rest on me.

"Katarina, I didn't intend to eavesdrop, but I couldn't help overhearing the conversation. There's something that I need to tell you about that night," Carlos says, walking into the room from the study.

"Dad, I overheard Chase talking earlier today and I know Jenny was exonerated because they found all the evidence in Ty's apartment. I never doubted he was behind it all," I say.

"Katarina, you are correct about Ty being responsible. He was Jenny's lawyer for a long time before they started dating. He had access to all of her personal information and was laundering money through her company for several years. That's about the only thing you've got correct though," he says, sitting down at the table beside us.

"What do you mean?"

"You need to understand something, Katarina," he says, dragging a hand through his mussed hair. "There are things that I've done in the past that I'm not very proud of and I have to live with the choices made as a young man. What happened in Miami is not one of them. I would do it over again in a heartbeat. As soon as Chase and I got confirmation on where they were holding your mom we spent a great deal of time planning the strategy of her extraction. Jay and his teams used infrared technology and we knew exactly how many people we were dealing with. We were able to get in and out fast, securing your mom, destroying a meth lab that was using fatal chemicals in their mix and hopefully instilled enough fear in those nine young men to clean up their lives."

"The news said the nine men were dead," I say.

"We needed it to appear that way to get them underground and help us shut down the other labs like this. You have no idea how much time and energy we put into identifying the men guarding the house before we went in. Many of these people get pulled into this by blackmail and that's exactly what was happening here. It's why we were able to change their position."

"Are you telling me that you got the men out of the house before you blew it up?" I ask.

"Yes, and that you are wrong about almost everything. You were right about the night Jenny was raped, at least partly. Chase did take matters into his own hands. Jay had his team go into Ty's downtown office and confiscate the material they needed to prove he was the one funneling money and using Torzial as a cover. They were able to trace the actual deposit routes and had substantial proof that Ty was responsible. After they were done, they set off the alarms knowing Ty would be contacted, using that to lure him out of his condo and into his office that very night. While he was there, Jay's teams were able to get into his condo and confiscate his personal computer files."

"This is the information they needed to ensure Ty could not blackmail Jenny in the future. If they had not succeeded, he not only would have been able to blackmail her, but, at any time in the future the information could have been used to initiate an investigation," I say, recalling Chase's words that night.

"Yes, everything would have indicated that Jenny was laundering money for multiple corporations. She could have been sent to prison for years," he says.

"Dad, I didn't know the details, but I knew Chase was responsible for getting her name cleared and I'm appreciative. I just can't condone the violence afterward. The stuff they did to him, it's awful. There were other ways," I say.

"This is what I've been trying to tell you. Jay's men never came into contact with Ty. You're right that Chase isn't innocent. In fact, after they got the information they needed to clear Jenny he was working to expose Ty publicly for the lying piece of shit that he really is. The intent was to do exactly what you said, put him behind bars for years, but he was attacked before Chase could do that."

"Wait Dad, you're saying that Chase's team wasn't responsible?"

"Katarina, that's exactly what I've been trying to say. Ty's assailants broke into his condo and you already know how brutally they beat him. The sole point of the attack was to draw very public attention to the fact that our family was connected to this. It worked, just as they anticipated," he says.

"I'm trying to comprehend all of this, but if Chase didn't do this, who did?" I ask.

"Katarina there were some pretty telling marks left on Ty's body. Someone wanted the police to believe my family, namely myself, was involved in this attack. Any detective worth his salt would have linked Jenny to her best friend and then to Chase which would have brought them right to my doorstep, which is exactly what happened."

"I don't understand how Chase being involved would have brought anything to your doorstep. Are you saying he told the police you did it?" I ask.

"The police made the connection they were intended to make. Once they learned of Chase's involvement, the rest was easy. He and his family have a strong and well-known relationship with our family and the marks I referenced would have brought them directly to the Larussio family door."

"The mafia markings," I say, swallowing at the implications.

"I'm afraid so, Katarina."

"So, someone is trying to make it appear as though you are responsible for Ty's assault?"

"That's what I've been trying to say. The police came straight to me as soon as they learned about the markings. Chase had kept me informed about what happened to Jenny."

"Who would want to do that and why didn't someone tell me what was happening?" I ask.

"It was evident at that point that it was someone in the family. Chase asked me not to mention it to you. Something about short term issues and long term trust. He's a hard one to follow sometimes Katarina, but he is clearly devoted to you. Chase and Jay believe your uncle Joey was responsible for Ty's attack. They have not been able to prove it, yet, but that doesn't surprise me. They would work carefully," he says.

"So the mafia markings stories are true and would lead police to the Larussio family?" I ask.

"Katarina, our family has a lot of history, some I am deeply proud of and some that I am not, but you have to believe me when I tell you that Chase and I were not involved in this. There is nothing that I would do to cause your mother worry and Chase has done nothing except assist in her rescue and your friend's exoneration. The only regret I have is that we weren't able to secure Alfreita."

"I recall Chase telling me that Uncle Joey wanted to take over control of the family empire. You think he's responsible?" I ask.

"Sadly, that may be the case," he says.

"Thanks for sharing this with me, Dad," I say, getting out of my seat to go and stand beside him, giving him a quick awkward hug as he stands up. "Now if you'll excuse me I need to find Chase," I say, sending a quick message to him to find out where he is.

"Katarina, there's one more thing that you need to know. You are not going to find Chase upstairs. He and Jay left about half an hour ago. They took the yacht and last word I got was they were going to be traveling off the coast of Brazil into the South Atlantic Ocean. That boat Chase has is Platinum and it's powered by four MTU diesel engines. The fastest money can buy, Katarina. It's probably upwards of twenty six knots by now."

"Why, where is he going?" I ask, looking down at my phone. There's still no response to the text, so I send one to Jay.

Message: Jay where is Chase?

No response from him either. My heart is now racing uncontrollably. "Where did Chase go? I thought Jay was going to have the teams get into United States waters and we were just waiting here until they did?"

"I'll let Chase explain the details later, but he had to be on the yacht to make things look legitimate. Alfreita's men are watching."

"What!" I exclaim. "The guy's been after Chase for the last year, kidnapped Mom, and he plans to use himself as bait?"

"There's no talking to him when he gets something on his mind. He asked me to take care of you while he was gone."

"Take care of me hell. I'm going after him!" I exclaim.

THIRTEEN

"They are in the middle of the ocean and you will never catch up to them, besides it's not safe!"

I just need a few moments to think about how to handle this. I know Chase wouldn't leave me without security, but my guess is they have been instructed to keep me where I am and I have no doubt they will run to Chase if they have so much as a hint what I have in mind.

"You're right, Mom. I think I'll go to my room and wait for him to call," I say, dismayed at how easily the deceit rolls from my tongue. My dad's eyebrows raise and at first I think he is going to call my bluff, but he does not.

Outside of their suite I pass security and Sheldon is glued to my side as I enter the elevator and push the button for the suite above. The elevator doors open and Sheldon takes vigilance outside of our room. "Thanks for your help today," I say as I enter my room and close the door behind me.

Once inside, I call the front desk and ask for the number of Mikael's catamaran service remembering Chase telling me about him giving the tourists helicopter tours and starting his own flight instruction classes.

"Thank you," I say, hanging up once I have his number and quickly punching it into the landline on the bedside table. A young woman answers the call and I ask for Mikael.

"I'm sorry, but he is with clients at the moment," she says.

"This is urgent. Could you please get a message to him? I am calling on behalf of Chase Prestian. We are in dire need of assistance to fly a helicopter," I say, again surprised at how easily the lies flow off of my tongue.

"Chase Prestian? Please, remain on the line and I will find him," she says, putting me on hold and subjecting me to eighties sounding elevator music. It seems like hours and hours, although the clock has barely moved moments before he comes onto the line.

"Mikael here, who am I speaking with?" he asks.

"Mikael, this is Katarina. We met on the catamaran with Chase Prestian. He's in trouble and I need a helicopter ride out to his yacht. They left about forty minutes ago. Can we catch them?" I ask.

There is a slight pause on the other end of the phone. "Mikael, I need to know now if you can help, otherwise, I will find someone else," I say.

"Yes, of course, I would do anything for Chase. I was only trying to determine which helicopter to take. If time is of the essence, we will take the one Chase owns and has here on the island this week. The Augusta 169 can move at about 311 kilometers per hour. We should be able to catch up to them fairly easily."

"I will come by taxi and be there shortly then, thanks Mikael," I say, hanging up and calling the number for the taxi listed on the hotel brochure. I look down at the sundress and sandals that I have on and quickly slip the only pair of jeans I brought, a tank top, a pair of flats, a hair tie and hat into my fashionably oversized purse and leave the suite.

"Sheldon, I'm going to go down to get a coffee and then can we drive the jeep out to the rocks? I'd like to take some pictures before we leave and maybe that will take my mind off of everything going on," I say.

"Sure thing, Kate," he says, texting a message presumably to someone that will pull the car around. I stop by the coffee shop, purchase a hazelnut decaffeinated coffee and then head into the restroom. Once in the stall, I divest myself of my sundress and sandals before I slip into the tank top and jeans from my purse. I pull my hair into a bun and tuck it into the purple crocheted beret that I brought for the trip home to Chicago. I shove my sundress and sandals into my purse and come out of the stall to look at myself in the mirror.

I toss my recently purchased coffee into the garbage, walk out of the restroom and purposely try not to look for security, only intent on reaching the doors and the awaiting taxi. I give the driver Mikael's address, and only after we are on our way do I dare to glance back at the Ridalgo entrance. No sign of security or anything suspicious. I sit back into the seat, breathing deeply, trying to steady the racing of my heart.

The cabby navigates the island drive easily and it is only a matter of minutes before he is pulling off the main road and toward a coastal drive. I thank the cabbie and pay him, before walking the short distance toward Mikael who is standing outside of his catamaran shop scanning the distance. "Mikael, it's me, Katarina," I say, taking the purple hat off and letting my hair down as I approach.

"Forgive me, I did not recognize you at first glance. We must hurry if you wish to catch up to the yacht. Chase is a very good friend and I wish to help however I can," he says as we head to the helicopter that has the Prestian logo emblazoned on its side.

There is already a pilot onboard and I look to Mikael in surprise, having assumed he would be flying and that there would just be the two of us.

"Chase had the helicopter stored here last week in the event it was needed. It's just a standby as his yacht is equipped with a small craft, but if Chase is in trouble I want Monty to fly. That will free me up to assist Chase once we are there," he says.

"I really appreciate your kindness and dedication to Chase. I'm sorry to have put you in this position, but didn't know who else to call," I say.

"Come, we need to get in the air," he says as we board and he speaks to the pilot in another language. It's not long before we are in the air, flying over the people dotted along the coast and veering out to sea. I anxiously scan the turquoise horizon for a sign of Chase's yacht and after what seems like forever am rewarded with the distant outline of a microscopic yacht in the distance.

"We're going to put down, but they want us down and back up in the air as quickly as possible," the pilot yells to Mikael.

"Roger that. I will get off with Katarina," Mikael shouts over the noise of the craft. The minute the helicopter touches the yacht's helipad he takes me by the arm, assisting me into the strong wind of the Caribbean which has been made worse by the whirling blades of the Augusta. We make our way across the deck towards Dereck, one of Chase's security guards, who is walking towards us. He takes my arm and hurries us along the deck and into the main cabin as the pilot lifts off and makes a turn to head back to the island.

"Kate, what are you doing here? We've got teams out searching the entire island for you," he says.

"I'm looking for Chase. Where is he?" I ask.

"Kate, he isn't onboard," he says, running his hand through his hair, looking from me to Mikael.

"What do you mean? Where the hell is he?" I ask.

"Kate, the team was never on the yacht. Everyone just assumed they were onboard, which is exactly what we wanted. I really can't say too much more," he says.

"I want to be with him, Dereck. At least, tell me how to get ahold of him."

"I have already sent Jay a secure message to let them know you are on the yacht. Jay wants you to remain below deck until further notice. The pilot didn't mention Mikael was with you, so they aren't aware of that," he says.

"Chase is a dear friend. If he is in trouble I want to help," Mikael says to Dereck.

"Thank you, sir," Dereck says to the older man. "We'll get things figured out and don't worry, Kate. Chase should call soon," he says.

I settle into the corner sectional and pull the blanket that is lying on the back of the couch around me, attempting to ward off the chill that has suddenly overtaken my body. I am filled with dread at the thought Chase may be in danger and furious I've been kept in the dark about his entire plan. I am pulled from my contemplation when Dereck brings me what appears to be a two way radio. "Kate, I have Chase on the line. I'll leave the radio with you and give you a little privacy while you talk," he offers after showing me how to use it.

"Don't bother, Dereck. He seems to ensure you know more than I do, so please feel free to stay," I retort, immediately regretting my outburst as a look of embarrassment passes between the two men.

"Katarina, what the hell are you doing on the yacht?" Chase says, as I put the obnoxious looking thing to my ear.

"I came to be with you, but you're obviously not where everyone thinks you are. What the hell is going on?" I ask.

"Katarina, we can talk about this later. Right now I need you to listen to me carefully. Jay and I are aboard the yacht that will be meeting the one you are on in about forty minutes. At that time, I need you to switch yachts without being recognized. There are people watching everything going on right now. Fortunately, your arrival did not raise suspicions. In fact, added a degree of credibility to the fact I am on that yacht and appeared to those watching that you were simply joining me. Dereck is going to give you an outfit to put on. Let's just say it will disguise your feminine qualities and make it appear as though you are a working hand helping with the transfer of goods from yacht to yacht. I need you to wrap your hair up and keep it under the hat he will give you. Wipe any traces of makeup from your face and do whatever you can to keep your face down so satellite cameras are unable to pick you up," he says.

"What the fuck! Satellite cameras?"

"Katarina, I'm pretty sure there is an appropriate punishment for such unladylike language, but right now, I just need you to follow instructions and stay off the cell phone. It's not secure."

"What about Mikael? He brought me here and wants to help," I say.

"Mikael brought you to the yacht?" he asks.

"Yes, we used the Augusta since it could get us here faster and, well, Miguel thought you were in trouble so it seemed like the wisest choice," I say.

"Katarina, you are supposed to be safe at the Ridalgo in the care of your parents and our security team, not in the middle of the ocean on a yacht that is to be ambushed," he grinds out.

"How the hell was I supposed to know that? Need I remind you, that if you had trusted me enough to tell me what was going on none of this would have happened and I would be safe at the Ridalgo in the care of my parents?"

"Katarina, we will make arrangements for Mikael to come aboard, too. Now for the love of God, please, just do what I have asked and make sure you act like a work hand coming aboard. We can't afford to raise suspicion right now," he says, before disconnecting.

"Your gear is on its way up. We'll want you disguised as deck hands as you switch ships. The crew knows what to do, stay with them, and keep your heads down until we pull aside the Temptress," Dereck says.

"The Temptress?" I ask.

"Yes, Chase has told me to fill you in on the details so you understand the gravity of the situation. The Temptress is the yacht that will appear to be transporting the merchandise Alfreita is after. It needs to look like the hands are transferring the product from yacht to yacht. Your uncle's crew will see the transfer of product and follow, intending to take it over, but when they do they will find nothing here, or Chase. The problem is you will be on board unless we can get you off quickly," he says.

"I'm sorry for all the trouble I've caused, Dereck. I was just worried about Chase," I say, more than a little embarrassed at my rash behavior and the situation I now find myself in.

A man I have not been introduced to comes down the stairs with two blue hoodies and bright yellow rain jackets. Dereck takes the clothing from the gentleman. "Here, put these on. Chase wants to make sure you have your hair tied up and covered so you aren't recognizable," he says to me.

"No problem, Dereck. He already told me," I say.

"Mikael, we'll want to make sure no one can identify you on satellite cam, either," he says. I grimace at the large yellow water boots which are at least two sizes too big but resign myself to the disguise, slipping off my flats and pulling on the rubber boots that extend past my knees.

We slip our hoodies on and secure the ties as tightly around our faces as we can before donning the outer yellow raincoat covers. I head into the bathroom to wipe any traces of make-up from my face. My heart catches as I look around and see the loofah hanging in the shower and all the personal items that Chase purchased before he brought me aboard the first time.

"Kate, we need to move," Dereck says, rapping at the door. I make quick work of washing my face before returning to the living room.

"Okay, we're getting ready for show time," Dereck says to us. "When I give you the word, I want you to head up the stairs. The crew will come in from the lower levels and keep you in the center of the group. They'll be moving quickly and you'll need to keep up so they can't get a lock on exactly how many went aboard. Once you are on the yacht, the crew will head downstairs. Jay will have someone onboard assigned to pull you both aside after that. I want you to wear these," he says, placing the familiar GPS band around my wrist and handing Mikael's to him.

"Tracking device," I say, in way of explanation as Mikael places it around his wrist.

"We need to go now," Dereck says, urging us to the stairway. At the top we are engulfed by a throng of deckhands, and are moved swiftly across the lengthy deck and onto the makeshift bridge between the two yachts.

I keep my face down as we cross onto the ship and are led downstairs. At the first bend, a man leads us down a hall and into the yacht's living space. As he takes off his raincoat I recognize Sheldon and grimace with embarrassment recalling how I eluded him at the resort. "I'm sorry about the trouble. I didn't think you would go with me and I wanted to be with Chase," I say.

"I'm over it now, although it's not every day someone slips out of my watch and I need to catch a private ride to find the boss's fiancée," he says, grinning widely.

"Thanks, Sheldon," I say grateful for his attempt to put me at ease. Where's Chase?" I ask, pulling off my raincoat and hoodie.

"He had to leave before you arrived. You'll be safe with me until all of this is over," he says.

"Where did he have to go, Sheldon?" I ask.

"Kate, you know I'm not at liberty to say," he says.

"Chase told Dereck that he should answer all of my questions."

"Kate, he wanted you to understand the severity of the situation. They're working as quickly as they can to wrap this up," he says.

"Do you know what a bunch of bullshit this is?" I state.

Sheldon has the good grace to look embarrassed at my outburst. "At least tell me something," I urge.

"He's just not in a position to take a phone call. We've got our best men with him and it'll all be over soon. Why don't you get comfortable and I'll let you know as soon as we hear from him. In the meantime, try not to worry, Kate," he says.

Mikael places a comforting hand on my shoulder and I realize that's all Sheldon is going to divulge. I walk across the yacht's living space to the leather sofa that faces the large glass window and lay my head on the arm of the soft couch, pulling the afghan over the top of me. The rolling turquoise sea is mesmerizing, the whitecaps are dancing in the distance and the lull of the gently rocking ship is strangely calming. Sometime later, the sharp crackling sound of the short wave radio startles me.

"Sheldon here," he says, pausing to listen to the person speaking on the other end.

"Roger that," he says, disconnecting. "We need to move both of you right now, Kate. I've got orders to get you onto that helicopter and back to dry land," he says, opening the closet in the far corner of the room.

"Is that where Chase is?"

"Kate, put these on and tuck your hair into the hat. We need to protect your identity at all costs," he says, disregarding my question. He hands me a green flight suit along with a matching cap as he forages in the bottom of the closet for a pair of men's black boots. These will have to do," he says, holding up two pairs.

"If you can't tell me anything else, at least tell me if Chase is okay?"

"I wish I could, Kate. Everything went sideways. Right now, I need to get both of you to a safe spot until we learn more," he says as I hastily pull the jumpsuit on over my clothing.

"Let's move, everyone. Kate and Mikael, you need to keep your faces down until we are out of surveillance range. It's critical no one can trace you back to this ship today," Sheldon says, as we are shuffled up the stairs, onto the windy deck and into the back of the spacious Augusta. The security men board last and it is hard to keep my eyes averted from the worrying firearms. I try to take in deep breaths and slowly let them out, attempting to reduce the anxiety that threatens to overcome me at the thought that Chase may be injured or worse.

FOURTEEN

It is a short flight to Oranjestad airport and as the Augusta touches down there is a flurry of activity on the ground around us. I recognize Chase's security men emerging from the limo and congregating around the helicopter as we get out. "There's been a change of plans. We're heading to the states," Sheldon shouts, trying to permeate the wind and noise of the blades still swirling above us. "Mikael, Chase wants you to stay on the island. We have a car waiting and the driver will see you home," he says.

Mikael gives me a quick hug. "Stay safe and give Chase my best," he says. Sheldon takes my arm and guides me toward the large jet on the runway, proudly displaying the Prestian Corporation logo. It is a massive plane, larger than anything we've flown in before.

"Where's Chase, I'm not going without him," I yell, as we reach the ramp to the plane.

"He had to leave, Kate, but will meet you stateside," he says, leaving me no recourse but to follow him up the ramp and into the jet surrounded by armed men and ammunition. As we enter the plane there are two rows of recliners with small tables in front of each that holds a computer screen. The security men in front of us take their seats in the cabin's seats. Sheldon guides me to the living space, closing the door behind him. It is an opulent living area with plush leather couches running parallel to the airplane windows, and recliners that are situated around a small table in the middle of the room.

"Better get buckled up. The pilot will be taking off as quick as he can," Sheldon says to us.

"What happened, Sheldon? Why isn't he calling me and where are my parents?" I ask.

"Kate, he'll explain everything to you once we're stateside. Your parents are on their way back to the states with Chase. For now, no cell phone communication. Let's get in the air and then you can get changed and relax. I believe you'll find some clothes in the back bedroom," he says.

I eye him broodingly, attempting to suppress the fear that something bad has happened to Chase as the pilot announces our takeoff. *Why wouldn't they have waited for me to fly back to the states with them?* As soon as we are in the air, I excuse myself, opening the door to the bedroom in the back of the plane. The master bed is proudly displayed in the center of the room, with a fireplace and sixty-inch television monitor across the room from it, two recliners by the window face each other over a small table and a mini-bar is situated in the corner.

I untie the offending boots, kick them off, and shrug out of the warm disguise before pouring myself a glass of wine and heading toward the shower. I strip out of my sweaty clothes, turning on the water and adjust the temperature before stepping under the refreshing feel of its spray. I reach for the shampoo and notice that all of my brands have been stocked and am unable to hold back the flood of tears. I sob uncontrollably under the gentle rain of the shower until I am emotionally exhausted and have no more tears to shed. A long white robe hangs behind the door and I run a finger over the luxurious material as I get out of the shower. *One at every home he owns.* I suppress the tears that threaten, wrapping my body in the comforting reminder of Chase before settling into the bed that feels overwhelmingly large and lonely.

. . .

I AM AWAKENED to the sound of the captain's voice, surprised that I have even managed to fall asleep. I dress quickly and head into the bathroom to hastily dry the rest of my hair and brush my teeth. Sheldon is in the living room, still working on his computer and looks up as I walk into the room.

"Were you able to rest?" he asks kindly.

"I actually slept for quite a while," I say, slipping into one of the remaining recliners and buckling my seat belt. "Have we heard anything new?" I ask.

"Nothing," Sheldon says as the pilot makes a smooth connection with the runway and we zoom down the strip. It takes only a matter of moments to taxi in but the wait seems like an eternity. I stand up as the plane comes to a stop, anxious to see Chase.

Sheldon opens an interior closet door and pulls out a parka. "Here, put this on, it's cold outside," he says, as we convene with the security guards before heading toward the ramp. There is a flurry of activity on the tarmac as Sheldon and the security guards usher us from the jet into the awaiting limo.

"Get us to Northwestern hospital as quickly as you can," Sheldon says to the driver.

"Sheldon, what's going on?" I ask, instantly filled with a bone-chilling dread.

"I'm sorry, Kate. Things went sideways and your father was hurt. Chase and your mom are with him, but my orders were clear. Get you to Chicago and not alert you until we landed."

I start to respond, but he doesn't wait. "Chase didn't want you to worry for hours," he says, trying to soften the message.

I take out my phone to text my mom, but Sheldon stops me. "Kate, no cell phones, yet. We'll be at the hospital shortly," he says.

The limo pulls up to the front entrance of the chrome and glass state-of-the-art hospital. I feel like I'm on autopilot as the security guard opens the door for me. The receptionist at the desk is looking down when I reach her.

"Excuse me; I'm looking for Carlos Larussio. He is a patient," I say.

The receptionist is still typing something into her computer, engrossed in whatever it is she is doing. It feels like seconds are hours in those moments.

"Please, where is the waiting room?" I ask, trying to hide my impatience.

"Can I have your name and your relationship to the patient?" she asks, finally looking up.

"Katarina Meilers," I say.

"She's the daughter of the injured party, miss," Sheldon says to the lady.

"In that case, take the elevators to the second floor, and the waiting room will be visible on your right. The surgeon will come out and speak to family members when the surgery is complete," she says.

I am escorted into the elevator, surrounded by security guards. Sheldon selects the second floor from the elevator panel and a few moments later we are exiting into a sprawling waiting area. My mom is in the corner; her slight frame appears so small, only her spiky auburn hair is visible, peeking over the top of the hospital blanket wrapped around her shoulders. Matt and a few other security men are seated around the room and acknowledge me with somber nods. She looks up and her eyes are red, swollen, and appear anxious as they meet my own. The tears begin to cascade down her face as I sit next to her hugging her close to me.

"The surgeon said they did everything possible, but it's in God's hands now. They'll let me know once he's in his room and awake," she says, gently sobbing.

"What happened, Mom? Sheldon hasn't told me anything," I say, gently rocking her frail trembling body.

"Your uncle and his men came after your dad. If Chase hadn't arrived when he did, your father would already be dead," she says.

"Mom, slow down, what happened?" I ask.

"Joey found out that the cartel learned he was responsible for turning in Alfreita's shipment last year. He and his men came after your dad and shot him. They stabilized him and flew him here for the surgery because of the complexity. The bullet was lodged in a precarious position and they wanted a specialized heart team available when it came out."

"What about Chase, where is he?" I ask.

"He's fine, Katie. One of Joey's men took a shot, but Jay put himself between the bullet and Chase."

"Oh, my God! Is he going to make it?" I ask, trying to absorb everything that has transpired.

"He was critical and Dr. Madeira had to have him flown to Brazil. Last I heard he was still in surgery, but that was quite some time ago," she says.

"Where's Chase?" I ask, looking to Matt.

"He's in the conference room down the hall. He was on an overseas call when I left him," he says.

"Why didn't he call or message me?" I ask my mom.

"Sweetie, he didn't say a word all the way home except to order people around. I'm pretty sure he's torn up over the situation with your dad and Jay," she says.

Sheldon guides me down the hall and towards the conference room but Chase is nowhere to be seen. I turn towards the nursing station. "I'm looking for Chase Prestian or the room they are taking my father, Carlos Larussio to after surgery," I say.

The young nurse in blue surgical scrubs and a long brunette ponytail comes from behind the station. "Follow me, it's a little bit of a maze on this floor," she says kindly, leading us down one hall and then to the right onto another more private wing. A code is called, overhead, *Stat nurse to room 611, stat nurse to 611.*

"I have to respond to that, but he's right around the corner, number 302," she says, before rushing down the hall. I reach the room and am just about to enter when I hear Chase talking quietly. "We had to get her off my yacht for fear they would blow it up, thinking I was still onboard. The teams transferred her to the Temptress and then got her back in the air before they overtook the yacht and confiscated the product. Jay was smart to have the backup helicopter and ammunitions ready," he says.

I can't make out what my father is saying from outside the door. "No, Carlos. Once I had confirmation the product was in Joey's hands, it was simply an honest phone conversation with Vicenti. He's aware that Joey tipped the police off to the Alfreita shipment last year, a clear attempt to gain a foothold in the cartel territory, and that Joey and Alfreita are working together, but not to what extent."

My father says something, but it is garbled and unclear. All I am able to make out is a hoarse whisper and the sound of my given name.

"I was hoping over time she would realize that I couldn't possibly do those things. I know she's wrestling with right and wrong. I love her, God help me Carlos, but she doesn't trust me and that's no way for a man and wife to live."

There is a garbled voice and then the beeping of the equipment grows to a pronounced intensity. Overhead I hear the announcement... code blue to 302, code blue to 302. I hurry into the room as I realize it's my father, but Chase draws me out of the way as the code team races in, pulling me into the corner of the room, holding me upright and steady, as they start emergency ventilations, apply pads and suction to my father's chest.

There is a scramble of activity around his bed and it's hard to make out what is being said. They are talking out loud and there is a scribe taking notes. "One milligram of epinephrine given before the physician arrives. No change.... Another man arrives in scrubs and begins barking orders. "Forty milligrams of vasopressin. All clear!" There is a pregnant pause and then, "all clear!" I can't make out anything else they are saying and after what seems like an eternity. "He's back!" he says.

"Oh, God, Chase, he's going to make it," I say, slumping against him.

"He's going to make it, Baby," he says, cradling me in his arms, allowing me to lean into his frame as he guides me out of the room and into the main hall where Sheldon has kept my mother detained.

"What happened, Katie?" she asks. Her eyes are red-rimmed and filled with fear and I wish we knew if the worst was over.

"He went into cardiac arrest but they've got him stabilized. Go be with him," I say, glancing at the nurses and hoping they will allow her in to be with my dad. Chase's arm is still around me and he pulls me into an embrace as we move into the main hallway.

"Katarina, look at me," Chase says, gently lifting my chin. "I know the events of the last few weeks have taken their toll on you and our relationship and I know you're struggling with everything that has happened."

"Chase, I know you didn't have anything to do with Ty and my dad told me what happened in Miami," I start, but he does not let me finish.

"I love your innocence and I don't ever want you to lose it. I want you to have the life you've always dreamed of and be able to trust the man you call a husband someday. I am setting you free, Katarina," he whispers, pressing a light kiss onto my forehead.

"Chase, you don't understand," I say, but my words trail off as two Chicago police officers approach. One is of medium stature and the other one is unusually tall. "Chase Prestian, you are under arrest for the illegal transportation of narcotics with intent to distribute and for the murder of Joey Larussio. You have the right to remain silent..." the tall police officer says.

"Take good care of her, Sheldon," Chase interrupts as the officer places him in handcuffs and the harsh sound of steel clicking resounds in my ears.

"You can't arrest him. He didn't do the things you are accusing him of," I say, barely able to choke the words out.

"I'm sorry, miss," the shorter man says before he and his partner walk Chase down the long hall of the hospital.

I watch them until they are completely out of my sight. My heart is aching and I am having trouble breathing and finding my voice.

"Sheldon, do something," I say, sobbing.

FIFTEEN

"Kate, I know this is hard. I need to touch base with the rest of the security team, but why don't we see how your parents are doing first," he says, guiding me down the hall towards my father's room. The Larussio guards are still posted outside his door and they nod at both of us as we enter the room. My father is sleeping peacefully and my mom is in a recliner next to his bed. Her eyes flutter and close again as we walk into the room and I turn around quietly so as not to disturb her.

"I don't want to wake them up," I say to Sheldon as we make our way towards the waiting area. There is a coffee pot in the corner of the room and I pour a little bit into a styrofoam cup, attempting to warm myself as Sheldon begins conferring with the other security guards.

"Kate, most of the security details you've gotten to know are still in Aruba and Brazil. Chase sent Matt and Dereck and their teams to be with Jay. Chris and his crew will stay with your parents."

"My dad has his own security with him, though," I say.

"Two of your father's security men were working for Joey. That's how they got into your dad's suite. Chase dedicated an entire team to your father and mother after the incident, so we're running a little short," he says.

I look around at all the guards. "Sheldon, surely we have enough men?" I ask.

"Not enough to cover all the perimeters and points of contact we usually guard," he says, shaking his head.

"Did someone call Keith?" I ask.

"No, who is that? Jay usually handled all the coordination."

"He helped Jay bring my mom back from Florida. Chase talked to him not too long ago and gave him time off for paternity leave, but he lives nearby. Chase trusts him," I say.

"If he's on the payroll, we'll find him," Sheldon says. "In the meantime, let's take you home to get some rest and then I'll bring you back in the morning," Sheldon says gently, guiding me out of the hospital with an army of security in tow.

The paparazzi swarm us as we exit and the security men clear a path for us as we make our way towards the limousine that has been pulled up as close to the entrance as it can be. The entire scene is reminiscent of the last time we left the hospital and I was with Chase. The reporters are yelling out questions about Chase's arrest and the shootings. I avert my face as I slide into the back seat and the door closes behind me. Sheldon gets in on the other side and sits across from me while the others pile into the seats in the front of the car.

"Sheldon, please take me to where they are holding Chase," I request.

"Kate, I'm afraid I can't do that. He's asked me to keep you away from the police station and to avoid the reporters as best we can," he says.

"Sheldon, we can't just leave him there, he needs a lawyer," I exclaim.

"Kate, Chase has the best lawyers money can buy. They were already working on the situation before it happened," he says.

"Then why won't you take me to him?" I demand.

"Kate, Chase asked me to help you pack and get you settled into your new condo on Park Street, before he returns," he says gently.

"I don't have a condo on Park Street, Sheldon," I say.

"Chase purchased it for you so that you would be in a good neighborhood and not too far from work. I'm really sorry, Kate, but I have orders to take you there. Would you like to stop at the house to pack your belongings or would you prefer to have Gaby and housekeeping do it?" he asks kindly.

"Sheldon, I'm not going to a condo. Chase doesn't think I believe he didn't do the things that he was accused of," I exclaim.

"Kate, Chase didn't tell me much and it's really not my business, but he did say that you were having a difficult time with all the violence that has happened recently, and he wanted to move you into a place that would keep you sheltered from it all," he says.

"Sheldon, either you take me to see Chase, or as soon as you let me out of your sight, I will take the first taxi cab to the police station. I'm not sure what the hell Chase thinks he's doing, but he's got a hell of a lot more problems than the charges he faces right now," I exclaim.

"Kate, he's not going to be able to have visitors. He's not even processed, yet. Let's get you settled into the condo and then I'll have someone pack your clothes and bring them over a little later," he says, glancing at me.

My body feels cold and numb. It's not long before we pull up in front of a high-rise, not far away from the condo that Chase has in town and within walking distance of Prestian Towers. The doorman recognizes Sheldon and waves us through, and Sheldon guides me to the elevator. "I've created a listing of all the passcodes you'll need and have left them on the kitchen counter," he says, entering a code into the panel.

I say nothing. The elevator does not stop until we reach the top floor and as soon as we exit it is apparent the penthouse condo is the only one on the entire floor.

Sheldon unlocks the door and gestures for me to go in first. The entire great room is a sea of windows overlooking the cityscape and winding river below. There are dual brick fireplaces in the living space and they are each softly burning with blue colored embers. I walk through the condo taking in the neutral colors throughout and the overwhelming starkness of the space. There are a total of four bath-rooms and five bedrooms, along with an office. A Macintosh computer sits on the highly polished cherry desk with a wall-size monitor across from it. A large vase of calla lilies sits on the matching credenza and they are too much. I feel the warm hot tears flowing from my eyes, faster than I can wipe them.

I pretend to take in the room's view, attempting to compose myself in the doorway, before turning to follow him down the hall. The master suite is just as hard, proudly boasting of tile steps leading up to a large corner whirlpool. All I can think about are the times we spent in a similar tub, completely nude, talking intimately and making love. I continue into the bathroom and there is a walk-in stone wrap around shower and all of my favorite brands are on the ledge. In one corner hangs a lone loofah sponge.

"Sheldon, is there a safe room?"

"No, Chase didn't have them put in the normal safety precautions. He knows you hate them and… well, you know," he says, trailing off.

"I know what, Sheldon?"

"I'm sorry, Kate. What I was going to say is that if you're not in a relationship with Chase, you won't need all of us constantly giving you grief," he says.

"I see," I say, swallowing as the reality sinks in. He would have never condoned me living in a home without a safe room.

"Are you getting an update on Jay?" I ask, as Sheldon reviews the screen of his cell.

"Yes, he's doing as well as can be expected. He's still in critical condition, but he's got the best surgical team in Brazil caring for him," he says.

"Does he have any family?"

"His dad and younger brother are still alive. Chase had both of them flown over and they're with him right now," he says.

"Good. I just got a text from my mom and my father is awake and seems to be holding his own. Sheldon, I need you to prepare the plane. I'm leaving for Brazil to be with Jay. He'll know what to do for Chase. Would you also contact Chase's lawyer and set up a conference call with me as soon as he is free?" I ask.

"Kate, I don't have the authority to send you to Brazil on the company plane. Chase left extremely detailed instructions for your care and you are to stay in the condo," he says, running his hand through his hair.

"Sheldon, if you don't have permission or can't get approval to have the plane readied, I will book my own flight. Also, two things you should be aware of since you've been given the unfortunate task of putting me up in this wonderful little apartment and keeping me safe. One, I wouldn't accept this condo if it were the difference between sleeping in a warm bed or out on the cold city streets tonight. Two, if I can't be with Chase, I am going to be with the person that saved his life. He is probably the only person in the world that knows what needs to done for Chase or how to get it done. Now, either tell me that we've got a plane ride or tell me goodbye so I can get things moving, Sheldon," I say.

"Damn it, Kate, you're not leaving me much choice here," he says.

"Exactly the point, and Sheldon, you and I both know that Chase is still calling the shots. Get a message to his lawyer and let him know I am heading to Brazil," I say.

Sheldon has the good grace to look guilty, but texts out a message in the standoff. His phone beeps and he grimaces. "Kate, his lawyer wants you to stay put. Brazil is dangerous, he can't say much more, but doesn't want you to go," he says.

"Tell him to let Chase know that things wouldn't have gone side-ways if security had not been moving me around. There would have been more men with my dad and Chase. I need to make this right. He will know all about that and hopefully he can respect my wishes," I say.

His eyes meet mine and I can't distinguish the emotion I see in them before he looks down at the incoming message. "You're not going on your own. Give me a few moments to make arrangements and then let's go see how Jay's doing. There's nothing that we can do for Chase right now, but Lloyd's with him," he says, giving me a wide smile as I step into what would have been my office, giving him a few minutes to make arrangements and open the gold embossed envelope nestled in between the green fern-like stems of the plants.

DEAR KATARINA,

You had my heart from the very first time I laid eyes on you, self-lessly saving another human's life. It's not hard to understand why life is so valuable to you and why the situations we find ourselves in are so difficult for you to comprehend. Please know that our time together has meant the world to me and that I love you, but I want you to be happy in the future. No constant security invading your space and privacy, and no doubts about the husband I hope you will someday find. I have every hope that you will find peace with this parting and know that I will always hold you dear in my heart.

Love,
Chase

I WIPE the tears that escape and attempt to fight the dam that threatens to burst. I remind myself of the family that I come from, people of power, used to giving direction and having those orders carried out. I compose myself and try to draw strength from that.

We are going to need someone to get a handle on the press. I text out a message to Jenny and her response is almost immediate. Sheldon walks into the room. "I just got confirmation that our flight crew is preparing and if we leave now we can be up in the air in about forty minutes. Traffic isn't too bad tonight," he says.

"Thanks, Sheldon. I'm ready to go, but I need specific clothes. I'll give you a list, but can you have someone bring them to the airplane along with a laptop from the house? I left everything I packed for Aruba at the resort, except for this," I say, pulling out the sundress that is now horribly wrinkled from my purse. He raises his eyes at me, but has the good grace not to mention my earlier deceit. "No problem, Kate," he says, taking the list.

"Jenny is coming with us. Would you have someone pick her up and bring her to the airport? She's thirty minutes on the other side of the city."

"Yes, will she have any issue if it's someone she doesn't know?" he asks.

"Thanks for thinking of that Sheldon. No, I'll let her know and she'll understand," I say, typing out a text to Jenny as we head toward the awaiting car.

"Your laptop is still in route from Aruba. It'll be with the next team that heads to the states. I'll have someone bring you a secure device and you can use that. We've got systems on the plane, but I'm thinking you're going to want to stay in touch at the hospital, too," he says.

"Thanks, Sheldon. What is Lloyd's cell phone number? I want to reach Chase," I say.

"Kate, I don't think that's such a good idea," he says.

"Sheldon, my perception is that Chase and Jay have an excellent relationship. I know for certain that Chase trusts him implicitly. He holds you in very high regard or he would not have entrusted me in your care. I am hoping to have the same relationship with you some-day, but that's only going to happen if we are on the same page," I say.

"Yes, ma'am," he says smiling.

"Now, I need Lloyd's cell phone number. I need to be in touch with Chase," I say, sliding into the backseat.

"The two of you are enough to give all of us heart attacks," he says, throwing his hands up in mock despair. "As soon as we reach the airport we'll have a safe phone ready for you. I'll give you the number then, but don't try texting him or Chase for that matter on your phone. It can and will be traced," he says.

My phone vibrates and it is a message from Jenny to let me know that her driver has arrived and she will meet us at the airport.

"Thanks, Sheldon," I say, as we pull into the Chicago traffic towards the airport. At this time of the night it is relatively quiet and the driver navigates through the city with ease. As we approach O'Hare the limousine pulls up as close as possible to the Prestian Corp jet. The car is sandwiched between two other smaller Lincolns each holding four men who get out and surround us as we make our way to the plane.

Another Lincoln pulls up and I recognize two more members of Chase's security team assisting Jenny to the jet ramp. I give her a long hug, so glad that she is with me and that I am not facing this without my best friend.

"Welcome aboard Miss Meilers. We have instructions to lift off as quickly as possible. You'll want to take your seats and buckle in right away," the flight attendant says, as we enter the plane.

As soon as we are seated I use the new phone I have been provided with and text Lloyd. It is clear by the immediate response that Chase is with him.

Message: Lloyd, going to see Jay.

Reply: Go to the condo!!

Message: I don't think so. Did you forget who I am?

Reply: Keep Sheldon nearby and text me when you land.

Message: You've lost the right to tell me what to do. I'm in charge of me now.

I power down my cell just before the plane's powerful engines roar and the pilot plummets down the runway, lifting off, bursting through the night's twinkling sky and leaving the vast array of city lights below.

"So are you going to tell me the real reason we are flying halfway around the world?" Jenny says as Sheldon heads into the security cabin.

"You know Chase was arrested. Interpol won't stop coming after him for the shipment last year. There's something that we're missing. I'm hoping Jay will know what to do to clear his name," I say.

"I've already connected with his publicity team. They are working on creating a strategy for handling the media, but he's instructed the team that they are not to comment at this point. In the meantime, we should bring Nate in. He'll want to help Chase, too," she says, reminding me of the journalist that writes exclusively for Prestian Corp.

"Jenny, there's more that I need to tell you. I thought Chase was the one that had Ty beat up the night they took him to the hospital," I say.

"He wasn't?"

"No, you thought he did?"

"Well, I wasn't sure, but it did cross my mind more than once. I didn't know about all the stuff with your family and that's the only thing that made sense," she says.

"And, you were okay with it?"

"I wouldn't say that, but I can't pretend that I held it against him," she says.

"I can understand that, Jenny. It sounds as though my uncle ordered Ty's injuries in an attempt to throw suspicion on my dad. You know, the mafia markings the story referred to," I explain as she lifts her eyes in question.

"Oh, now that's making sense," she says.

"I think we've exhausted everything we can do for now," I say, skimming the internet for the latest stories.

"Anything new?"

"No, just rendition after rendition about Chase's arrest, making him out to be this horrible person," I say.

"I wonder why he won't let his team respond. I just got a message from Nate that he was under the same restriction," she says.

"I don't know, but that's the first thing we find out when we land. Listen to this one," I say.

Northwestern
Chase Prestian Arrested on Drug Smuggling Charges
Bruce Tyler, Freelance Journalist

CHASE PRESTIAN, CEO and Owner of Prestian Corporation has been arrested today after a year-long investigation into a drug smuggling charge. He was apprehended at the Northwestern Chicago hospital while visiting Katarina Meiler's father, Carlos Larussio, who many have linked to an organized crime syndicate on the East Coast. Carlos sustained gunshot injuries in the same confrontation that led Chase Prestian to shoot and kill Joey Larussio. He was flown from Aruba to Chicago due to critical lodgment of the bullet in his heart muscle. He is in the intensive care unit and his family anxiously awaits his recovery.

"WELL AT LEAST that one is factual, even if it doesn't accurately paint the picture," Jenny says as I continue reading more about the history of the Larussio family in New York City and begin developing a list of questions for Jay.

I wake as the plane is landing, realizing that I've fallen asleep in my seat. Jenny is reading a paperback and I scurry to turn my cell phone on.

Message: Lloyd, we just landed.

Reply: Thank you for making me aware.

I realize immediately that Lloyd is no longer with Chase by the response and try to contain my disappointment.

A black SUV is waiting as we disembark from the plane and I recognize some of the security guards that helped my mom in Florida. It seems like years ago, rather than weeks.

"Sheldon, did you arrange all of the security?" I ask, as we get into the back seat and realize that we have teams positioned in front and back of our car.

He raises his eyebrows and doesn't have to say another word. Even from across the world, and most probably in a jail cell, Chase has the power to control everything. I sit back into the plush soft black leather of the limo's interior and Jenny squeezes my hand from the seat next to mine.

The drive to the hospital is relatively short and the sun is just starting to come up, pink and blue swirling hues blending with the magnificent puffy white clouds in the sky. The tall majestic palm trees are lined along the roadways, swaying in the breeze on our drive to the most renowned hospital in Brazil. The facility is an impressive sky-rise of glass and white stone overlooking the turquoise backdrop of the sea.

"Kate and Jenny, we need to place your hair underneath these," Sheldon says, handing me a beret and Jenny a scarf that she quickly wraps around her hair and neck.

"When we go in let me do all the talking. I don't want to elevate suspicions," he says.

I raise my eyebrows at him in inquiry. "Please Kate, trust me.... not a word until we get in the room. It's amazing what raises questions here and having two American women walk into a hospital to see a gunshot victim most certainly would," he says, as he and one of the security guards each take our hands, guiding us to the reception area.

The woman behind the desk seems friendly, greeting us in what must be the native tongue. Sheldon speaks with her in her own language, fluently, and we are soon on our way through the hospital, along corridors and elevators that lead us to Jay's room.

As we enter, my heart catches, seeing him lay so lifeless on the bed, recalling all the times he has saved me from danger. I am filled with a pang of guilt, knowing I was at least partly responsible for the deviation of a security plan that Jay probably had worked out to the finest detail.

Matt and Dereck stand up as we enter the room, shaking hands with Sheldon as he gestures for them to remain silent. I have never met the two security guards sitting in the corner and they stand as Sheldon begins speaking.

"How is he?" Sheldon asks, referring to Jay and closing the door behind him.

"He's better. They just moved him to this room from the intensive care unit and changed his status," Dominick says.

"Yes, better," Jay says, opening his eyes and taking in the surroundings.

Sheldon puts his finger to his lips alerting Jay that he should remain quiet. He tries to sit up. "Where's Chase?" Jay asks hoarsely.

"He's fine," Sheldon says, putting a finger to his lips and gesturing to the ceiling.

Jay nods, and I pull my Mac out of my handbag. "This should help," I say, turning the notebook around for their review. They peruse the list of questions and Matt takes my computer and animatedly begins responding.

Chase met with the cartel, Vicenti. Who and where do I find him? He is still in Brazil. Unable to give you a last name, but Jay knows. Jay nods his confirmation as he peers over the computer.

Where is Alfreita? On his yacht headed south. He wants to connect with Vicenti to make plans to transfer the product, but doesn't know he's still in Brazil.

I turn the notebook and type out one question.

What product, I thought it was all fake? Matt looks from me to Jay and Jay nods. Matt begins typing furiously: It was ALL fake, but Alfreita doesn't know that. He thinks we confiscated the stuff he was trying to get to Vicenti last year. It's poisonous- will break down tissues from the inside out. That's the product your dad wants off the market and Alfreita was trying to deliver to Vicenti instead of what he ordered last year. We just need to prove it.

I turn the notebook and type out one more question.

Why do we need to prove it? Vicenti knows that it was Joey who tipped off the cops and not Chase. But, Vicenti doesn't have a reason to want Alfreita out of the picture. Vicenti doesn't know the entire shipment Alfreita and Joey conspired to move was toxic and the product was intended to be distributed under Vicenti's name. They would have been responsible for killing millions of people.

I turn the computer and begin to type furiously, my mind processing through the various scenarios.

So he still believes Alfreita was just attempting to get merchandise to his buyers when my uncle blew the whistle and had it confiscated and nothing about the product's quality? Bingo.

So when Jay leaked the information about this year's supply, it led them to believe it was the same product that Interpol had confiscated last year? That's why it drew them out so fast? Exactly, we counted on it.

So we need to be able to prove this to Vicenti to leverage his assistance in helping Chase? Jay takes the computer and types.

Not we, us- meaning, not you! I ignore the remark and type out my next question.

Why don't we already have proof? It happened over a year ago. Jay turns the computer and begins to type. We had it, but Chase wouldn't use it to clear his name because he didn't know how the Larussio family was involved and his dad is friends with Carlos.

He knew all this time and didn't say anything? He shrugs his shoulder at me as he types his response: Now that we know it was Joey who was responsible for the leak and that he was working against and not for the Larussio family, it's a new ball game. Chase couldn't be sure other members of your family weren't involved when he met with Vicenti.

Set up a meeting with myself and Vicenti. He needs to know exactly what has happened.

"Yes, ma'am," Matt says aloud.

Jay begins to protest from his bed and Matt begins to type showing both Jay and I.

Chase has been arrested for the transportation of the product. If I don't go with her she will only go by herself. She's not going alone, Jay.

Jay nods, shakes his head and begins to type.

If you are going to Vicenti you need to take the proof that Alfreita knew the shipment was poison last year and in a way that makes it clear Chase was protecting him. I have the tape you need. At the time, the police didn't have enough evidence to pin it on Chase, and he had me wipe it off the system because the Larussio family was involved, but I made a copy just in case.

Jay continues to write providing Matt and Sheldon the contact numbers and instructions on where to find the communication recording.

We visit with Jay for a while longer and he insists that Matt and one of the teams with him at the hospital accompany us. The men say their goodbyes for a few more moments before Jay's father and brother who have been breakfasting in the cafeteria return. Sheldon lowers his voice introducing us to them, but instructs Jay's father to tell anyone inquiring that his other two sons and daughter-in-laws were visiting.

Sheldon and Matt escort Jenny and me out of the hospital and settle us into the back of the limo, taking seats across from us. Sheldon is working intently on his phone the entire drive across town.

"Vicenti has a home in Rio de Janeiro. He has agreed to meet with you later this afternoon," Sheldon says, as the driver pulls under the front entrance of a towering contemporary sky-rise. The bellmen are in immediate attendance and I watch as our security men interact with them. They leave nothing to chance, not allowing them to come close to Jenny or me as we enter the prestigious hotel. The floors are made of crisp white marble, patterned with intertwining strands of gold. There is a magnificent floor-to-ceiling man-made waterfall, designed entirely in stone that cascades water down its length to the lush green tropical plants housed at its base.

Matt checks in with the desk attendant and we are immediately escorted to the penthouse suite. The living room window covers the expanse of the wall, allowing us a panoramic view of the city, white sands that sprawl out to the brilliant blue coast below, and mountainous ranges as far as the eye can see.

"It was a long flight and I'm starving. Is anyone besides me hungry?" Jenny asks the group.

A resounding yes is heard from the group and she begins taking orders and calling for room service, while I review the information that Jay has provided us about Vicenti.

There is a knock on the door and I stand up intending to answer it. "No Kate, the guards will take care of it," Sheldon says as they open the door and go outside before returning with two silver carts laden with food and begin handing the plates out to the group. There are only six seats around the dining room table and most of the security men take their food and disperse into the living room to talk while Matt and Sheldon stay with Jenny and me.

"I want to go over the satellite image of Vicenti's estate while we eat," Sheldon says, focusing us on his iPad. He acquaints us with what to expect as we arrive and leave the estate. We review the interior of the home, reason for me being here, and discuss potential questions that Vicenti may ask. I stare down at my barely touched pancakes, eggs, and fruit willing my nerves to stay at bay.

My cell phone vibrates and I look at the incoming message. The screen displays Lloyd's phone number.

Message: What the hell are you doing?

I frown at the message and type a response into my cell.

Reply: Making this right.

Message: Katarina, I don't want you anywhere near Vicenti.

I turn off my cell needing to concentrate on the task at hand and excuse myself to go and get ready.

I change into a short black skirt that barely skims the top of my thighs, a silver silk camisole, and black suit jacket. I put on the four-inch black Louboutin stilt heels with straps that crisscross around my ankles and grimace, walking around the room to get acclimated to their height. I twirl the magnificent princess cut diamond ring that represents my engagement to Chase, a lie in every sense, but Vicenti cannot possibly know this. I freshen up my makeup and brush out my long auburn hair until it is glossy and shimmering.

I take a last turn in front of the mirror as Jenny walks in and whistles. "Kate you look hot. Like one of those executives you see on the cover of magazines," she says.

"I sure hope so. This man is in charge of the entire drug empire in South America, Jenny."

"You are going to have him eating out of your hands," she says, nodding her head in approval.

"He could have me taken out with a snap of his fingers," I say nervously.

She sits on my bed cross legged. "Don't let him see even the slightest bit of fear. You are bringing him information that he needs."

"You're right. I hope what Chase did will be viewed as honorable," I say, still navigating the pending conversation in my head. Jenny slides off the bed and gives me a large hug. "It's your job to make him see that. You should have no problem since you look like a frikken billionaire's fiancée and a mob boss's daughter," she says.

I hug her to me holding my best friend tightly. "This is it, I better go," I say.

"You've got this, Kate," she says.

Sheldon has had the car brought around for us and the driver is waiting under the expansive stone pillars as we exit the hotel. Sheldon opens the back door and I settle into the back seat of the limo and he and Matt slide into the seats across from me. He glances at his cell phone and scowls.

"What's the matter?" I ask.

"Nothing, but you really should turn your phone back on," he says, shaking his head.

"Chase?"

"Yes," he says, typing a message into his phone.

"What does he want?" I ask.

"A minute-to-minute update," he says, shaking his head as he types a message into his cell phone.

"Sorry, Sheldon," I say.

"Any chance I can get you to turn on your phone?" he asks.

"No, I need to concentrate right now. I'll talk to him when it's over," I say, leaning into the plush black leather seats for the thirty-five-minute drive to Vicenti's. As we get out of the city and closer to the estate my heart begins to race. I try to slow its beat, breathing in and back out deeply. The driver finally veers off the highway and we follow a winding road that takes us through a dense path of palm trees. The vehicle slows drastically as we approach a guard station.

"Sheldon, are we okay?" I ask, taking in the men with machine guns standing outside of the small little station in front of us.

"Don't worry, Kate," he says as our driver speaks with the guardsmen for a few moments. The gates to the property open and we are waved through by the security men. In a half mile, a sprawling mass of contemporary white stone pillars and glass comes into view, set amongst palm trees, bamboo and green tropical plants which are all blowing in the warm ocean breeze.

SIXTEEN

The doorman shows Sheldon and me into a grand sitting room. The sheer opulence of the room would have once intimidated me. The vast floor-to-ceiling windows give the impression of walls made of glass, overlooking the brilliant blue sea and palm trees below. It is not long before a dark haired man of medium height with a sprinkling of grey, lean and trim enters the room. He is wearing black dress pants and a tan-colored polo. His eyes are steely grey, almost the color of ash as he regards me. His laconic gaze is somewhat unwavering, taking me in.

I meet his eyes, capturing them with my own, trying to remember who I am, daughter of the head of the East Coast crime syndicate and fiancée to one of the wealthiest men in the world.

He holds out his hand and I extend mine thinking that he wants to shake hands, but instead, he takes it to his lips, brushing a light kiss over it. "You must be Katarina," he says and his voice is gentle, not commanding as I would have expected.

"I am and you must be Vicenti, I've heard much about you in the past few days," I say.

"It's lovely to meet you in person. You are every bit as beautiful as your mother," he says.

"Thank you. I appreciate you seeing me on such short notice," I say, trying not to show surprise at the reference to my mother.

"I can't think of anything I would rather be doing at the moment. In fact, you have my curiosity peaked," he says, gesturing me to the couch.

"Thank you. I know your time is precious and I will get right to the point. I am aware that Chase has already shared some information with you recently, but I believe there is more that you need to be aware of now," I say.

"I'm quite intrigued, Miss Meilers," he says, a slight smile crossing his lips.

"May we talk openly in this room?" I ask.

"We can," he says, nodding to the security man that has taken up vigilance next to Sheldon at the doorway. He and Sheldon depart, closing the door behind them, leaving the two of us alone in the large room.

"I appreciate that security has been dismissed, but in terms of satellite communications?" I ask.

"You can be assured my compound is completely protected," he says.

"Good. I would not want what I am about to share with you captured on tape by anyone," I say.

He raises his eyes in question. "Please proceed, Katarina," he says.

"I'm sure you recall the shipment of merchandise confiscated last year on Alfreita's ship."

"I do," he says.

"I also believe Chase has recently informed you that my father's brother, Joey, was the one responsible for alerting the authorities about its location. Unfortunately, Chase was aboard the ship, meeting with Alfreita regarding an entirely different matter, but Interpol thought he was responsible given his financial status," I say.

"Miss Meilers, while I greatly enjoy hearing you speak, this is not new information. Your fiancé and I have been in communication as of late and I am also aware that Alfreita kidnapped your mother in an effort to coerce Chase into moving product. This was a terrible mistake on Alfreita's part. Carlos Larussio, as you know, is not a man to cross, especially where Karissa is concerned," he says.

"Yes, I'm aware that Chase has been in contact with you, but I'm not sure, however, if he's shared the situation he now faces or how that impacts you directly," I say.

He gives nothing away, reminding me of that hooded and controlled look on Chase's face when he is in the middle of negotiating a situation. "Please continue," he says.

"As you referenced, Alfreita did kidnap my mother. Chase and my father were in the process of drawing him out of hiding this week. Joey, my uncle, found out that Chase and my father had discovered he was behind the leak last year and that he was systematically trying to move into your territory, attempting as well to take over as head of the Larussio family."

"It would appear it has been quite a week, but I am still not sure how all of this is connected to me," he says.

"Yes, I am just coming to that very important part of the story," I say.

His eyebrows raise and he nods. "Carry on, Katarina," he says.

"What you may not be aware of is that last year Chase's security team intercepted a communication between Alfreita and Joey that would have freed him of any involvement with the shipment."

"I'm not sure I understand. Why is it that Chase did not come forward with this when he was all but indicted last year or when we spoke last week?" he asks, standing up and walking to the window.

"Chase did not use the communication because he did not believe Interpol had enough to make the charges stick at the time, which as it turns out they did not. More importantly, he was not interested in bringing trouble to your door or to that of the Larussio family," I say.

"My door," he says, turning towards me once again. His steely eyes are intimidating, watching me, and I find it hard to concentrate. I slowly stretch my leg, crossing it over the top of my left thigh and his eyes follow the gesture giving me a brief reprieve from the intensity of his stare.

"You see Joey and Alfreita were discussing the shipment intended for you. The entire load was full of subpar product, in fact poisonous merchandise that Alfreita had acquired from Joey with the specific intent of discrediting you when people learned of the product's effects," I say.

"And how is it that you came across this information and in what way does it impact me?" he asks.

"Chase became aware of a communication picked up over the waves which included a pretty pointed conversation that would seem to suggest you, or at least those in your employ, were aware of the product's deadly side effects."

"You're going to need to be more specific," he says, walking towards me.

"The conversation would implicate you in trying to poison innocent people. We're talking about a drug so powerful that it will kill someone within days of consumption," I say.

"I just spoke with Chase and he did not reference this," he says.

"He didn't mention it because he is an honorable man and has no intent on using the tape to clear his name. Chase asked his security team to destroy the tape last year not wanting to turn evidence on one of the Larussio family members or yourself. His father and Carlos, my father, have been great friends for years."

"Ah, yes," he says, rubbing his finger across his chin. "I do know the fathers go back a long way. Chase is a brilliant investor and has done very well for himself throughout the years. He has a keen sense in business and inherently understands how things work in the world. So, what is it that I can do for you Katarina?" he asks.

"Well, as you know my father is recovering in the hospital from the shooting and Chase has been arrested. My father and Chase were trying to draw Alfreita out and made it look as though they were transferring product from one yacht to another. The police have surveillance footage of that and believe they can use it to make the charges hold from last year. Chase won't come forward with the communication. In fact, he thinks it was destroyed since that is the order he gave his security team."

"It was not destroyed?" he asks.

"It was not, but no one is interested in turning the investigation towards you. However, the tape could be altered slightly and used to prove that Alfreita was behind the shipment."

"I admire your fortitude, Katarina. I have no doubt that while you have inherited your mother's beautiful looks you have also inherited your father's sense of nobility and shrewd business sense. I take it you came with a copy of the communication for me to review?" he says.

"I did. Jay, his head of security, will have to answer to Chase for that when the time comes," I say, handing him the audio copy that Sheldon provided from the backup system.

I watch as he listens to the conversation I have heard multiple times by now, memorizing the part that proves not only did my uncle and Alfreita know they were intending to give the poisonous product to Vicenti's group, but can be heard talking to someone from Vicenti's team who knew the product would be poisonous and planned to pocket the difference in price between that and the higher quality product Vicenti typically moved.

"This tape, if ever placed into the hands of Interpol would have the ability to bring you and Alfreita to prison for the rest of your lives. This is why Chase chose to deal with the accusations himself," I say.

He is solemn as he shuts the device off. "I take it there are copies?" he asks.

"Our security team can procure whatever you may need," I say.

"I have no doubt, Katerina. Let me put your mind at ease. I would never have distributed a product of this quality, as your father can attest. He and I have a great respect for each other, which is why we have never attempted to encroach in the other's space. Your uncle was a greedy, evil man that apparently went to great lengths in his attempts to discredit both of our families. It is disheartening that someone in my employ knew of and allowed the endangerment of thousands of people, besides putting my reputation at risk."

"It is indeed," I say, trying to process what he has told me.

"I admire the way Chase navigated through this situation and have the utmost respect for the young man. It would please me greatly to repay him for protecting my name. I'll meet with my team and reach you in the morning with a plan," he says.

"Just what would that entail?" I ask him warily.

"Rest assured. The situation will be handled with the utmost of diplomacy and you will not regret coming to discuss this with me. In fact, I appreciate greatly that you came to see me, Katarina," he says as I stand. He raises my hand to his lips before guiding me to the front door of his home where Sheldon waits for me.

Vicenti shakes hands with Sheldon. "Thank you for bringing Katarina. I take it you'll be on your way stateside as quickly as possible?" he asks.

"Yes, sir. We need to stop at the hotel and then run by the hospital. Chase's head of security is recovering from surgery and will be here until he is strong enough to be flown home," he says.

"Very well, I'll have my men accompany you and ensure that you get up in the air safely. Please exercise all precautions with her on the way home. The ties between Interpol and Alfreita are concerning," Vicenti says.

"Thank you, sir," Sheldon says, not referencing the teams which surround the large estate, in the event we were followed or something went awry.

We are soon navigating the lush tropical road back to the main highway. I turn on my cell and review the messages from Chase telling me not to talk to Vicenti. We are barely at the entrance of the hotel when the vibration on my phone signals an incoming message.

Message: Where are you?

Reply: Back at the hotel. All is well.

Message: When do you arrive stateside?

Message: I am leaving for the states within the hour.

Message: Good.

Poor Lloyd, having to deal with what I am sure is a contentious and bad tempered Chase. We stop by the hospital and I don a scarf as Sheldon reminds me not to discuss anything except Jay's health. He is sitting up in bed with his cell phone in hand when we walk in. He shakes his head as he puts it onto his bedside table.

"A message from Chase?" I whisper, knowing all too well that it is.

"I think we're all going to catch a little hell when we get home. You probably more than anyone," he says. It is good to see Jay smile and feeling a little better.

"I'll be flying back to Chicago as soon as the physician clears me. It sounds like Lloyd has been bothering the physicians here constantly. They're probably anxious to get my butt out of here," he says laughing. We visit for a little longer, scribble down a quick update and then say our goodbyes before leaving the hospital.

The driver navigates the busy traffic and it is not long before we arrive at the hotel. Jenny and the security men are waiting for us as we pull into the covered entrance. The hotel porter places our bags into the trunk and she slides in next to me while the other men get into the car directly behind us.

"How did it go?" she asks.

"He's working on a plan to get pieces of the tape released," I say.

"I worked with Nate while you were gone. He's got all the preliminary information and is ready to release once the tape goes live. You'll have to call him though. He wants you or Chase to approve it," she says.

"Okay, no problem," I say, sending a text to Nate as the limo heads towards the airfield. The Prestian Corp jet is waiting as we approach and I breathe a sigh of relief that there is no sign of paparazzi. The security team moves us quickly from the limo to the plane and once we're boarded I text my mom.

Message: About to take off. How's Dad?

Reply: Good, stable. Lloyd, Chase's attorney made plans to have your dad flown back to NY tomorrow.

Message: Poor guy!! I hope Chase is paying him well this week.

Reply: I'm sure he is!

Jenny reviews the rest of the social media plans she and Nate worked on while I was at the hospital and I'm duly impressed that everything has been laid out in such a methodic manner before exhaustion finally takes its toll. We pull the hideaway bed out from the seats adjacent to the window and I give her a pillow and blanket from the overhead before making my way into the plane's bedroom.

I wake to a knock on the door and glance down at the time on my phone with a start. I've slept so long that there's no time for a shower before we land. I slide into a pair of yoga pants, sweat shirt and boots, brush my teeth and twist my hair into a messy bun. I am barely seated and buckled in before the pilot announces the final decent and touches down at the O'Hare airport. As we get into the back of the awaiting limo my cell phone rings.

"Good morning, Katerina," a gentle voice that I immediately recognize as Vicenti says.

"Good morning. I wasn't expecting to hear from you so soon. We just landed," I say.

"I spoke with Sheldon earlier and he informed me you were still sleeping or I would have connected with you sooner. The men have been working through the night to get the communications dispersed. The stories have already hit the Associated Press and many of the local releases will have it included as part of their headlines this morning due to the time difference," he says.

"What should I expect?"

"While clearly exposing Alfreita and your uncle, the release will completely absolve Chase from any of the events last year. If Interpol has not destroyed the product from that shipment, they will be able to test it and Alfreita will be convicted for the rest of his life, if not worse," he says.

"You can't know how much I appreciate this. Thank you so much," I say.

"Katarina, unfortunately we are still working through a few things. It was one of the largest product shipments ever so there's a chance it was taken straight to the infirmary, although we are counting on the fact they wanted Chase's indictment and held it to use it as evidence. Secondly, Prince Alfreita has significant and powerful connections with highly positioned agents within Interpol. We will see how this plays out, but that aside, the tape's release absolves Chase and the Larussio family of any involvement. You will most certainly be accosted by reporters and paparazzi as word continues to leak. I'm sure I do not need to mention that discretion is expected," he says.

"No, of course not. If there is ever anything I can do to assist you, please do not hesitate to contact me," I say.

"Likewise, I'm glad we had a chance to meet and do give my best to both Chase and your father," he says before disconnecting.

"Vicenti?" Sheldon asks.

"Yes, it would appear everything has been taken care of. He told me that you and your teams worked through the night to clear Chase and put Alfreita behind us. I can't tell you how much I appreciate that," I say.

"No need to thank me, Kate. That's what Chase pays me to do. Although this week has been a little adventurous even for us," he says as the driver comes to a stop in front of Jenny's complex.

"Jenny, with everything going on Matt will stay with you, at least for a little while," Sheldon says.

"That is really not necessary," she says.

"Boss's orders. Chase wants you to have round the clock security. I'll get a hold of you with long range plans," he says.

"Thanks for everything you did to help Nate and just for being with me," I say, ignoring her upraised eyes and hugging her to me.

"I seriously wouldn't have missed all the excitement for anything. I'm just glad things are working out so well for everyone," she says, squeezing me tight before she gets out of the car.

"Sheldon, take me to the police station. I want to see Chase."

"Um, Chase has been in contact. I'm to have you safely back to the house and as quickly as possible," he says, looking slightly embarrassed.

"You heard from him?"

"Lloyd," he says, splitting off from the city traffic onto the highway that leads to the country house. I contemplate how long it will take for them to release Chase and what we'll say to each other as Sheldon's cell phone rings breaking through my reverie.

"Yes, we're home. I'll let her know. Yes, I understand," Sheldon responds before hanging up.

"Was that Lloyd?"

"You must still have your phone on silent," he says. I rummage in my purse, pull out my phone and check the messages. There are three missed calls, none of them with a voicemail, and three texts.

Message: Where are you?

Message: Where are you?

Message: I am coming after you!

I break into a full laugh as I see the messages he's left and the ache in my heart lightens knowing he must have already been released.

"He's out? I ask Sheldon.

"Yes, ma'am. He's on his way home," he says, grinning into the rearview mirror.

"Oh, my God. We did it, Sheldon! Thank you so much for all your help," I say as some of the tension begins to subside.

"Most welcome, Kate. Besides, there was no way I was going to explain to Chase how you managed to give me the slip twice," he says.

"I hope I didn't put you in too bad of a position. I'll talk to Chase if I need to," I say.

"It's fine, Kate. I probably have more explaining to do for taking you to Brazil than for you giving me the slip in Aruba," he says.

"Why are you wearing such a big smile then?" I ask, feeling all the tension in my body begin to subside.

"You need to ask?" he says.

"Hmm, maybe not. I'm probably in more trouble than you," I say.

"Well, I would certainly hope so."

"Sheldon!" I say, as he is waved through the gates.

"If it's any consolation the entire team was pretty impressed with the way you went in and got things done for Chase."

"Thanks, Sheldon. It's the very least I could do."

"No problem, Kate," he says, pulling up to the entrance.

SEVENTEEN

Gaby greets us at the front door and after talking with her for a few moments I run upstairs to take a shower, relishing in the warm water and the smell of chamomile scented soap gliding over my body. My face is upturned letting the warm water cascade over me, soothingly rinsing the soap, along with the worry of the day from my hair and my face.

I sense him, before I feel him. The touch is light; a mere finger pressing gently against my spine, starting at the top of my shoulder blades and gliding sensually down the length of my back. My nipples harden under the contact and I feel goosebumps rise on my sensitive skin.

"Hi," I say hoarsely.

"Hello, Katarina. I see we have work to do on your listening skills. Clearly a just punishment can be found for a wayward fiancée who decides to leave her boyfriend hanging without any inclination of what she is doing, coerces his own security guards into assisting her and takes his jet to travel across the globe and go fraternize with the head of the largest cartel in the world," he says.

"Chase, it wasn't like..."

"Shh, Baby. I'm sure it was exactly like that," he says, capturing my wrists and securing them to the shower head with soft cuffs as he spreads my legs apart with his own. The rigidness of his cock presses against me from behind and I moisten at the feel of it, skin on skin. He pushes my hair from my shoulder, lightly caressing the sensitive spot between my ear and neck, nuzzling me with his mouth, sending shivers throughout the length of my body. I squirm but he does not let me escape, suckling, driving me crazy with desire. He runs his hands along the curve of my hips slowly tracing the length of my ass before reaching beneath me to insert his finger.

"Katarina, you are so wet, already. We've just begun, Baby," he says, working two fingers slowly in and out of me. My hips respond shamelessly, but he holds me in place, with a firm hand on my hip, controlling the friction my body is able to create while he continues to nuzzle my neck.

"You are a bad, bad girl," he whispers.

"I want you to turn around and remain absolutely still while I get washed up," he says, pulling his fingers out of me, leaving me bereft and aching for his touch.

He swivels me to face him. His body is sculptured and hard, sinewy muscles ripple and I am mesmerized by the erectness of his cock. He washes his hair, taking his time, letting the suds rinse him as he lathers his upper body.

"Your breathing is starting to change, Katarina," he says as I watch his soapy hand glide across his abdomen and trail down the patch of fine dark hair below. His deep green eyes capture mine, like magnets appraising me. He reaches up and lets one of my hands out of the cuffs.

"Touch yourself, but don't cum," he instructs quietly.

My hand glides across my stomach and through the soft auburn hair that lies below, parting it, rubbing lightly, and the deepening passion in his eyes is enough to push me over the edge.

"If you cum, I will punish you," he says hoarsely, running his lips along my shoulder, trailing over my chest before capturing a taut nipple with his mouth. He suckles, lingering, and rolls the other one firmly between two fingers as he does.

I softly moan as he squeezes, feeling it deep in my core. I let my fingers glide back and forth over the swollen area, now aching with desire. "Honey."

"Not yet, Baby," he says, deftly securing my hands above me again. He runs his fingers up and down my slickened opening, and then in one steady thrust, lifts me and brings me down atop him so that he is rooted deep inside of me. My legs wrap instinctively around his back, pulling him close. I feel the intensity of his rigidness, but he remains still, building my desire and body's urge to grind against him. He lifts me slowly, and then pulls me atop him, penetrating deep as I clench around him.

"Still, Baby," he says, holding my hips so that I am unable to move on my own accord.

My hands are above my head and he bites my erect nipples as he lifts me over his cock, agonizingly slow, tormenting me, driving in deep, holding my hips steady, and then pausing, allowing my heated desire to cool before he begins again over and over. I hear myself softly moaning aloud with longing and frustration.

"Enough?" he asks after what seems like an eternity.

"Yes," I pant as he brings me down faster and harder, rubbing against that special spot deep inside of me, building the ache until I can no longer hold back and begin trembling around his cock at the same time he finds his release deep inside of me. He kisses me gently on the lips as my legs unwrap and extend to the floor. He does not untie me right away, but instead rubs each of my still erect nipples, suckling them and kissing each one in turn, before returning to my mouth and slowly untying me.

He takes my face between his hands and kisses me harder, brushing my hair out of my face and leads me naked to the whirlpool, bending down to turn the water on. I pour a little of the chamomile scented bath salt that is sitting on the ledge into the water as it begins to run. He kisses me gently on the lips, and holds onto my arm as I step into the bubbling water and sink into its swirling bliss.

"Would you like a cup of coffee?" he asks.

"Yes, please." This is what I crave, intimacy with this man, sexually and emotionally. He secures a towel around his waist and leaves me alone with my thoughts. I sink into the water's depths letting it relax me before he returns with our coffee, placing the one with hazelnut and cream on the ledge in front of me. He lets his towel fall to the floor with a flick of his wrist. He is completely erect and I marvel at the lean sinewy muscles in his body and the power in his thighs as he steps into the whirlpool and slides into the water beside me.

"Do you have any idea how worried I've been about you?"

"Maybe as worried as I was about you when I couldn't find you," I respond.

His eyes raise in question and his lips quirk in response, but the smile does not reach his eyes. "You were halfway across the world and there wasn't a damn thing I could do about it," he says.

"Chase, I had to go. It was the only way to get you free," I say.

"I was worried sick thinking about what could have happened to you," he says.

"Everything worked out, Chase. Vicenti was grateful that you had kept his name protected and he did the right thing," I say.

"I need to know why you went to Vicenti, Katarina?" he asks.

"If I hadn't followed you there would have been more security at the resort. I feel responsible for a lot of things that happened that day," I say.

"None of this is your fault, Katarina. Tony has been working to overthrow your father for quite some time now. I'm just glad Jay figured it out and we arrived in time. There was a plan in place to bring Vicenti up to speed. I need you to trust that I have things under control and not put yourself in danger like that," he says.

"Chase, I did trust you and you told me that you wouldn't keep me in the dark anymore, but you did. Maybe you should have told me there was a plan in place? You were the only one I told about Ty. You told me that you were going to make sure he couldn't blackmail Jenny anymore and then the police find him beaten half to death. You had to think that I would assume you had something to do with it unless you told me otherwise. Why didn't you?"

"I shouldn't have needed to, on either count."

"Chase, let me get this out. It's been bothering me for a long time. You told me there were going to be stories about the Miami explosion, but if you had told me what really happened, I would have believed you. When my mom recounted the story it was different than what you told me. You left me no choice but to doubt what happened."

He rubs his hands through his hair; his eyes are hooded and controlled and there is a storm of emotion that plays over his handsome features. "Katarina, this is not how I saw this conversation playing out. You doubted what happened because of how it appeared. That is not what I consider trust. I need more, to know that when things are swirling around us that you trust me implicitly, not just sexually, but in all things. I can't tell you how many nights I've lain awake wondering what I should and shouldn't share with you, knowing that at any time something may trigger you to leave on principle. I want to shelter you from the ugly realities and have no doubt there will be others," he says.

"There's nothing ugly about you making sure we got my mom back, or ensuring that we got the evidence back from Ty that would have convicted Jenny. You did absolutely nothing to be ashamed of, I just didn't know it because you didn't confide in me and I guess that's what I was looking for," I say quietly.

"Katarina, those particular situations just happened to go well. Not everything will go so smoothly which is the fundamental issue. I would have done or will do in the future whatever it takes to keep my family safe. We haven't even talked about the fact that I killed a man. All the things you say I didn't do? I killed a man, shot him in the fucking heart, Katarina."

"Chase, you saved my dad's life. How could you ever feel like I would think badly of you for that? The surgeon said that if the bullet had been just a hair closer he wouldn't have even made it to the hospital. My dad told me what really happened with Ty, too," I say.

"Katarina, I told you when we met the work I do brings dissention to areas around the world. You've only seen a glance. Look at what happened last month. All the rioting and the injuries were a direct result of the decision made not to concede to their demands. I want to keep you protected from all of that and trust that I am doing what has to be done for the right reasons, good or bad. If you can't, it's no way for either of us to live."

"I don't want a life without you, Chase. I want to marry you and spend the rest of my life sharing it with you and our children," I say, looking into the deep green pools that are now holding me captive with their intensity.

He crushes my lips with his, capturing them, parting them so he can explore the warmth within, sealing our love and commitment as he picks me up and pulls me onto his hardness.

EIGHTEEN

We say our goodbyes to Gaby and Sheldon drives us to the airport so that we can fly to New York for the funeral. "You sure you're okay with this?" I say, taking in his solemn features as we get situated into our seats on the aircraft.

"I'm trying to be, Katarina. We need to be there to support your father, but it's not going to be easy looking at the family your uncle has left behind," he says.

"I can only imagine, Chase. Dad said he talked to most of the family and they understand that if you hadn't taken things into your own hands my father is the one we would be burying and the family business would be at jeopardy."

"Yes, he talked to me about it and I appreciate him sharing that with me," Chase says.

"I was surprised the family wanted the funeral in New York. Mom told me he's been living overseas for the last ten years, but their father would have wanted him buried in the family vault," I say.

The trip to New York City is quick and uneventful and when we arrive at the large Catholic church we are greeted by a crowd of family members I know, in addition to many friends of the family who I have not met. They appear to hold no ill will toward Chase and I am touched by the overwhelming comfort and gratitude expressed to both of us.

Security teams from both the Larussio and Prestian family hold vigil in an attempt to keep reporters at bay as members of the family enter the church and take their seats. My father's eyes are moist with emotion after the priest's words as he takes the stand to provide the eulogy for his younger brother. He shares memories of their younger days and all of the accomplishments his brother achieved in his lifetime. Family and friends alike are moved by the recantation. I take Chase's hand, squeezing it tightly. An award winning opera star sings a few renditions of classic Italian ballads before Ave Maria is sung which brings the congregation to tears. The coffin is slowly wheeled outside to the awaiting hearse and we leave the church.

The tension radiating from him is palpable as our limousine makes its way forward, near the front of the processional. The police, along with the Larussio security men, work side by side to ensure disruptions to the line do not exist, but when the hearse arrives at the private gravesite the security team has everything they can do to keep the paparazzi at bay. It is a somber hour as the family pays their last respects before he is laid to rest in the private vault and a final prayer is said. Chase is unusually quiet and I wish there was something I could say or do to ease his pain.

A large family gathering is planned at my parents' home after the service and close friends and family have been invited to spend time with each other. It is late evening before we say our goodbyes and Sheldon navigates the limousine back to LaGuardia for the flight home. Chase's favorite jet is awaiting our arrival. We board and he spends a few moments talking to the pilots before we enter the living area of the plane. The fireplace is on, spreading a warmth and coziness throughout the cabin. He settles into the large leather couch and pulls me into his arms and kisses me gently. We are not even in the air yet before Chase's cell goes off.

"Chase here," he says, shrugging out of his suit coat.

"Dammit! No, just get more people on it. Until then we'll be working from home. Didn't I tell you to take some time off?" he asks, his brows furrowing, pausing to listen to the caller on the other end.

"Thanks Jay, but I want you to get some rest now. Sheldon has everything under control and when you come back we'll move him full-time to Katarina's detail. If he's interested that is. You know she can be pretty hard to handle," he says, smirking at me.

I lower my eyes at him and give Sheldon, who has come into the cabin and is seated in one of the reclining chairs by the window, a smile. He disconnects just as the pilot begins making his way down the runway.

"Alfreita has gone into hiding again. Every indication would lead you to believe that he is being aided by his family members in the Middle East and Interpol," Chase says.

"It scares me that he's still out there," I say.

"We have a team investigating his relationships with Interpol, but we haven't learned anything of use, yet. Jay just wanted to let us know security has been ramped up at home and what we should expect when we get to the airport," Chase explains.

"That's why you said we would be working from home this week?" I say.

"Just precautionary, and it's a short week with Thanksgiving on Thursday," he says.

"Remember Mom and Dad will fly in for Thanksgiving. I told them we would have the Boys and Girls Club over for the day and they seemed happy to spend it with the teenagers."

"Good, I'm sure the kids will enjoy it, as well."

"Mom asked me about traveling to New York the week between Christmas and New Years to celebrate the holidays," I say.

"It sounds like a good plan, Dad and Emily would be pleased, but let's not finalize anything until we learn a little bit more about Alfreita's plans. I don't want a repeat of last time," he says, kissing my lips gently.

"Sheldon, can you get ahold of the team for a conference call once we get home? I'd like to discuss short and long term plans with them," he says.

"Already done, Chase. Jay thought you would want to pull everyone together. He plans to sign on even though I told him we had it covered," Sheldon says.

"Jay's a good man. I told him not to come back for a month, but we'll see how that plays out. Thanks for the update and taking care of things in his absence. I'll leave you to the logistics then," Chase says.

"There's frenzy on the tarmac," I say to Chase as we touch down at O'Hare.

"The paparazzi were alerted to our arrival so we've got security and police officers onsite," Chase says, as we make our way from the plane to the limo. Sheldon climbs into the front seat after making sure we are safely in the back, and I notice that vehicles have been positioned both in the front and back of us. I am reminded of another time when this would have scared me. Right now, I feel blessed they are keeping us safeguarded from this maniac who would like nothing better than to profit from poisoning thousands of people, do us harm, and is being protected by Interpol.

Once we get on the highway, it is not a long trip to the country house since Sunday evening traffic is relatively light. We find Gaby bent over at the counter going through recipes as we walk into the kitchen. She looks up with a start as we enter the room.

"I didn't hear you two sneak in," she admonishes, coming round the table to give us a quick hug. "I bet you're absolutely famished," she says, bustling over to the crock pot. As she lifts the lid the delicious aroma of thyme and slow roasted chicken fill the air.

"You bet I am, absolutely starving," Chase says, winking at me.

"What do you have in that pot, Gaby?" he says, pulling out a chair for me at the small oval kitchen table.

"Chicken dumpling soup," she says, ladling two soup bowls full.

"It smells delicious," I say, as we sit down to eat.

"Gaby, Katarina's parents will be spending Thanksgiving with us," he says.

"Wonderful, the more the merrier," she says and the twinkle in her eyes is unmistakable. The soup is wonderful and as we near the bottom of our bowls she brings us each a piece of freshly baked bread adorned with Irish cream butter and honey. I spend a few minutes chatting with Gaby about the holiday menu and as she's talking look down at an incoming message on my phone.

Message: I've been waiting all day to get you upstairs.

I chat with Gaby for a few moments before excusing myself for the evening and slowly walk past Chase while responding to his message.

Reply: Inquiring minds want to know what you have planned?

Message: A punishment, fit for all the worry and anguish you've caused me.

My heart skips a beat. We have not experimented like that since before we went to Aruba and he proposed.

Message: When you get upstairs take off all of your clothes. Leave on your bracelet and necklace. Text me when you are ready.

Everything south clenches at the thought and I feel myself moisten as I reread his message. I make sure Gaby is not looking before I slide my tongue through the honey and butter mixture, swirling it through the creamy sweetness, watching as his eyes follow my movements, before saying goodnight to Gaby.

I head upstairs and twirl my hair a few times, sliding it into a clip to hold its length, before I strip out of my clothes and slide underneath the warm water of the shower. I have a heightened awareness of my body's anticipation, his message stirring me, causing me to moisten, and my nipples to become hard and erect as the warm droplets of water rain sensually over their tips. I wash my body, gliding the loofah over my skin, eagerly anticipating the night to come. I turn off the water and spritz the Aruban Aloe moisturizer on my skin, deeply inhaling its scent and relishing in the soft, silky way it leaves my skin, before drying off with one of the Kashmir towels.

Message: Out of the shower.

The swoosh of my cell phone alerts me to an incoming text.

Message: Walk nude into the bedroom. Open our toy drawer. Take out the gift box.

My body is wired, wondering what he has purchased, and what the night will bring. I open our nightstand and look into the drawer. The package is at least twelve inches in length, rectangular in shape and wrapped in black wrapping paper with a red bow. There is a small card that simply says, "Katarina."

Message: I found the package. Can I open it?

Reply: Patience, Baby. Take it to bed and wait for me there.

I do as he asks, propping two pillows behind me, cushioning me as I sit upright against the headboard.

Message: In bed, nude, waiting...

Reply: Unwrap the package, Baby.

My fingers are shaking as I untie the red bow wound around the rectangular box. I set the ribbon aside and begin unpeeling the black wrapping paper, revealing a plain white oblong box below.

Message: I have finished unwrapping the package. May I open the box?

Reply: Very good, Baby. Yes, open the box and let me know once complete.

I slide my fingers along the seams and unseal the container. Inside is a large, rectangular shaped wooden handled paddle. I take it out of the box, running my hands over its shape. I feel myself moistening, but apprehensive as I contemplate its intent, setting it aside while I continue to explore the contents of the package.

Message: The package is opened.

Reply: Have you read the note?

Message: Not yet.

Reply: I'm impressed with your restraint. Read it and follow its instructions.

Katarina,

Sex of this nature should only occur between lovers who have complete trust in each other. Partners who know they will not only be taken to newly found heights, but will not be pushed beyond their boundaries. Do you trust me?

I contemplate the hard thick rectangular shaped paddle and reread his note again. I pick up my cell and type a single word.

Message: Yes

Reply: Lie down on the bed, and spread your legs for me.

Message: Done.

Reply: Let the lubricant drizzle over your clit. Slide the vibrator in nice and slow.

I am dripping with anticipation and slide down in the bed, propping my head on the pillows as I trickle some of the lubricating oil over my newly waxed mound, gliding it through my folds before I rub the end of the vibrator against my clit, and further south, allowing it to unhurriedly explore my depths before sinking it slowly and increasingly deeper within me.

The door opens and I continue sliding it in and out, panting, as he very slowly closes the door behind him and approaches the bed. "Don't stop, Baby," he says, as he pulls his shirt over his head, exposing a broad muscled torso and lean waist, tossing it over the top of the reading chair before unfastening his dress pants and allowing them to fall to the floor.

"Keep sliding it in, slowly, and now turn the vibrator onto its lowest speed, but don't cum or your punishment will be worse," he instructs.

I slide it in further, deeply rooting it, before pushing the button which ignites the gentle pulsing sensations that I can now feel radiating against me.

"Flip over on your stomach and lay on top of the pillows," he says, adjusting them as I turn. My ass is now elevated and the vibrator is held firmly in place by my weight and the pillows, lightly pulsating, igniting a slowly developing need within me.

"I have wanted to do this ever since I found out you took off from the resort. Then when I found out you took my jet and flew off to Brazil, I had exactly this vision in my mind. No ties, just you laying completely at my mercy of your own accord," he says, drawing a line down the bottom of my spine and over my exposed rear. "I contemplated many punishments, but then I came across this lovely little paddle," he says, tracing it along the path of his fingers. It is cool in contrast to my heated skin as it circles the cheeks of my ass.

"It's important for you to tell me if it is getting too intense. Can you do that, Katarina?" he asks, trailing the implement over my cheeks, and top of my thighs.

"Yes," I say, turning my face to the side. I can feel the flush of my cheeks; my body is having a difficult time not rubbing against the vibrator for relief. If I move, I am not sure if I will be able to control it. It is pulsating up and then down, causing an ache deep inside of me.

"Very good, I think a paddle to the ass for each day since we returned from Aruba will do nicely," he says, circling the paddle against my skin. I quickly do the math in my head; almost two weeks. Thirteen times? I swallow, trying to diminish my apprehension.

"Now you are going to be punished, Katarina. Your responsibility is to ensure you do not cum until I allow you to or for you to tell me it's getting to be too much. Are you ready?" he asks.

"Yes," I say, trying to keep my ass cheeks from clenching as I anticipate the whack of the paddle. It is slow coming and connects with a loud cracking sound. It does not hurt as badly as I anticipated, but instead, propels my raised body deeper onto the vibrator; its friction against my clit causes the intensity in my desire to ignite. The second, third and fourth come succinctly, in the same fashion. It is all I can do not to moan aloud as he continues, my body rubbing against the droning end of the vibrator with each connection of the paddle to my body. I finally get my breathing in sync after seven, eight and nine, forcing myself to think of something else, warding off the intense desire of orgasm that threatens.

"You're doing well, Katarina. Breathe through it, Baby," he encourages. I am beyond heated, my body screaming for release, but we have to be near the end. I have lost count and just as I do not believe I can hold on any longer he says, "Very well done," sliding me onto my back, turning my body so my legs are hanging over the edge of the bed on either side of him. He slowly pulls the vibrator from my body, and with one rigid thrust penetrates me. The heat from his body is intense compared to that of the vibrator and as he moves, the desire within me ignites. I softly moan, knowing I will not be able to hold on much longer, but not wanting to give in. My body clenches around his tightly, my legs entwine around his waist, pulling him in as deeply as possible.

"Cum for me, Katarina," he says, and my body responds shamefully to his command, trembling around him as he releases deep inside of me. We lay together for what seems like an eternity as we catch our breath. He lies on his side and pulls me into his arms, kissing my lips as he brushes a strand of hair out of my face. "I love you, Baby," he says, holding me tightly against his beating chest, sealing my lips with a deep kiss before I can respond.

"I love you, too," I say, barely able to speak yet.

"You look absolutely wrecked. Let's get you into a warm bath and washed up before you fall asleep," he says, getting up to turn the whirlpool on in the bathroom. I hear the water running and walk nude into the living room to pour us each a glass of white wine before heading into the bathroom. The smell of chamomile wafts through the air and I inhale its scent deeply. The lights are low and one single candle burns on the stone ledge of the tub. He turns the water off as I set the glasses down and holds out his hand, assisting me into the warm depths as I sit in front of him. I stretch my legs out over the top of his, entwining them as I lean back against his chest. He pushes my hair off my shoulder and kisses the sensitive skin of my neck.

"You did very well today, Katarina. I didn't think you would last," he says.

"I didn't know if I would at first or near the end. It was pretty intense. I wasn't expecting that," I say.

"What didn't you expect?" he asks, still rubbing the skin along my neck with his lips.

"Well, I thought the punishment was the paddle," I say, glad I am not facing him since I can feel the warmth of my blush rise to my cheeks.

"So you thought it would hurt?" he asks.

"Well, the thought crossed my mind. It looked pretty intimidating in the box and you did say you intended to punish me," I say.

"Indeed, I did. I think I also told you the very first time I spanked you that by punishment I intend to drive you absolutely crazy, not hurt you. Did I not?" he asks.

I smile as I recall asking him to spank me the first time, wanting to know what it would feel like. "Yes, you did and that did cross my mind," I say.

"Were you scared, Katarina? Did you think I might hurt you?" he asks softly.

"A little apprehensive may describe how I was feeling, but I knew I could stop at any time. I didn't want to give in once I figured out what the punishment was, but I wouldn't have made it if you hadn't encouraged me to breathe through it," I say, taking a small sip of my wine.

"Yes, your breathing had changed," he says, turning me around to face him, straddling my legs on either side of his thighs.

"You knew I was getting too close," I say, running my finger across his lower lip.

"Baby, when we're playing like that it's my responsibility to know exactly where you are both physically and emotionally. I have to be aware of those things so I don't push you too far. Was it too intense for you?" he asks, concern showing in his eyes as he searches my features.

"It was very intense, and it was a punishment. You know I don't like it when you keep me hanging like that, especially when it's that hot," I say blushing.

"You were intended to feel the difficulty of waiting, holding back while things were swirling out of your control, but not more than you could take, Baby," he says.

"It took everything I had to control my response. And you intentionally led me to believe that I was going to get spanked hard," I exclaim.

His eyes are full of laughter as he contemplates this. "I do admit, I intended for you to think about it, hoping that you would trust me enough to play," he says.

"Devil," I exclaim, as he lifts me up and onto his rigid cock sinking me onto his hardness until he is fully rooted inside of me.

"Well it was meant to smart a little, maybe I took it too easy on you," he says, cupping my ass with his hands as he captures my lips with his own.

NINETEEN

I wake up early Wednesday determined to assist Gaby with preparations for the forty teenagers from the Boys and Girls Club and my parents who will be joining us for Thanksgiving dinner. I throw on a pair of yoga pants, wooly socks and a long sleeve Henley, pull my hair back into a pony tail and head downstairs.

"Kate, we have more than enough help, really. Chase always has so many workers brought in that it's enough for me to keep them all busy. I think he knows the young ones from town use it for extra Christmas money," she whispers to me with a twinkle in her eye.

"I know, Gaby, but I'd like to be in the kitchen," I say.

"Well, just remember that you asked," she says, tossing me an apron.

We have been working all day and I am in the middle of grinding whole cranberries for a cranberry and orange zest relish when Chase walks into the kitchen, pausing to chat with the local women who have been helping for the last few days. His dark green eyes are alight with mischief as they find mine and his mouth quirks.

"What?" I mouth silently.

"Gaby, Katarina's parents are coming in tonight, instead of tomorrow. They'll be staying for dinner. If you don't mind I'd like to steal Katarina away for a short while," he says.

"Yes, I've been trying to scoot her out from under foot all day," she clucks.

I raise my hands in mock despair playing along with their little joke and narrow my eyes at Chase who seems to be enjoying himself immensely at my expense. I cover the relish and wash my hands before following Chase into the living room.

"Is something wrong?" I ask.

"Nothing at all, Baby. I just wanted to spend a little time with you before everyone arrives," he says, pulling me into his arms.

"The room looks so inviting. Gaby and the ladies did a wonderful job decorating," I say, looking around at the two stone fireplaces which are blazing with crackling wood and decorated with cornucopias, baskets of pinecones and twinkling lights for the holiday. The view through the picture window is of snow laden pine trees—a magical winter wonderland— and holiday music is playing lightly overhead.

"Dance with me," he says, spinning me around and pulling me close into his arms. He leads, his powerful thighs a guide for my own, dancing with me until the end of the song.

"Baby, I'd like nothing better than to be able to call you my wife by the holiday season next year," he says, pulling me close as the next number begins.

"I was going to tell you after the kids left... I know I said I wanted to wait, but that was before I almost lost you and my dad. Life is too short. I know everyone probably expects you to have a huge ceremony with the who's who of Chicago in attendance, but, how would you feel about having a quiet ceremony and getting married at my parents' home next month?" I ask.

"Baby I don't care where you want to get married. I just want to make you officially mine," he says, gently kissing me.

"Then it's settled. You propose and I'll accept," I say.

He laughs out loud, pulling me close. "Katarina, why the change? I thought you wanted to wait awhile and get married in Aruba?" he asks, watching me, still guiding me to the soft holiday music playing overhead.

"I was looking through some old family albums and found my parents' wedding pictures. There was a photograph of a journal entry in my mom's diary from years ago. I saw an entry that referenced their home was finally built and it would become the place they would marry, see their children married and watch their grandchildren grow," I say.

"Baby, do you want a different home? One that wasn't mine before we met?" he asks, lifting my chin so he can look into my eyes.

I shake my head. "No, I absolutely love this home. We will spend years enjoying the traditions you've established and making new ones as our family grows," I say.

His eyebrows rise slightly. "Just so I'm prepared, how big do you anticipate our family becoming?" he asks, smiling down at me.

"Definitely more than one, maybe two- better yet, maybe four," I say, laughing at his raised eyebrows.

He pulls me close. "Baby, you've made me the happiest man in the world. I better ask Carlos to marry you again, though. There was a little hesitancy when I told him we were contemplating a ceremony in Aruba. I couldn't quite put my finger on it then, but maybe he was reflecting on your mom's diary entry," he says.

Our moment of privacy is soon broken up with the arrival of my parents who come bearing gifts of wine, cheese, and fruits baskets. We spend the next hour visiting, enjoying the fireplace, view of the falling snow, and holiday music.

"Carlos, I think it's time to refresh our drinks," Chase says, taking our wine glasses as he and my dad head out of the room.

"Mom, I know this is sort of sudden, but I'm wondering if you would be open to having Chase and I get married at your home on Christmas Eve."

"This Christmas Eve?" she asks.

"I know it's soon, but I don't want to wait anymore," I say.

"Katie, nothing would make me happier, but seriously, do you not know how long it takes to organize a proper wedding?" she asks.

"Mom, I don't want a large wedding. Just family and a few close friends and a lot of the family planned to come back to New York for Christmas anyway," I say.

"That's true, Katie, but there's not even time to have a dress made. Then there's the catering, the flowers, and not to mention the cake," she laments.

"I don't care about all that stuff. I want to walk down the staircase and see Chase waiting at the bottom for me. I also need to talk to Dad and find out if he'll give me away. It will be absolutely perfect, Mom," I say as her eyes fill with unshed tears.

Chase and my dad come back into the room with a glass of wine for each of us and we chat a little before moving into the smaller dining room since the ladies are still putting the finishing touches on preparations for tomorrow's holiday festivities in the large dining room.

"Don't you have something to tell your dad, Katie," my mom says as we have barely taken our seats.

I shake my head at her half contained excitement. I'm pretty sure Chase has already talked to Dad, and as if reading my mind, he gives me a confirmatory nod from across the table. "Dad, Chase and I are planning to get married on Christmas Eve. I know it's short notice, but we would like nothing better than to get married at your home. Most of the family will be home and I'd be honored if they could see you walk me down the same staircase you had built for Mom years ago," I say.

My father's eyes moisten for the second time in as many weeks. "Katarina, you couldn't have made me and your mother any happier. We'd be delighted for you and Chase to marry at our home," he says.

The kids arrive just before lunch on Thanksgiving Day. Gaby has outdone herself with roasted turkey, mashed potatoes, gravy, stuffing, a cauliflower and cheese casserole, scalloped corn, green bean casserole, cranberry sauce, and an assortment of Jell-O salads, bars and pies. Chase spends time talking with the young adults as a group, but also with each individually, introducing me as his fiancée and drawing me into the conversations. I learn many of the children are from the community and not surprisingly, Chase is supporting many of them in their educational goals. My parents are drawn to the kids' outgoing personalities, as they tell stories and we play board games throughout the afternoon.

"Who's up for a bonfire?" Chase asks as night falls. The suggestion is met with resounding approval and we follow him through the french doors and down the deck stairs to the snow cleared path below. Several men have started quite a brush pile and chairs are set out in a circle around the fire.

"Here pass a few of these around," Chase says, tossing a couple bags of marshmallows to the teenagers closest to him. The kids are lively and animated passing them out, slipping the large white puffs onto the silver skewers that have been placed around the fire. They take turns toasting them until golden brown.

"You want one, Katarina?" Trey, one of the quieter teens, asks.

"I thought you would never ask," I say.

"Coming right up," he says, grinning while he attempts to load his skewer with four marshmallows.

I am seated next to Chase and take his hand. "Good?" he asks, looking into my eyes.

"Unbelievably good."

After a while servers arrive with a round of hot cocoa for everyone and the group talks about the ice fishing outing planned at the cabins for next month, until it is time for the bus to return them home. It's been a magical day all around and it is with sadness that I watch them leave.

"It was an amazing evening. I think the Thanksgiving holiday just took on a greater meaning for all of us," I say to Chase on the way up to our room.

The rest of the weekend flies by. Mom and I spend much of the time between Friday morning and the time they have to leave on Sunday evening preparing for the wedding while Chase and my dad stay secluded in the study with Jay and the security teams in an effort to track Alfreita.

The four of us are just finishing a late supper of lemon pepper salmon, served with baby Yukon Gold potatoes and green beans when Sheldon peeks his head into the kitchen. "The helicopter will be ready shortly and they have the jet preparing for departure at O'Hare," he says.

"Perfect timing, Sheldon. We're all packed and ready to go. We'll say our goodbyes and be right behind you," Carlos says, standing up from the table and pulling back my mother's chair for her.

"Chase, thanks for having us for the weekend. We had a great time and we're looking forward to many more holidays with the two of you in the future," he says, coming around to give me a hug.

"We look forward to it, Carlos," Chase says, before turning to whisper something to my mom.

"What are you two up to?"

"Don't spoil your surprise, Sweetie," my mom says, giving me one last squeeze.

"Alright, we'll see you in a couple weeks," I say, lowering my eyes at her as Jay peeks his head in to hurry my parents along. We wave one last time as they get into the helicopter and Chase puts his arm around me, before closing the door. "It was a nice weekend, but it feels good to have the house back to ourselves," he says, kissing the top of my head.

"I couldn't agree more. Seriously, I've never spent a more enjoyable holiday, ever. It was amazing," I say, hugging him to me tightly.

"Let's go upstairs," he says, scooping me into his arms as we reach the elevator and he hits the keypad to the upper level. The elevator opens as it reaches our floor and he lets me slide down his body slowly, pressing me against him as my feet find the ground. "Baby, raise your arms. I want to see your body," he says, sliding my skirt and panties past my hips, letting them drop to the floor. He raises my hip-length sweater past my waist, over my chest and head, leaving me completely naked before him with the exception of a white lace demi bra with a front clasp.

"All of you," he says, pushing the clip that separates the small amount of material that when opened leaves me completely bare. "Do you know how much I want you right now?" he asks, smothering my reply with his kiss.

"Let me undress you," I say, slowly unbuttoning his shirt. I slip my hands beneath it at his shoulders, sliding the material over them and down his arms. He is taut with sinewy muscle and I kiss the tip of each erect nipple as I let his shirt fall to the floor, watching the color of his eyes turn from light hazel to dark molten green. My fingers release the hook closure on his dress pants and then his zipper, sliding it down slowly, while he watches me with a passionate intensity. My hands slip under his waistband and he steps out of his pants as they join his shirt on the floor. He is gloriously male, powerful and erect, and the way he is watching me takes my breath away.

"I want to feel your body against mine," he says, pulling me down with him atop the large white fluffy rug at our feet. We are mere inches from the floor to ceiling stone fireplace. The fire is gently blazing, crackling and popping with the sounds of real burning hardwood and the warmth engulfs our nude bodies. He curls my body against him and his powerful thigh separates mine, entwining my legs with his own, while cradling my head in the crook of his arm.

"Do you know how much you have come to mean to me?" he says, pushing my hair out of my face.

"I feel the same, Chase," I say, kissing his lips lightly.

"You enjoyed the holiday?" he asks.

"It just dawned on me tonight how much they can mean. My mother and I have always celebrated them, but you know- it's just been the two of us. It's hard to explain how I feel right now," I say, curling into his chest.

"I want nothing more than to make you my wife, start a family and traditions of our own," he says.

"Even if I was serious about four children?" I ask.

"I'd be more than happy to oblige, but perhaps some practice is in order," he says, rolling over the top of me, sealing my mouth with his own as he begins to make slow and unhurried love to me.

TWENTY

In the morning, the security guards escort us to the helipad where the pilot is on standby ready to take us to Prestian Towers. It is the same bright blue helicopter we rode in New York, with larger, more spacious accommodations and a custom, sound-proofed living area.

"I thought you were leaving this parked at LaGuardia?" I ask.

"I purchased two. This one will remain here and we'll keep the other one at the airport in New York," he says.

I shake my head still trying to wrap my head around the magnitude of his wealth.

"It's only money. Don't let it bother you, Baby. I'd like to avoid the reporters if we can and right now the Prestian Towers helipad is secure," he says.

The pilot lands on the rooftop and the security guards who have been in the cabin behind the flight crew assist us out and onto the roof. I am prepared for the paparazzi, dressed in a short professional skirt, blouse, blazer and Louboutin heels since the announcement of our wedding plans for Christmas Eve has hit every tabloid in the United States and rumors from unplanned pregnancy to it was always planned for Christmas Eve abound. As we approach the private elevators that go directly to the penthouse suites the doors open and Jay steps out.

"What are you doing here?" Chase asks, bursting into a wide smile as he shakes Jay's hand.

"Can't keep me down for long and besides can't let Sheldon have all the fun," Jay says, nodding to Sheldon. I know that even though Chase has given him time off until the end of the year with pay, he will not be taking it.

"Do you mind if we look around the Torzial floor? Jenny texted me last night and wants us to see how they set up the space," I say.

"Let's stop by then," Chase says, pushing the button for the private entry to the new Torzial space which now comprises an entire floor of the Prestian Corp towers. Jay seems to have recovered nicely, and he, Chase and Sheldon converse on the way down in the elevator.

As we walk into Torzial I gasp at the sprawl of employees and their stations that have been created. All of the hard work and our plans are finally becoming a reality. "I'm so excited," I say to Chase.

"You and Jenny should be proud," he says, pulling me close and kissing the top of my head as he guides me toward the administrative areas and into Jenny's office. As you walk into the space there is a panoramic view overlooking the sky-rises and lake below. She is working on her Mac when we arrive and squeals in Jenny fashion when she notices the two of us, jumping up from behind her desk and catching me in a large hug.

I can barely control my laughter at her exuberance. "Jenny, it's amazing. We walked through the floor and everything is perfect," I say.

"Well, you helped develop the structure. The rest of it was just logistics," she says, shrugging off her part in the creation of the space. "All the employees are moved in, but a few aren't slated to start until next week. Design and maintenance are still working to get their space prepared before they start," she says.

"Jenny, you have done an incredible job with the space. We're going to need the entire team onboard, very quick. If Katarina hasn't told you already we've got the two facilities here in the city, two in southern Illinois, and we're in negotiations for two in New York."

"She did, and while they are going to be larger than the one here in Chicago, we'll gain a lot of productivity efficiencies utilizing what we've learned from Texas and Chicago. The hospital in Houston is not only reducing readmissions, but they're at the point now of preventing the admission from occurring in the first place," Jenny says.

"Yes, quality is increasing and the cost of healthcare is going down. I couldn't be more pleased with where we're headed," Chase says before his phone vibrates and he looks down at the message. "Ladies, if you'll excuse me, I'm sure you need time to catch up. Brian just arrived upstairs and we need to discuss a few things before our next meeting," he says, kissing me soundly on the mouth before he and Jay head toward the elevator.

Sheldon stays behind with me and I know there are a multitude of security men surrounding the building and keeping us safe from afar. Jenny pours three cups of coffee, giving Sheldon a cup to take back to the space he's claimed outside of her office as we settle in to discuss the Torzial expansion.

"Everything is going according to the plan we developed before we left for Brazil. As you can see everyone seems to be settling in nicely to their new roles here in Chicago. We still have a lot of work to do in New York though, especially since they are already negotiating contracts. I didn't anticipate that happening until next spring," Jenny says.

"I didn't think the requests for other healthcare organizations would come in as quickly as they did either, but the clip from the Houston design and the impacts to quality and service scores are most likely driving some of that. Chase and Brian received multiple national requests after that video went live. Health care organizations can't afford to wait, and everyone wants to get ahead of this before the reimbursement models change," I say.

"It sounds like we're going to need to expedite expansion plans to the East Coast. I'd like to take a quick trip out there and meet some of the department heads since most of the legalities are almost complete. Chase said we can use the same methodology we used here in Chicago as we expand into New York. They'll provide us with a floor at the

Prestian Corp towers and will wrap it into the overall start up," she says.

"I think it's a good idea to go see the space. I didn't expect everything to take off quite this quickly either, but it's exciting. I've been focused on getting the two facilities in Chicago ready for state approval, but I did manage to screen most of the facilitator applications human resources passed on to me. We have some great candidates. I'll interview them as quickly as they can be scheduled," I say.

"He told me a large healthcare organization in Los Angeles contacted him last week," Jenny says.

"Yep, it sounds like on the business side everything is escalating. Sort of like the personal front," I say.

"How so?" she says, raising her eyebrows.

"Well, after everything that's happened lately, Chase and I decided to get married Christmas Eve," I say.

Jenny's squeal is ear piercing as she jumps out of her chair to wrap her arms around me.

"Oh, my God! Congratulations," she says as I laughingly try to catch my breath at her exuberance.

"Jenny I would love it if you could be my maid of honor, but it's Christmas Eve and it's going to be in New York at my parents' house. I know you weren't quite sure what your holiday plans were," I say tentatively.

"Kate, I wouldn't miss it for anything. I can always get a flight afterwards and still spend Christmas night with my mother," she says.

"That would be perfect! My mom is already talking about dress fittings," I say, rolling my eyes skyward. "We could probably combine business with dress shopping as I am pretty certain no one would be able to make a dress in a month, much to Mom's dismay," I say.

"Absolutely! We'll go dress shopping and get a little business done, we've got this," Jenny says.

"My parents are ecstatic. Chase and I talked to Don and Emily on Thanksgiving and they were thrilled, too. New York just seemed to be the right place, with all the history and the fact that both our parents live there. Most of Dad's relatives were planning to return for the holiday and they'll stay in guest houses that he has on the property. There's more than enough room if you want to stay for the holidays, too."

"Let me see what I can work out with my family, but in the meantime it sounds as though we better book a trip to New York so we can go shopping for a dress," Jenny says.

"I was so hoping you would say that!" I exclaim.

"I'll text you with details then," I say, hugging her before I head back upstairs to find Chase.

I wake on Friday morning excited about our impromptu trip to New York City. Chase has early meetings and is already gone, but has arranged for the corporate Jet to take Jenny and me from O'Hare to LaGuardia to meet my mom for shopping.

"About ready?" Sheldon asks, peeking his head into the kitchen as I finish breakfast.

"All set," I say, following Sheldon and the other security members to the awaiting helicopter. I curl into the soft leather seat by the window and text Jenny.

Message: I should be at the airport in 30 minutes. Let me know when you get picked up!!

Reply: Ride just arrived. See you soon!

Message: Chase gave me an open credit card. More lingerie!

Reply: I hope this time you just said thank you!!

I smile at her message and send Chase a quick note as we lift off over the dense pines.

Message: Thank you for the shopping card!

Reply: You are most welcome. Enjoy yourself, but stay close to Sheldon! We are about to land and I text Jenny.

Message: Doesn't look like the paparazzi have gotten wind of our departure.

Reply: That's definitely a good thing. You'll have more than your share of that soon.

· · ·

JENNY'S LIMO pulls up and we board the awaiting Gulfstream and are soon taxiing down the runway in preparation for lift off. The trip between Chicago and New York City is becoming routine. Jenny and I pass the two-hour flight poring through bridal magazines that she has brought along.

It is barely nine in the morning when we land and Mom is waiting for us, along with the security team my father and Chase have assigned to her. The limousine we transfer into is spacious and Jenny and I take our seats in the back across from my mom. Sheldon slides into the passenger seat up front and the two other team members get into the far back section of the stretch limo while the rest of the team disperse into cars in front of and in back of us.

"Dad certainly rides in style," I say, raising my eyebrows at the over-the-top extravagance as the privacy glass in front of and behind us slide into place.

"It's custom made for privacy," my mom says shrugging, seemingly embarrassed a little herself by the opulence. The driver veers into the vast lanes of traffic and I'm awed by the sheer magnitude of the city as we drive right through the heart of it. Mom pushes a button on the side of her door that engages the internal speaker system, giving instruction on which shops we'll be stopping at.

I am swept from one bridal boutique to the next in search of the perfect dress. It is hard not to get caught up in their exuberance and after hours of shopping and laughing, I find the perfect mermaid style dress. "Mom, this is the one," I say, staring at the gown in the window.

"Could I try it," I ask?

"The dress in the window is just a design. We do not have that particular dress in any size but the one on display. It may be close, though," the seamstress says, assessing my size.

While not the perfect fit, it is everything I could have imagined. It has long white lacy sleeves, connected only by the sheerest of tiny straps that connect at the shoulder, and then crisscross down my back to the top of my hips, leaving my back completely bare. It has a flowing train that swirls around me, and I am absolutely in love with it.

"Dear, turn around now," the seamstress says, tucking and measuring as we talk, sharing that the dress was handmade by a new designer who provided it as a window display in hopes that someone would like the design. After another hour of fittings, I am assured the dress will fit me just as though it were costumed tailored and be done in plenty of time for the wedding.

We are just leaving the bridal shop when my phone rings and I answer recognizing my father's number. "Hi Dad. I'll check with her. She might have left it on silent or in the car," I say, gesturing to my mom's purse.

"How's the shopping coming?"

"Excellent, I found a dress, but I think they are going to drag me around to a few more shops," I say, feigning dismay.

"Well, have fun and let your mom know to respond to my text when she has a chance," he says.

"Will do."

They proceed to drag me to Dolce and Gabbana for lingerie, Chloe for a couple stylish dresses and shoes, and just for good measure we shop in Gucci, Louis Vuitton, and Prada at Saks Fifth Avenue. We have had a great day, but I am thoroughly exhausted of shopping.

"No more," I say, slumping into the cool interior of the limo.

"Now you can say you've shopped New York City," Jenny says, laughing at me as we all slide into the middle section of the limo.

"Oh my God, that's my shopping trip for the year!" I say.

"I was pretty impressed with Sheldon's team. They were pretty good at staying within range, but letting us have our own space," she says.

"Definitely. Did you see Matt deal with the reporter outside of Gucci?"

"Yep, pretty smooth," Jenny says.

"You know at one time the level of security we have in place would have made me crazy, but I'm really thankful for it," I say, sending Chase a message.

Message: Found a dress. Almost to my parents' house.

Reply: Excellent. I can't wait to see you in it.

Message: Not until Christmas Eve!

Reply: Still planning to be home tomorrow?

Message: Yes, Dad's taking us out for dinner tonight. Jenny and I are going to Torzial in the morning to scope out the space.

My phone begins playing Chase's ringtone immediately.

"Where are you going for dinner? Jay didn't mention it to me earlier," he says.

"My mom just mentioned it to me before I texted you," I say, rolling my eyes upward for my mom and Jenny's benefit. "You'll also be pleased to know that I sent a text to Sheldon before I messaged you. I think he's working with Jay and Dad's team on the logistics for tonight. Everything is fine," I say.

"You're halfway across the country and that maniac is still out there somewhere," Chase says.

"Chase, we've been shopping all over New York City today. Security was with us the entire time. We're going to dinner, that's all. I'm sure Sheldon has it all under control," I say, hoping to reassure him.

"I'll give him a call," he says.

"So, I think between my wedding dress, designer outfits, and hot lingerie I managed to do some damage to that card you gave me," I say, changing the subject.

"Hot lingerie, huh?" he says.

"Nothing you can see until our wedding night, though," I say, turning away from Jenny and my mom who are in animated conversation paying absolutely no attention to me.

"Do I take it you've now come to appreciate the pleasure of anticipation, or do you just enjoy teasing me from halfway across the country?" he inquires. His voice has lowered and I feel myself moistening at the seductive quality of his voice.

"That would certainly call for some sort of delicious, torturous punishment," I reply, whispering hoarsely.

"It would indeed. When you arrive, go upstairs and take all of your clothes off. I love talking to you when you are completely nude," he says.

"Hang on, we just arrived," I say into the phone, before climbing out of the limo as we arrive at the estate.

We enter the foyer and Mom offers to show Jenny to her suite so she has a chance to get freshened up for the evening. "I'm going to take a quick shower before we head out for dinner. I'll catch up with you in a short while," I say to them as I make my way up the shiny white and black marble staircase to the guest quarters that Chase and I share when we are visiting.

"I'm back," I say breathlessly, reaching the top of the stairs before closing the door to our room and stripping down to nothing.

"Are you undressed?" he asks huskily, as I walk into the bathroom. The shower is black granite, encased with a circular door of glass. I open it, placing my phone on the speaker before turning the faucet to warm and allowing the showerhead to cascade water over my body.

"I'm interested in finding out which delicious, torturous punishment you find most appealing, Katarina?"

"Well, maybe being tied up while you use the nipple clamps that you gave me last week," I say, lowering my voice, although no one can hear me with through the privacy of the shower and bedroom door except him.

"So you were thinking about them this week," he says.

"You have no idea," I say.

"Indeed, Katarina. I think while at first I would leave you nude with the exception of your pretty little white thong, eventually that would have to come off, too. Tied up, and completely at my mercy to do with as I please." he says.

"That sounds very nice," I say.

"Your nipples are so sensitive, Baby. The nipple clamps would certainly account for some degree of punishment. First I would barely touch them, tracing lightly with my finger, then with my tongue, allowing them to grow erect, swollen with need while I begin stroking your clit. When I know you're ready, I would place one nipple clamp on at a time, slipping my finger deep inside of you to take your mind off the initial discomfort. Then I would torment you with my tongue, running it through your sweetness, tugging at the little silver chain connected to your nipples, teasing, but not allowing you to cum. Would that suffice for delicious punishment, Baby?" he asks.

"There's only one problem. You're not here," I say hoarsely. My breathing is uneven and my body is flushed with excitement at the sound of his voice.

"I don't want you to cum. I want you to think of that until I see you next, Katarina," he says.

"Chase," I moan, knowing now that he is going to make me wait.

"Patience and anticipation. I can't wait until I see you again," he says before disconnecting the line. I stare at the phone on the ledge of the shower and place my head under the water, relishing in its warmth, trying to suppress the desire our little game has created. I desperately miss him and contemplate asking Jay to have someone fly me back to Chicago tonight but dismiss the thought, knowing how much my mom is looking forward to us all having dinner together.

I get out of the shower and dry off, slip into the dark grey v-neck sweater dress, clasp the diamond necklace back in place, and slide the silver and diamond bangles back over my wrist before sliding into my silky thigh highs. A present from Chase, they are like pure silk and I run my hands along them before slipping into my heels. I finish my hair and makeup contemplating our little game. *Two can play this game, Let him think he's won this round,* I decide, ignoring the growing urge to message him back.

Message: Jay is security set for tonight? Chase was worried when I talked to him.

Reply: Sheldon and I have everything covered. He's on the phone with me now.

Message: Thanks, Jay! I figured as much. Tell him to relax!

Reply: Yeah, right now I'm not getting a word in edgewise!

Message:

I head downstairs to find my parents and Jenny waiting for me. Dad has made reservations at one of their favorite restaurants in New York. We have a security team in front of and behind us, escorting our limo into the city. Sheldon is up front in the passenger seat, something I've now become accustomed to. The driver steers through the heavy New York traffic navigating the large Lincoln with relative ease before pulling up to the entrance of a two-story building that has a red brick exterior with an expanse of white trimmed windows. It is a small quaint restaurant and Mom told us earlier that reservations are almost impossible to come by, but the hostess knows my father by name as we enter.

"Good evening, Mr. Larussio," she says before escorting us to a private table in the back of the restaurant.

"Your server will be with you shortly, and I'll let Mr. D'Angelo know that you have arrived Mr. Larussio," she says.

"You'll love the food here," my mom says to Jenny and me as my dad discusses wine preferences with the young man who has stopped at our table. "The shrimp scampi and linguine are my favorites," she says as we peruse the menu before the server returns. Mom takes a sip of her red wine and murmurs her appreciation and agreement with Dad's choice. I taste my own; delicious, a little sweet, but not overpowering, medium bodied with a crisp finish.

"Next time you're in the city we can take you to Maka's," my dad says as he reviews the menu. It's Omakase style, meaning the chef's choice," he explains.

"Really?" I ask.

"Don't worry; the food is absolutely to die for and it's flown in fresh from Japan. It really does take the hassle out of deciding what to order," mom explains, catching our furtive glance. A gentleman places a woven basket covered with a white cloth onto our table. As he lifts the cover, the scent of garlic and parmesan cheese escapes. My dad passes a basket full of a variety of breads around the table. The freshly make bread is still warm to the touch. We have no sooner passed the basket before he returns with a loaf of crusty bread and knife sitting atop a cutting board, along with olive oil and bruschetta which he sets in front of us before taking our dinner order.

It is a relaxing atmosphere and we are filling my dad in on our day of shopping when a man of medium stature and grey hair joins our table, shaking my father's hand as he greets us.

"Carlos, so good to see you and your lovely family, my friend," he says.

"You know Karissa. My daughter Katarina and her friend Jenny are in New York for a couple days shopping for the wedding," he says, introducing us both to his friend, Antonio D'Angelo.

"It's a pleasure to meet you both and please call me Tony. My wife and I were just reading the wedding announcement. You must be sure to bring Chase and Don around for a congratulatory meal," he says.

"Thank you, Tony. We would enjoy that very much," I say, before he leaves our table to stop and talk to another guest.

"He's been a friend of mine and Don's for a long time," my father explains as the waitress refreshes our wine glasses.

"I talked to Don earlier and he said to let the staff know when you arrive at Prestian Corp tomorrow and he'll give you a tour of the Torzial area personally," he says to Jenny.

"That was nice of him to offer to do that. I'm looking forward to meeting Chase's dad," Jenny says.

"You'll like him a lot. He's really not much different than Chase," I say.

"That intense?" she says, lifting her eyebrows and I wonder if she's nervous about meeting him.

"Relax Jenny. He's seriously one of the most laid back people I've ever met," I reassure.

"That he is, Jenny. Nothing to worry about where Don's concerned. If you've survived Chase, you'll be just fine," my dad says as our dinner arrives. The women have opted for shrimp scampi, while my dad has chosen a dish of manicotti. "Tony started his restaurant business years ago and made all the pasta by hand. Today he owns six restaurants throughout the state along with a manufacturing plant that produces fresh pasta for each of his restaurants, many of the nation's hotels and much that is packaged and sold commercially," he says, clearly proud of his friend's accomplishments.

The scampi is sinful, sautéed in real butter and minced garlic with a hint of white wine and lemon juice, and is sprinkled with fresh parsley. It is every bit as delicious as Mom promised and then some. We are just finishing the meal when Mr. D'Angelo stops by to make sure everything was to our liking and to wish us a great evening.

Our limo is awaiting curbside, and as we exit the restaurant, Sheldon and a few members of our security team join us as we proceed to the car. I catch the raised brows of my father as we pile into the limo and Sheldon slides into the front seat. My father has his cell phone out and is texting someone. *His own security?* The silence and tension in the car is palpable as we pull into the heavy evening traffic of downtown New York. We ride like this for a short distance until my curiosity gets the better of me. The privacy glass is down and I turn around in my seat to face the front of the car.

"What's going on Sheldon?" I ask, breaking the uncomfortable silence that has dropped over the group.

"We don't know much right now, Kate," he says, turning in his own seat to face those of us in the back.

"Sheldon, if there is something happening we need to be aware of it," I say, catching my father's uplifted eyebrows from the corner seat.

"We've received word that Alfreita's men may be in the city. Right now, we're just taking extra precautions, Kate. That's all we know right now, it hasn't been confirmed and we just didn't want to worry anyone needlessly. My job is to make sure you get back to Mr. Larussio's house safely."

"You know I hate being kept in the dark," I say.

"We haven't known for long, Kate. Otherwise, Jay would have insisted that we alter plans for dinner," he says.

"I'll give Chase a call when we get home and find out what's going on," I say as much to myself as the others in the car. The ride home is anti-climactic and I find myself relaxing a little once we're in the gated compound and I see the lights of the Larussio mansion in the distance. I didn't realize that I was tense after learning that Alfreita might have men in the city. *Were they watching us?*

Our chauffeur drives us to the front of the estate's entrance before bringing the car to a halt. The men in the car in front of us climb out, walk to our car and open the passenger doors for us. Sheldon and I get out at the same time. There is a loud noise overhead, and we immediately look into the sky as the distant thwup...thwup...thwup sound of rotating blades cuts through the night. Goosebumps form at my neckline as I recall the last time helicopters canvassed the air in this very same place. No one is moving.

"Sheldon, what's happening? Shouldn't we go inside?" I ask as the sound of the rotating blades becomes even louder.

"We're expecting it, Kate. Nothing to worry about," he says as the lights and outline of the helicopter come into view over the tops of the trees.

"More security?" I ask, as it heads toward the landing pad.

"You could say that," my dad says as the helicopter lands and three men get out. I would recognize the shadow of that man anywhere. I look on in shock as the lights of the helicopter illuminate the three figures steadily making their way toward us.

"Looks like someone has come to protect you himself," Jenny says, nudging me as the men come into full view.

"So it would appear," I say, dumbfounded as Chase walks up to us and shakes my dad's hand. "Good to see you again, Carlos. Karissa, Jenny, I hope you had an enjoyable evening. Sheldon, thanks for seeing them home safely," he says, before putting his arm around my shoulders.

"Hi," I say at a complete loss for words.

"Hello, Katarina," he says, kissing me lightly on the lips as everyone begins heading into the house.

"What are you doing here?" I ask.

"I felt the need to finish what we started earlier," he says quietly.

"You are absolutely incorrigible," I say, giddy that he has flown all this way to be with me.

The fireplace is blazing in the great room and my father pours wine for everyone as we make ourselves comfortable. Chase pulls me into a love seat facing another leather couch, putting his arm around me as we talk. My father places a wine glass in front of each of us before offering up a toast. "To a wonderful evening spent with friends and family. We are richly blessed," he says. We spend the next hour visiting and recounting our day for Chase and my father. I am curious to learn more about Alfreita, but decide to ask Chase when we are alone.

"Your father offered to meet Jenny and me at Prestian Corp tomorrow and give us a tour of the Torzial space," I say to Chase.

"He mentioned that when I talked to him earlier. If you don't mind a little company tomorrow, we can take the helicopter over to Prestian Corp in the morning and then head to the airport from there," he says.

"Sounds fine to me," Jenny says before thanking everyone for a wonderful evening and retiring to her room on the second floor.

I attempt to stifle a yawn, but it does not go unnoticed. "Carlos, Karissa, thank you for a nice evening. I think Katarina and I are going to retire, as well. It appears you have worn my fiancée out shopping, Karissa," he says smiling.

She laughs. "Yes, it has never been her favorite pastime. It's a miracle we got as much accomplished as we did. She and I still need to go over some of the wedding preparations tomorrow, but we can do it at breakfast before you leave," she says, hugging me goodnight.

"Thanks for everything, Mom," I say before Chase and I climb the stairs to our suite upstairs.

As we enter the living area of the suite, Chase takes me into his arms, capturing my lips with his own. "You are a bad, bad girl. Teasing me when I'm halfway across the country," he murmurs.

"Yes, horribly rotten of me," I murmur against his lips.

"I think I have just the punishment for such a bad girl," he says, leading me into the bedroom and closing the door behind us.

"This dress is lovely, but it's quite clingy, low cut and provocative. It took everything I could do to focus on conversing with your parents instead of picking you up and carrying you upstairs tonight," he says, lifting it over my head and tossing it onto the reading chair in the corner. He lightly runs his fingers over the crest of my breasts which are peeking out from the top of my white lacy bra. "So lovely, Baby," he says, his eyes passionate, watching mine before he unclips the front clasp exposing my already erect nipples to his gaze. He runs his finger over each of them, eliciting a soft moan as I feel myself moisten in response to his caress.

"The thought of you like this has been driving me crazy all evening," he says, sliding his hands down to the top of my thigh highs. I think we'll leave these and your heels on for the moment," he says, cupping my ass cheeks as he kisses my lips.

"Now, I don't think you get to see anything more for the moment," he says, pulling a little mask from his pants pocket and slipping it over the top of my head, securing it around my eyes. I feel oddly exposed, standing in the middle of the bedroom half nude, and unable to see. I can feel him moving about the room, and hear a zipper, but nothing else, until I feel the warmth of a single finger trace the path from my neck to one of my nipples. They are erect and the slight touch sends goosebumps down my thighs. "I love how your nipples get so hard," he says, suckling one while caressing the other. He takes my hands in his own and I feel his fingers unclasp the bracelets dangling on my wrist before he raises my arms over my head. I hear the faint click and feel of the cold metal against my skin, as he affixes them to something that keeps my hands suspended in the air leaving me completely at his mercy. He lifts my hair and unclasps my necklace, sliding the weight of the diamonds across my heated flesh. The touch of cold against my nipples leaves me moist, anticipating the feel of clamps around my sensitive skin. He teases me, rubbing the roughness against me and I lean into it as I feel the sensation in my lower region.

"Your breathing has changed, Baby," he says, capturing the sensitive skin of my neck, suckling and kissing it, rubbing the cool strand of diamonds across my navel and tracing his way back up to my breasts. My body heats with need. I inhale audibly at the thought of what he will do. He lets the silver glide over my skin, cooling it, creating anticipation and desire. He traces a finger over one of my nipples, lightly skimming its erect tip before kissing it and suckling it with his mouth. "It will be different initially without the ice. Focus on the pleasure that comes, Katarina," he says, sliding the clamp of the chain around my nipple, gently allowing it to close, letting me acclimate to its feel. I hover between the slight pressures of discomfort before I feel myself moisten, desire turning more intense as he places the second clamp, letting the coolness of the long slim chain trail from them to my navel.

"Tell me if it becomes too intense, Katarina," he says, leaving them in place while he traces a light pattern from my navel down to the top of the lace on my panties. He rubs me through the silky material and I press into his hands. "Let's get you out of these, Baby," he says, drawing both sides of the material over my hips, cupping my ass cheeks as he slides them down. I lean on his shoulder and step out of them. His finger traces patterns from the top of my heels, over my calves and up my legs until he reaches the inside of my thighs. The pulsing in my nipples is causing a resounding ache deep inside.

I softly moan as he caresses the delicate skin between my legs with his tongue, tracing patterns between my thighs while his hands gently caress my hips and ass. He pulls me closer as he nuzzles and kisses my mound. I push into him but he stills me, grasping my hips to keep me positioned where he wants me, teasing me leisurely before finally allowing his tongue to find its mark. I am close and he knows it, a brief gentle flick of his tongue, then it's gone, nuzzling the newly waxed skin around it, driving me crazy before finding it again, teasing me... stroking just off the mark. My nipples are becoming heated under the pressure of the clips causing intensity in desire that I've not felt before. I move to find his tongue, but he holds my hips at bay.

"Baby, is this the punishment you wanted?" he asks, tugging gently on the chain, sending a shooting mixture of pleasure and pain to my nipples and igniting the flame between my legs.

"Chase," I moan, grinding unashamedly against his evasive tongue. He captures my clit in between his lips and nips with his teeth. He gently licks while pulling slightly and then in one quick movement he releases the clips causing me to cry out and tremble uncontrollably on the end of his tongue.

"So delicious, Baby," he murmurs, trailing kisses up my body, around my navel until he stands to caress my nipples with his tongue, one at a time, before finding his way to my neck and releasing my wrists. He picks me up laying me onto the bed and wraps my legs around his waist. He reaches up and pulls the mask from my eyes.

"I want to see you, Baby," he says, pushing inside of me. I feel myself clench around him. "You're so wet for me," he says, shifting my legs higher around his waist. He is already in so deep and the change in position causes him to sink deeper. "Oh, Honey," I hear myself murmur.

He draws back. "Not yet," he says, watching me intently, as he pushes against that special spot inside of me. I am building again, and he does it over and over, never taking his eyes from mine. I am too close, about ready to lose control. He can tell. "Cum with me, now," he instructs and I am powerless as he drives even deeper causing wave after wave to crash over me while finding his release deep inside of me. He lies beside me, taking me with him, pulling me to his chest before kissing me tenderly on the lips. "You look completely wrecked, Baby," he says, slipping my panties between my legs, and adjusting the comforter to cover me.

"I'm glad that you came, Chase," I say.

"You couldn't have kept me away," he says, pushing the strand of hair that has fallen over my eyes.

"Chase, they said Alfreita's men may be in New York," I say tiredly.

"Shh, Baby, I'll tell you all about it in the morning. Right now, you need to rest," he says before sleep takes over.

TWENTY-ONE

When I wake, the sun is shining into the windows and the bedside clock registers seven a.m. Chase is already gone and I stretch, smiling to myself at the tightness of my muscles from last night's exertions. I pull myself out of bed and jump into the shower, luxuriating in the warm water as it cascades over me. I rummage through my clothing options, quickly dress, and get ready for the day before packing my bags. I place them next to Chase's before heading down to find him and the others. Chase and my dad are having coffee at the kitchen table and look up when I walk in. "Good morning," I say.

"Good morning, Katarina," Chase says and I try to avoid the mischievous glint in his eye and upturned mouth.

"Morning, Katarina. We just finished eating, but your mom should be down shortly for breakfast. We haven't seen Jenny, yet," my father says.

I pour myself a cup of coffee and glance through the paper while Chase and my father talk. I miss some of the conversation, but perk up when Chase mentions Brian leaving. "I didn't know Brian was leaving the company," I say to Chase.

"Brian's dad passed away about five years ago and left him the sole heir to the largest shipping industry in the United States. Brian is an astute young man and wanted to finish his degree and learn more about global industries before he took over. I had an opening at Prestian Corp in our New York office at the time and hired him on. He's sat in on every negotiation we've done in the last five years and then put operational structures and processes in place to support them. He wants to take what he's learned and expand his family's business globally," he says proudly.

"Wow. I would have never guessed. He works as hard as you do," I say.

"That he does. He's just like his father and he's excited about the expansion of the Carrington shipping industry."

"So, where does that leave you?" I ask.

"He'll continue to do both jobs and help with the interviews. We've already posted the position and started national screening and recruitment efforts. I'm not worried. Things will fall into place," he says as my mom joins us.

A slightly older woman with greying hair brings a tray of croissants and fresh fruit to the table. "This is Maddie, she has been with the family for years and is in charge of most things around the house," he says.

My mom regales us with stories of the wedding planners she has been working with as we eat. I'm thankful she is taking care of all the details and I dutifully answer each of her questions. Chase rolls his eyes at me across the table and I narrow mine at him, trying to pay attention to my mom.

Jenny comes into the kitchen and Maddie returns, refilling our mugs while offering Jenny a cup of coffee. Jenny takes a seat and my mom offers her breakfast as we finalize the last of the wedding preparations.

"Ladies, we're going to take the helicopter over to the Prestian Towers and then head to the airport from there. Jay and Sheldon are getting things prepared as we speak," Chase says. As if on cue, Sheldon walks into the kitchen to let us know the crew has the helicopter ready and is waiting.

Chase says goodbye to my parents, hugging my mom and shaking hands with my father. I embrace my mom, holding her close. "Thanks for taking care of all the wedding arrangements. I don't know what I would do without you," I say.

"She's having the time of her life," my father says, wrapping me into his arms in a quick hug.

"Thank you both for having me and for giving me a place to stay for the wedding," Jenny says.

"You're very welcome. We wouldn't consider letting you stay anywhere else," my mom says.

Sheldon and Jay assist us aboard and then climb into the front of the helicopter behind the pilots after closing the door to the private cabin of the Augusta. My phone beeps and I look down at the incoming message from my work email and scowl. I type out a message and hit the send button. I feel his gaze upon me and look up, my eyes drawn to the steely green ones watching me intently.

"Why do you let them bother you? The land is purchased, the facility is designed and we'll go to state for building approvals on time. The model works, don't let them make you second guess this."

"Why do you think I'm second guessing things?" I ask as we lift off.

"Why, you've been recalculating numbers and replying to messages that should have just been deleted all week," Chase says.

"Maybe they're right? We haven't been able to get through the pharmaceutical costs, yet," I say.

"We are working with the pharmaceutical companies on a bundled price. It will just take time. In the meantime, stop worrying."

"Anyone ever tell you that you are extremely bossy?" I ask.

"If I recall, it was you," he says, raising his eyebrows.

"You are absolutely incorrigible..." I say, feeling the warmth of a blush rise on my cheeks.

"Probably," he says, kissing my lips lightly with his own. I ignore Jenny's smirk.

"I told you when we started this project it was not going to be popular and may shake up things in the industry. We're starting to see some negative movement now that the outcome measures are looking so good. Until they came out, there was nothing for the big industries to fear. Now, all the health organizations across the nation are taking notice. Try not to let the emails worry you, Baby," he says.

"I'll try," I say, looking out the oblong windows of the helicopter. The city below is breathtaking and there is a lump in my throat recalling the skyline that used to include the Twin Towers. It is a crisp clear day and the pilot easily navigates us around the city to land on the helipad across the street from the Prestian Corp towers. Sheldon and Jay assist us out of the helicopter when we land, walking beside us as we enter the prestigious underground passageway that leads us to the Prestian towers elevator. Chase inserts his passcode and just like in Chicago, when we step out of the elevator we are in the administrative areas of the complex.

He chats with the receptionist for a few moments, introducing us, while we wait for his father. We are not left waiting long as Don strolls through the waiting area and shakes Chase's hand. "Good to see you, Chase," he says.

"Katarina, you are looking lovely and this must be Jenny," he says, raising my hand to his lips before reaching out to shake hands with her.

"Dad, this is Jenny Torzial. Her company will be taking occupancy as they expand to support the Prestian Corporation Medical Center facilities," he says.

"It's nice to meet you. Chase and Katarina have told me such nice things about you. If you're interested in seeing the layout, I'll give you a quick tour," he says, smiling.

"I'd love it," Jenny says as he leads us through the facility, stopping to introduce us to those who are working.

"It's empty right now but I think you'll find the space and location appealing," Don says as we take the elevator a few floors down.

"It's absolutely perfect and what a fantastic view," Jenny exclaims, walking toward the perimeter offices which offer a majestic view of the bay and Manhattan city skyline beyond.

"Do you mind if we take some pictures, Don?" I ask.

"Anything you need," he says as Jenny and I leave the men to explore the arrangement of the floor and snap a few shots of the space configuration, conference room layouts, and cubicle spaces.

He and his dad stop their conversation short as we walk back into the room and I attempt to hide my annoyance as we visit with his dad.

Jay looks down at his phone. "Flight plans are cleared and the jet should be ready to go by the time we reach the airport, Chase," Jay says.

We are escorted from the helipad to the awaiting jet once we get to LaGuardia and as we enter the Gulfstream, Chase spends a few moments talking to his pilot and copilot before we take our seats in the living area of the cabin and prepare for takeoff. The flight is relatively short and Chase works on his Mac, Jenny is engrossed in a book, and I sign on to the internet to skim through email. Most are quick reads that bring me up to speed on the Prestian project. One of the largest facilities in L.A. is requesting cost and quality data from the medical facility project. I quickly calculate the projections and square feet for the new buildings before responding and copying Chase into the correspondence so he has the most up-to-date figures.

TO: KMeilers@TorzialConsulting.org
  From: CHPrestian@PrestianCorp.org

IMPRESSIVE! I love you, Baby.
  C. H. Prestian
  Chief Executive Officer, Owner
  Prestian Corporation

TO: CHPrestian@PrestianCorp.org
  From: KMeilers@TorzialConsulting.org

DEAR MR. PRESTIAN,

I love you, too, not only for your considerable prowess and physique, but also your most amazingly intellectual mind.
  Kate

. . .

KATE MEILERS
Project Consultant
Torzial Consulting Firm

TO: <u>KMeilers@TorzialConsulting.org</u>
From: <u>CHPrestian@PrestianCorp.org</u>

MY CONSIDERABLE PROWESS? Indeed.
C. H. Prestian
Chief Executive Officer, Owner
Prestian Corporation

TO: <u>CHPrestian@PrestianCorp.org</u>
From: <u>KMeilers@TorzialConsulting.org</u>

IN FACT, just thinking about it makes my panties wet.
Kate

KATE MEILERS
Project Consultant
Torzial Consulting Firm

TO: <u>KMeilers@TorzialConsulting.org</u>
From: <u>CHPrestian@PrestianCorp.org</u>

. . .

CAREFUL, Baby, before I decide not to be such a gentlemen in front of company and take you into the bedroom.

C. H. Prestian
Chief Executive Officer, Owner
Prestian Corporation

Our fun is broken up by the pilot overhead. "Chase, we've been asked to delay landing and circle out to the private air field," the pilot announces.

"I'll be back shortly," Chase says, getting out of his seat to go and speak with the captain.

"What do you think is wrong?" Jenny asks.

"I'm not sure. I know security was increased, but we haven't had a chance to talk about it. All I know is what Sheldon told us yesterday about the possibility of Alfreita's men being in New York," I say as Chase returns to his seat.

"Ladies, it's nothing to worry about. Our intelligence team picked up a group of Alfreita's men in New York City, which is why we put everyone on high alert. Unfortunately, a few of that team is staked out at O'Hare. We seldom use our private landing runway, but Jay wants us to land there today. He'll have the pilot call in a last minute flight change to throw them off and have a team meet us at the air strip and escort us home," he says.

It is another long forty minutes before we land. Chase is on the radio with Jay almost constantly during this time. "Jay, I trust you implicitly, set it down," he instructs, before disconnecting. "Buckle up ladies," he says.

"Holy shit," Jenny says.

It is not long before the pilot announces our impending decent. It is quick and deliberate and he sets the plane down with perfect precision and we begin taxiing down a long runway in between vast forests of green pines covered with heavy snowfall.

"Chase, where are we?" I ask.

"We're not far from our house. We just never use this strip," he says as the jet comes to a stop.

"Ladies, as soon as we get the all clear I want you to move quickly," Chase says, guiding us to the plane's ramp. "Jay's got security in place, but it's imperative we follow their direction," he says as security falls in around us, shielding us as we proceed from the jet to the awaiting limo. The rifles at their sides demonstrate the gravity of the situation and my heart is beating rapidly as I think about the implications, but we are soon tucked safely into the long black stretch limo. There are two cars in front of us and two behind us all the way to the estate and we arrive home and are escorted inside the complex without incident.

Gaby greets us with unabashed concern and admonishment as we walk into the vast foyer. "I'm so glad you are both okay. I was worried sick when Jay called to let me know what was happening and told me to make plans for the two of you to stay here all week. There's never a dull moment working for you," she says, ushering us into the kitchen.

"It's been an interesting day, that's for sure, Gaby. Security is just taking precautions. Nothing for anyone to be alarmed over," Chase says.

"Thanks for everything, Chase, but I really should get going. I still need to get a lot of work done and pack for my trip. I thought we would be landing at the airport and I was planning to take a cab back," Jenny says.

"What trip?" Chase asks.

"I told my parents that I would come visit them for a couple weeks and spend a little time with them since I'll be with you and Kate on Christmas Eve and most of the day on Christmas," Jenny says.

"In all honesty, I would feel better given the circumstances, if you stayed with us for a few days, Jenny."

"Chase, I appreciate your concern. After everything that happened today, I wouldn't mind if you had security follow me back to my house while I get packed and onto the road, but then I should be fine," she says.

"Your parents live seven hours away on a good day by car. You're not driving. I'll arrange a team to fly with you to your parents. It's highly unlikely anyone will follow you, but you were with Katarina on her recent trip to Brazil and you were also with us in New York, so I want to be certain," he says.

"Chase, really, I don't think it's necessary," she says.

"You are Katarina's closest friend, and as such, getting to you affords them a way to get to me. You won't even know they are around once you get to your parents," he says.

"Very well, Chase," she says, rolling her eyes at me and I can't help but laugh.

"I saw that," he says, narrowing his eyes at us.

"I actually think it's a good idea and besides you're not likely to win this argument. Have a piece of coffee cake while they make the arrangements," I say as Gaby sets a glass dish on the kitchen table in front of us. It smells deliciously of cinnamon and has nuts and a swirling cream cheese frosting covering it.

"Jay is assembling a team who will be ready to leave for your house in about ten minutes. They're having a loaner jet prepared for takeoff from JFK, just to be certain we don't have tails," Chase says, reading a message on his phone as he joins us at the table.

"I'm already packed. I'll plan the next two weeks with Mom and Dad and then I'll work at Torzial Monday and Tuesday, probably work from home Wednesday morning, and then fly into New York that afternoon or evening. I can help you and your mom with any last minute details before Friday," she says.

"Jenny, Matt will be your key contact while you're visiting your parents. You'll clear all plans through him. Just be sure to give him advance notice if you and your parents are going out. He'll arrange to have you flown home, too."

"That's amazingly kind of you, Chase. I don't think it's necessary, but I have to admit it sounds much nicer than dealing with airport check-in and delays around the holidays," she says.

"Good, then it's settled. Just let Matt know the details and he'll take care of all the arrangements. Looks like the teams are in place and are ready for you," he says, glancing down at his cell.

"Thanks for everything," Jenny says.

"You are most welcome. Ladies if you will excuse me I need to take a call," Chase says, heading towards his study.

"I'll see you in a couple weeks. Make sure you call if there's anything you need help with before the wedding," Jenny says, giving me a hug goodbye.

"Are you serious? Something my dear mother hasn't thought of?" I say, walking to the entrance with her.

"That's true," she says laughing.

"Remember to text me when you know exact times for certain," I say.

"Will do," she says, waving as she is ushered to the helipad by Matt and I go in search of Chase.

"I'm giving you my advice, Chase. You asked me for it and that's what you pay me to do," Sid says. I am at the door, but don't want him to think I have been eavesdropping or that I have to stay for the conversation. I motion that I will come back, but he shakes his head, urging me in with a wave of his hand gesturing for me to close the door. He is behind his desk and a look of consternation mars his hand some features.

"Sid, if we do this, will it end for good?"

"It's the only thing that will."

"Have a plan ready for my review first thing in the morning. Thanks, Sid," he says, disconnecting and running a hand through his hair.

"Do you have any idea how much I love you and how crazy it makes me that this lunatic is out there," he says, kissing me with an unleashed ardor that leaves me breathless.

"I think you should show me," I murmur against his lips.

"Story time first, Baby," he says, taking me by the hand and guiding me upstairs to our bedroom. "I know you're dying to know what's happening. I didn't want to say too much in front of Jenny," he says, throwing his suit jacket over the ottoman and loosening his tie before he begins unbuttoning the cuffs of his shirt. He starts to loosen the top button of his dress shirt, but I place my hand on his.

"Let me undress you," I say.

He tries to suppress the quirk but the glint in his eyes gives his enjoyment away. I watch as his irises turn dark as I begin to slowly unbutton his shirt, brushing my finger through the light chest hair, traveling under the shirt and over his erect nipples, teasing as I trace down the length of his torso and through the patch of hair above his dress pants.

"Baby, if you keep this up, this is only going to end one way," he says, as I push the shirt off his shoulders and pull it from his frame. I lean forward and brush kisses on his nipples relishing in their hardness and his masculinity. My fingers find their way back over his navel and unzip his dress pants, letting my hands rub against the rigid bulge in his pants before letting them fall over his slim hips and onto the floor.

"Honey, you're right. This is only going to end one way," I say huskily before I slide my fingers into the sides of his briefs and pull them over his hips and slowly past his muscular thighs, before letting them fall to the floor. He is gloriously nude and I run my hands over his thighs, around his muscular ass exploring with my hands as I push him back towards the bed, reaching up to capture his lips with mine.

"Now that you have me undressed whatever are you going to do with me?" he asks against my lips.

I push him back onto the bed. "Watch Honey," I say as he positions a pillow under his head so he can look down at me.

"Oh, Baby, I couldn't take my eyes off of you if I wanted to," he says.

I feel myself moisten further as I gaze at his rigidness laying the length of his lower abdomen, its tip against his navel. I remove my sweater and toss it atop his suit jacket, lift my tank, slowly sliding it up my belly, past my ribs and leisurely moving it past my breasts and over my head, tossing it, too, onto the pile. I run my hands over my breasts, teasing my nipples through the sheer black lace, but decide to rid my skirt first letting it dramatically drop to the floor.

"Baby, sheer black bras, black fishnet thigh highs, black thong and four-inch heels are what dreams are made of," he says as I walk slowly away from the bed allowing him full view of my thong, before bending over and turning back around. I am purposeful, walking slowly towards him, watching the smoldering of his eyes. The intensity of his look is an aphrodisiac. I reach up and unclip the silver clasp, allowing it to fall to the floor, freeing my breasts to his gaze as I reach the end of the bed.

· · ·

I STRADDLE his thighs and he takes me by the waist, lifting me over the top of him, sliding my thong aside to pull me deep onto him. I relish in the feel of him inside of me, riding him slowly, swiveling my hips, loving the groan of pleasure it elicits.

"Baby," he moans, grasping my hips and pulling me deeper.

"Slow Honey," I say, mimicking his words from a few weeks ago. "I want to feel you deep inside of me, slow," I say, rocking my hips to take him in deeper before slowly gaining rhythm and speed.

"Baby," he says, pulling me down hard and then back up again, and then pulling me deeper as he helps me gain momentum. I feel myself climbing as he continues rubbing that special spot inside of me, building and building until I crumble around him and feel him release deep inside of me. He holds me tight, kissing me on the lips as we both catch our breath, and I collapse on his chest.

"Chase, I trust you. I don't need to hear whatever it was you were going to tell me."

"Katarina, you don't know what the plan is, and the players involved. If we do this it's going to greatly impact your parents, the entire Larussio empire, and life as you know it will drastically change. Are you willing to take that risk?"

DOWNLOAD a free copy of my exclusive story, "A Promise" to receive updates, sneak peeks and fun and games through my newsletter.

HOPING FOR A HAPPILY EVER AFTER? Read Degrees of Power to find out what happens in this exciting conclusion!

THANK YOU

Thank you for reading Degrees of Control. Reviews help other readers connect to books they may love. Would you be willing to help your fellow readers learn what you love about Chase and Katarina? If so, please leave a review.

ACKNOWLEDGMENTS

Wayne, my husband, thank you for always believing in me, supporting my passions, and helping me make my impossible dream come true.

My parents and family have been a steady reminder that you can achieve your goals with determination, hard work, and commitment. Thank you!

Karla, my dear friend, who read the first book first and encouraged me to keep going, and who recommended getting other beta readers, because "You can only read a book for the first time once." Thank you for your unconditional support through all the insanity!

A special thank you to all the people who diligently bring all the aspects of these novels together. It takes an army, and I may be a bit biased, but this team is fantastic!

Debbie, my amazing street team, and all the groups, bloggers, and book lovers who spread the word about these stories, thank you!

Via's House of Vixens, is a "private" Facebook group for readers and fans to connect. If you would like to be part of this group, request to join for loads of fun!

I hope you continue reading Degrees of Power to find out what happens next with Chase and Katarina!

ABOUT VIA MARI

Contemporary romantic suspense author Via Mari likes to keep her readers on the edge, fanning themselves as the action unfolds and the heat rises. Her books, featuring the most handsome, intense males, exemplify extreme romance, with powerful men who will stop at nothing to protect the women they love.

Via was raised in both the United States and United Kingdom. Since childhood, she has enjoyed reading books that carry you away. In fact, you can still find her in the early hours of the morning, curled up in an overstuffed chair by a crackling wood fire, reading a page-turning novel, especially during the harsh winters of the Midwestern United States.

When not writing, Via spends her days with her husband. She enjoys gardening, shopping at the local farmers market, and walking in town or around a big city. And she loves traveling to research her next novel.

She also loves interacting with her readers, so feel free to connect with her on the following social media sites! If you want to stay updated on the latest releases and claim a copy of an exclusive story, **sign up for her newsletter.**